THE MUSHROOM GATHERER

THE CZECH LIST

VIKTORIE HANIŠOVÁ

The Mushroom Gatherer

TRANSLATED BY
VÉRONIQUE FIRKUSNY

LONDON   NEW YORK   CALCUTTA

Seagull Books, 2025

First published in Czech as *Houbařka*
by Viktorie Hanišová

© Host — vydavatelství, s. r. o., 2018

First published in English translation by Seagull Books, 2025
English translation © Véronique Firkusny, 2025

ISBN 978 1 8030 9 569 1

British Library Cataloguing-in-Publication Data
A catalogue record for this book is available from the British Library.

Typeset by Seagull Books, Calcutta, India

The Mushroom Gatherer

01

I hated it. The dusty-rose dress with frills was too tight around my waist, my toes were cramped in the white patent-leather ballet flats, I sat on the upholstered theatre seat, my back straight as a candle, and if I hunched the slightest bit, there came a jab between my shoulder blades: 'Sit up!'

Out of the corner of my eye, I could see my brothers turning up their noses, making faces, now and then spitting out a dirty word. They were about as eager to be going to the opera as pigs on their way to being castrated, and would have much preferred to go to a movie or stay at home and watch television. They might not have felt such disdain for a show at the Alfa, but that was out of the question. We were obliged to attend the Grand Theatre in the Smetana Gardens. The only 'real theatre in Plzeň'. A proper stage with a large orchestra, elaborate set designs and classical composers—Prokofiev, Verdi, Smetana. My mother had a thing for classical music.

I couldn't wait for the lights in the auditorium to dim and the buzz in the audience to die down. As soon as the first strains of the violins cut into the silence, my eldest brother snuck his CD player out of his pocket, inserted one earbud into his own ear and offered the other to his younger brother. Even my father, who sat on a side seat, relaxed a bit in the darkened box. He let his shoulders droop, leaned his head against the wall, and sometimes crossed one leg over the other. I would lower my shoulders millimetre by millimetre, until my chin touched the balcony railing, and I could finally rest my cheek against one hand and with the other fish out the opera glasses from my purse. I liked to watch the people in the audience more than what was happening on stage. Within the visual field of the opera glasses, women with violet-tinted bouffant hairdos would trade places with young men, their cell phone screens glowing in their hands, and with tourists who had come wearing jeans and applauded wildly after each solo.

But what was most interesting was happening behind my back. Never have I seen anyone so consumed by what was taking place onstage. Some of the spectators in the lenses of my opera glasses held their breath, others even shed a tear, but compared to her performance that was nothing. My mother sat on a stool, her back straight as a ruler, her hand on her chest, her mouth slightly open. She looked as if someone was performing an exorcism ritual on her. Every word from the stage, every stomp on the hollow floorboards resonated in her face, at every loud noise she would get startled, widen her eyes, or narrow them. During the love scenes her cheeks were on fire, and if something unpleasant was happening onstage, she would cover her eyes with her hands and watch the performance through the gaps between her fingers. I could have sworn that I heard her heart pounding. I could observe her intently for the entire performance, I probably could even have pinched her thigh—she wouldn't have noticed at all.

My mother was the spectator that every proper theatre deserves. She was as much a part of the Grand Theatre as the ushers with the programmes and the carefully painted sets. In fact, she was more than that. My mother was the best actress in the house. Her performance was worthy of long, standing ovations. Brava! It was her moment of glory. My father, the head of the household and our sole provider, next to her, looked like a mere appendage, a supporting actor serving as a foil to the real star.

My mother was an artist who empathized so fully with her character that she couldn't turn it off even after the performance was over.

And so, no one could blame her for bringing the sweeping theatrical gestures even to her death bed. Her final hour was reminiscent of a classical tragedy, worthy of Sophocles.

Shortly after six in the morning they called me to come as quickly as possible. My mother appeared to be very weak, they feared the worst. For a moment I hesitated, the sun beyond the windowpane was urging me to head into the forest, but with an effort I scrambled out of the rumpled bed, got dressed in a hurry and set off for the train station.

I got to the hospital just before ten.

Both of them were already waiting outside her room. Evžen was standing up straight with his hands behind his back, looking out of the window. Milan, half a head shorter, was leaning against the white wall. He gave me a slight nod of greeting and a cautious smile, but when he saw Evžen turn to him with a sour expression, he quickly drew down the corners of his mouth.

What are you doing here? Evžen barked at me.

I didn't answer, opting instead to make a beeline for the door, but by then Milan already had me by the shoulder.

Hold on, Sisi, we can't go in yet.

He cleared his throat into his clenched fist, on which his knuckles had turned white, and dropped his gaze to the floor. The muscles in his face were tense and droplets of sweat glistened on his forehead.

I sat down in silence on the leatherette bench outside the door to the room. It was only after a few minutes had passed that I realized why I hadn't been allowed to go in. The door to my mother's room opened and into the hallway stepped a nurse wearing blue rubber gloves, a cart with a dripping basin and a pile of rags in front of her. She motioned to us that she had finished.

I won't disturb you, she whispered and pushed the cart towards the nurse's station. The wheels of the cart squeaked like a mouse caught in a trap.

I entered the room last. I wasn't the least bit nervous, I was absolutely certain that this was yet another false alarm. Not even Evžen and Milan, despite their best efforts, could manage to hide their annoyance. It wouldn't be the first time that we had dragged ourselves here for nothing. Twice this past month alone our mother had summoned us to her already.

As soon as I saw her ashen face, however, and looked into her glazed over eyes, their whites a toxic yellow, it was instantly clear to me that this time she wasn't leading us by the nose.

Our mother, whom the nurse had purged of all disagreeable smells, lay theatrically sprawled on the hospital bed with a white blanket draped over her body like a scene in a painting by Rubens. Beneath the fabric, however, was no young, voluptuous body. The sagging skin on our mother's white, fleshy arms fell in folds over her forearms and armpits, creating unsightly creases, her overgrown, dishevelled hair stuck out in all directions, the corners of her mouth were stuck together with yellowish spittle. The air in the room reeked of old age, disinfectant and pathos.

Squinting up at the ceiling with her reddened eyes, our mother didn't seem to be aware of our presence. For a while we just stood there, then Milan stepped towards her, lightly touched her hand and spoke to her, but his words didn't penetrate the confused expression on her face, they rolled off like drops of water on glass. He shrugged his shoulders, curled his bottom lip and returned to us.

We three sat down on the vacant bed next to her. None of us felt like talking. Milan was fiddling with his cell phone, Evžen staring fixedly out of the window and I was swinging my legs under the high frame of the bed. Not one of us wanted to look death in the face. We sat side by side like three people who had randomly settled on the same park bench, hardly anyone could have guessed that we were siblings.

I had no sense of how long it took, it might have been several hours, or just a few minutes. Finally, our mother stirred on the bed and turned her head slightly in our direction. The misty film was gone from her eyes. She looked at us.

Children, she rasped. The enormous goitre beneath her sallow skin quivered. I noticed her breathing was very shallow. The monitor above her head flashed.

Mother swallowed with difficulty, blinked several times, spread her arms and opened her palms. We understood that she wanted to spend the last moments of her life feeling connected to her loved ones.

Two hands, three children. A choice, even on her deathbed. We exchanged awkward glances, no one wanted to make the first move. Milan indecisively rubbed his chin, Evžen was biting his lip, I preferred to stare down at my worn-out hiking boots.

Eeny meeny miny moe...

It was obvious from the beginning who would drop out. Evžen glanced around a few more times, slid off the bed and gingerly approached his mother's right hand. Immediately after him, Milan began to pick his way through the IV tubes, electrodes and monitor cables. He brushed against the urine bag, emitted a contrite 'Uh-oh,' but in the end successfully assumed his place on his mother's left.

Our mom clasped the hands of her two sons and again rasped something. The words that slowly struggled to come out of her mouth were punctuated by dry coughs. My brothers were looking into her eyes and nodding in agreement. I was sitting too far away to make out what she was saying. For a moment I thought I might join them, might try to embrace her and kiss her forehead, after all I too was one of them, my mother's only daughter, her little girl, but I didn't want to disturb the perfect symmetry. There wasn't enough room for me at her bedside anyway. Evžen caressed her hair, leaned towards her and whispered something into her ear. Mom briefly lifted the corners of her mouth and her eyes gleamed in a barely perceptible way. Even Milan bent down to her and stuck his cheek against hers. I had the feeling that, holding each other so closely, they had turned to stone. The image moved me deeply. This is how one should die, I thought to myself, embraced by one's family, this is how a real tragedy should end. It was a catharsis in every sense of the word. The exalted atmosphere was spoiled only by the presence of me, the voyeur, for whom there was no hand left to hold.

My brothers remained with my mother like that for several minutes. Every now and again, she would still mumble something. I looked out of the window at the rooftops, on which the sun sparkled. I would have preferred, by now, to be back in the Bohemian Forest.

When I next looked back at them, it was all over. The monitor above my mother's head had gone off and the nurse came rushing into the room, this time no longer wearing rubber gloves. She threw back Mother's voluminous draperies, placed her hands with interlaced fingers on her waxy skin and shouted at my brothers to step back. They obeyed, alarmed looks on their faces.

A brief attempt to resuscitate her was made, for form's sake, but there was no point. The love triangle between the mother and her two sons was broken forever.

'Death occurred at 1.56 p.m. . . .'

None of us fell to our knees in despair or pulled out our hair. We, who had remained in the room, tried not to show what we were really feeling at that moment. Relief.

We closed the wide door and left our mother, her face covered by a white sheet, forever behind us. We exchanged condoling smiles and shook hands.

'We'll let you know when the funeral is. We won't burden you with anything, we'll take care of everything for you, sis,' said Evžen by way of goodbye. Milan shook my hand and then gave me a brotherly pat on the back. I stood where I was and watched the pair disappear down the hospital corridor. Evžen walked upright, with dignity. Milan swung his arms, trying to keep up with his brother's brisk stride. Just before the staircase, he briefly turned back towards me and waved.

02

The funeral took place a week later. I almost missed it. The train got stuck on the tracks between Mileč and Nepomuk, another suicide who had shown no regard for others. After a half hour I gave up on waiting and tried to hitch a ride, since I didn't have enough money for a taxi. I fared no better in Plzeň. At the stop near the main train station, I accidentally got on a bus that let me off at a shopping mall instead of at the Central Cemetery, so I had to run all the way down the slope.

I was among the last to enter the chapel, my sweaty turtleneck sticking to my back. It might have just been a feeling I had, but as soon as I crossed the threshold, a murmur seemed to ripple through the room. As if a wasp had infiltrated a beehive.

Almost all of the pews in the crematorium chapel were full, people were pressed up against the sides of the room. The number of people was staggering.

I managed to get a spot in the last row. A heavily perfumed woman in her forties on my right gave me a hostile stare. I searched my memory in vain to put a name to her face. But as for disapproving looks from people, those I had grown used to long ago.

The door cut us off from the fresh air and sun, and the buzz in the room was blanketed by a hushed silence, pierced by muffled coughs. After a moment the opening notes of Beethoven's *Moonlight*

Sonata spread through the space. Everyone stood up as if on command and the darkened hall blossomed with white handkerchiefs. The music ended and everyone sat back down. The first speaker ascended the podium, our father's long-time faculty colleague and family friend. He stood at the lectern, gave his scribbled-on pages a shake, and began: 'Esteemed ladies and gentlemen, my fellow mourners...' He went on to speak at length about hard work, respect, and traditional values, making deliberate pauses between each word.

'She was the wife of a *great* man,' he declared meaningfully to the room, looking up from the papers and nodding his head.

I felt embarrassed by his speech. Not that he wasn't right, because my father surpassed my mother in more ways than one. Mother, with her unremarkable education, work experience and background, was nowhere near his level, and furthermore, was almost two heads shorter. But this was, after all, her funeral, it had nothing to do with our father, he had had his parting moment of glory already two years ago. I wanted to stand up and point out to the speaker that in the coffin to his right lay not my father, but my mother. I looked around the hall, but the guests assembled around me were all politely wringing their handkerchiefs, their eyes fixed on the orator. They never even deigned to look at my mother's photograph.

It struck me that all of these people hadn't come together to pay their last respects to my mother, but rather to pay tribute to him— my father, and by extension to his oldest son. To profess to Evžen, who had inherited not only our father's looks and bearing, but also some of his influence, their loyalty to our family. My mother's funeral was just a pretext.

'We bid farewell to a wonderful wife, mother and friend,' the speaker concluded, his voice breaking dutifully.

I was on the verge of shouting at him: And what about Magdaléna Tichá, born Mináčová, don't you want to bid farewell to her?

The people stood up again. The music resumed, but this time more subdued and wistful. I tried to catch a glimpse of my mother's coffin over the mounds of backs, wreaths and flowers, but without much success.

I wondered what she would have had to say about this opulent ceremony. If just this once, for the final time, she would have preferred to step off the main stage, slip out the side door and run away home? Maybe she would have liked a modest funeral, perhaps back in her birthplace, a village at the foot of the Tatra Mountains. A small cluster of relatives around her coffin with a priest up front, a three-person band and then a little spot in her native soil next to her old mom and dad. Instead, they would cremate her and pour her into a gaudy brass urn.

The mourners formed a queue, waiting to speak to my brothers, the main actors in this tragedy, who in perfectly tailored suits and polished shoes stood shaking hands and exchanging small talk with each guest. Apart from a resemblance in their faces, they seemed to have nothing in common. Although they were only two years apart, Milan looked ten years younger. Not one wrinkle on his forehead, a strand of his gelled hair had come loose and was hanging across his face. I noticed that he had opened the top button of his shirt and that the hem was protruding from under his jacket. Evžen, on the other hand, looked perfectly groomed and sterile. With each acknowledgement of heartfelt condolences, the furrow between his eyebrows deepened.

I could spare myself this scene, and made my way directly to the coffin. In the packed room, it looked downright desolate.

I asked myself why my brothers had opted for a closed casket. My mother's body was surely well preserved, and undertakers today could work wonders. The deceased person's face could be so plastered with makeup that the inert body barely looked like a corpse. Maybe my brothers were ashamed to let everyone see her swollen countenance and massive, wrinkly neck. In fact, right beside the coffin on an easel was a huge photograph of Mother from a time when she was still beautiful.

Inside there could have been anyone, yet I felt her presence intensely. My body began to tingle, the mere thought of her dead body concealed beneath the lid made me feel anxious and ashamed. But somewhere beneath the layer of resentment, revulsion and suffocating memories I felt a deep tenderness. That dead mountain of flesh and bones had once been my mama. I stroked the coffin in the place where, beneath the inlaid poplar wood, which would soon slide into the furnace with her, I sensed her face might be. I bent down to the coffin, shut my eyes and breathed in. Now came the moment for which I had long been preparing myself.

Just then, someone knocked into me from behind. I'm sorry, apologized a bald, sweaty man, motioning with his hand, by way of excuse, behind him. I realized that the queue had shifted away from my brothers to the coffin. For a moment I wasn't sure which way to move, but it was pointless, the bald man had ruined everything. I let the coffin be and quickly left the room.

I ran down the steps and once outside, took refuge in the shadow of a relief of a female figure holding a torch. I looked at my watch—if I left within a half hour, I could just make the train to Horažďovice. I'd stop at the cottage, shed my black turtleneck, pull on my boots, and could still manage to head into the woods.

Instead, I stood as if bolted to the ground. With the tip of my shoe, I kicked over a red remembrance candle that was lying at my feet. The candle rolled away onto the sun-drenched walkway in the direction of our family tomb. Before long they would place the urn with mother's ashes on the imposing headstone.

A slap on my back snapped me out of my musings. 'So, sis,' came Milan's voice, 'It's good that you made it.' He pulled a blue pack of Gauloises from his jacket pocket, tapped the top of the carton and pulled out the middle cigarette, running his tongue over it before sticking it into his mouth. There's a bum who hangs around in front of the wine shop on the square in Sušice who does the same thing. He too thinks that it looks cool and sexy. In town they call him a lech or the village idiot, it depends. When Milan finished his smoke, he offered me a ride to the train station.

'That way you don't have to run yourself ragged, Sisi,' he said, but it wasn't about that.

I was just about to nod and thank him when something in me suddenly rebelled. Wasn't I one of the three closest relatives? Wasn't my name on the bereavement card right after the names of my brothers?

'I'll come with you,' I shot back and Milan awkwardly scratched his head.

'Whatever you want . . .'

The guests filed out of the chapel, the women hooked into the arms of their husbands, seemly expressions of sadness plastered on their faces, the men in dignified silence. The only thing marring the perfect picture was the warm spring sunshine, rain would have been more appropriate.

We climbed into Milan's black Beemer and joined the tail end of the convoy of cars. The whole way home my brother smoked one cigarette after another, running his fingers through his gelled hair without saying a word. 'Damn,' he finally hissed, when he realized that the other cars had blocked his entrance to the garage.

He parked on the next block, never even looked at me, and set off in hurry towards the house. I could barely keep up with him.

As I approached our fence, the old familiar feeling came over me. Facing the majestic shadow, my knees were shaking. But I managed to stay on my feet.

Our two-storey villa is one of the most beautiful homes in the Bezovka quarter. Our parents weren't among the newcomers to the Plzeň-Bory district, the nouveau riche who purchased houses here in order to stamp their freshly acquired status onto their calling cards. My father was an old-time resident, as deeply rooted to the place as the one-hundred-year-old oak tree in the garden. He had inherited the villa as the firstborn son of his father, who in turn had inherited it from his own. My grandfather, a prominent city councilman, had had it built in the 1920s. He took great care to make sure it looked grand but not ostentatious. In terms of architectural design and scale, it was perfectly integrated with the surrounding buildings, standing just a hair taller than the other houses. Even today, almost a hundred years later, our villa inspires admiration. While the surrounding houses were flashing their brand-new loft conversions, wrapping themselves in polystyrene, grinning in toxic colours, their windows aglitter with new vinyl shutters, one could depend on our house to remain exactly the same. The sandy yellow facade that gleams through the branches of the spreading oak tree, to this day, makes an impression of understated elegance. Only a nitpicking fanatic would on close inspection notice that the paint in the corners was peeling and that the cracks in the facade were sprouting black mould.

We passed through the gate and went up the steps towards the inlaid front door, which in its workmanship rivalled our mother's coffin. From the vestibule we stepped directly into the largest room of the house—the living room, which we called the great room. This is where guests were always greeted with a glass of fine champagne, and silver spoons would stir coffee in porcelain cups rimmed with gold.

I can see it as if it were today. Dad's colleagues from the faculty and various sponsors settle into the leather sofa and armchairs and discuss politics, culture and football, with a tumbler of expensive scotch—'Where did you find it?'—on the coffee table in front of them, their hands holding a cigarette and resting on the armrest of the leather sofa.

'And what is your opinion, Mr Tichý?'

Dad leans back in his chair, takes a sip from his glass and looks out of the window at the English garden. He takes care to make sure the pause isn't too long, but long enough to be sufficiently dramatic. The guests are nodding their heads even before he begins to speak.

I lost sight of Milan in the crowd of people, and remained standing on the threshold, observing the scene in the living room.

The guests dressed in black were standing and sitting around the room, a cup of coffee or a glass of wine in hand, dropping reminiscences about my parents, and examining old photographs.

How long had it been since I was last here? Since I ran away from here, intending never to return? Seven years already. From that time nothing had changed. Not a thing. The furniture was in the same place, the old familiar pictures were on the walls, a distinctive smell was infiltrating my nostrils. Except instead of my father, it was Evžen who sat enthroned in the fine armchair. The resemblance was incredible. He was of the same stature, with a slim build and a slightly bulging belly. His hair had started to recede, he had almost as little hair as our dad when he died. He crossed one leg over the other, holding a glass of wine in one hand and keeping the other clasped to his chest, a solemnly downcast expression on his face. But I could see perfectly well that he was surreptitiously keeping an eye on everything happening around him.

He could feel satisfied, he had succeeded in staging an atmosphere of perfect mourning. All of the invited guests were whispering reverentially and examining the photographs on display on the walls and cabinets. In the presence of Evžen, a prominent Plzeň businessman and freshly minted city councilman, no one wanted to tarnish their reputation by laughing or sobbing out loud. And yet for a long time it had seemed that Evžen would never walk in his father's footsteps. When he didn't get into law school, Dad had bombarded him with insults and reproaches. Evžen, the 'disgrace of the family', then pulled himself together and left for Prague to study at the Polytechnical

Institute, but even then, he only made it as far as a bachelor's degree. At the time of my departure from home, it had been several months already that, as an undereducated engineer, he hadn't been able to get near a proper job. It was only after my downfall that things began to look up for him. He returned to Plzeň, set up an IT company, and business began to pour in. After that, evidently even Dad took him back into his graces.

As soon as I took a few steps, the mourners parted like a flock of sheep. For a moment I regretted that I hadn't left the funeral and gone straight to the train station. I poured myself some tea, waded through the guests, deliberately greeting those who turned their faces away from me, and holding out my hand to those who were staring down at their shoes. And when I got tired of parting the crowd, I returned to the vestibule and climbed the winding wooden staircase to the second floor. I wanted to walk through my former home one more time, brush against the past, caress the memories.

I walked slowly, unhurriedly, savouring every step. In the little hallway on the second floor, flat IKEA boxes were scattered about. Shelves, cabinets and a desk. In just the one week since our mother's death, Evžen had accomplished a lot. Or had he already moved in sooner, while she was still in the hospital? I ran my index finger over the handle of the third door.

My room was the smallest of the three, but I liked it the best. Even after all these years it was still *my* little room. The creaking of the parquet floor radiated in all directions, the sound travelled all the way to the bare walls, and because there was nothing to absorb it, bounced off them and made its way back. All my things, books, clothes and even pictures, were gone. Evžen had had the furniture and curtains removed, the room was ready to be repainted. And ready for the arrival of the firstborn, that my eldest brother would no doubt soon beget. It would be a son, of course. I lay down on the parquet floor, shut my eyes, and tried to take in through my nose what was left of the scents that I remembered. Through the open window I could hear the noise from the street. For an instant I was transported back to the time when I was happiest here. A time before I celebrated my tenth birthday. I knew that I would never come back again.

As I descended the stairs, a bearded man in his forties, with a camera that had a big lens swinging from his neck, approached me. He had been asking every guest to allow themselves to be photographed and to write a few words in the condolence book, as a memento for the family. Could he ask me as well? And, by the way, who was I?

I glanced into the living room. His Excellency Evžen was sitting in Dad's fancy armchair in exactly the same position, except for having re-crossed his legs the other way. Behind him stood his wife, her hand resting on his shoulder. Both were staring at me.

'I'm nobody. I'm a total *zilch*. I don't belong here at all,' I answered, my eyes still fixed on Evžen.

'Then what are you doing here?'

I just shrugged my shoulders, waved my hand, sailed through the room and out the open front door.

Before I opened the gate, I looked back one last time. For the past several years, I've been haunted by a persistent dream, that one day I would come knocking, my mother, with my father and my brothers, would open the door wide, and we would all shake each other's hands, maybe even embrace and kiss each other on the cheek. We would explain everything to each other, maybe shed a few tears together and with the wave of a hand, be done with the past. That, which had happened, had been just a simple misunderstanding, a brief interlude that could be erased. This impossible dream was so alluring that its odour crept into my nostrils even now, after they were both dead.

On the steps the first drop of rain landed on my forehead. I couldn't get the gate open, not even on the third try, the hinges came loose and the metal frame rubbed against the brick post, I didn't have the strength to slam it shut. Evžen will have to get it fixed.

I got back to Dvorce only after eleven. There was no time for dinner, I grabbed a handful of nuts from a jar and jumped straight into bed, without washing up or brushing my teeth, just in my underpants and tank top. I finally managed to fall asleep by early morning. In my sleep, the thought that I had failed continued to oppress me. I hadn't managed to whisper through the thick poplar wood into my mother's ear what I had wanted to say.

I forgive you.

Even so, it had gone better than last time. 'It's all your fault, Sisi,' my brothers had said at our father's funeral. This time they were content to remain silent.

03

Early every morning I pull on my father's leather hiking boots in the hallway, grab the basket and the dishcloth, and set off on the *path*.

My 25-kilometre route is perfectly mapped out. I know in which woods I'll find plenty of mushrooms and where, on the contrary, I won't come across even a puffball; through which opening I can best slip into a dense thicket; where I can ford a stream; and where I can squeeze through the fencing in the cow and sheep pastures.

Some might imagine my path as a narrow trail through a dark and mysterious forest, in which my feet brush through dewy grasses and I leap from boulder to boulder across mountain streams, scramble up rock faces, and balance over deep ravines full of trees broken after a storm. But they would be wrong. At the edges of the Bohemian Forest National Park there are sparse woods interspersed with meadows, cottage villages and camping sites, and the area is teeming with local inhabitants and tourists. It's a long way from pristine nature. But when I'm on my path I really do feel like a lone traveller in the middle of the wilderness. When I get into the vicinity of an RV site, I feel like I've scaled the jagged peak of a high mountain. When I'm crisscrossing the bike paths, it's like being in hostile territory full of hungry wolves, waiting in ambush for their prey. And along the stretches of asphalt, which are unavoidable, I become a pilgrim on the 1,000-kilometre journey to Compostela, making my way up and down the rocky hillsides.

This is also why on my excursions I keep my eyes fixed with sacred reverence on the ground. I don't care to look into the faces of random passers-by. But most of all, I don't want anyone to see *me*. I prefer to be a shadow gliding through the forest.

Yet should someone notice me on my route, they would see just an ordinary girl wearing a baggy sweatshirt of nondescript colour. My face isn't remarkable, my hair is neither short nor long, and is of a dull shade. I camouflage myself like the most delicious mushrooms. I am not memorable.

My days have an unvarying schedule. When, shortly after seven, I head out from Dvorce, I feel a pleasant tickling in the soles of my feet. With the first findings between Stráž and Nuzerov, the tension climbs farther up my leg, and by Krušec my calves start to go numb and my thighs grow stiff, which is why I like to step up the pace, to make sure I make it through the whole mission. Around Hartmanice I never spend much time in the woods, I just peek under a few spruces, then impatiently veer eastward and take the woods near Kundratice by storm. By the time I get to Vatětice, I feel a tingling and a stitch in my lower belly, my destination, the conifers just past Annín, are a mere stone's throw away. I know exactly under which spruce I'll find porcinis and where in the grass the tallest parasol mushrooms grow. It was my dad who taught me, and I'm grateful to him to this day.

I run from spot to spot, from the slope of red cracking boletes to the parasol meadow, from the chanterelle patch to the matte boletus moss, I scour the hiding place of the brittlegills and the orange cap bolete nook. I bend down to the fruiting bodies and examine their multicoloured and less conspicuous caps growing out of the stipe. The taller and stronger the stem, the better. I grasp the stipe in my fist, encircle it with my fingers and pull one protruding mushroom after another out of the earth. I lean over the roots of trees and quickly straighten up again, beneath the spruces I feel a twinge in my side, by the larches I skip for joy, arriving at the pines my heart is beating in my throat.

Once I've criss-crossed the entire forest, my body is groaning in pain and I feel butterflies in my stomach. My sweaty clothes stick to my body. I'm hunched under the weight of the basket and gasping for breath. On the bank by the river, beneath a gnarled pine, I finally sit down on a double stump and give my swollen lungs and stressed organs a break. I set down the basket, rest my elbows on my legs, hide my hot cheeks in my hands and breathe deeply. Just like the mushrooms in the basket at my feet, I need to spend a few minutes being still before my pulse goes back to normal and the rushing water drowns out the sound of my ragged breathing. Then I slowly get up, stretch my slack body and head for Sušice. As I make my way north along the Otava riverbed, exhaustion trips up my feet. But even so, I can't resist, and now and then will stray into the thicket bordered by thick blackberries or stinging nettles and add something to the basket.

Around five o'clock I'm already knocking on the back door of the Toadstool and handing over the spoils. Part of the money I stash in the inner pocket of my wallet, and with the rest I buy myself something to eat and then drag myself home. I usually get back to Dvorce around seven o'clock, gulp down some dinner, and kill time until the moment when I go to bed.

That's how it goes from April, when the winter mushrooms are still growing and the morels and wrinkled thimble caps are beginning to appear, right through November, when, with a bit of luck, I might come across some honey mushrooms or Heralds of Winter. I basically stick to my route, adjusting it only slightly according to the season. In the spring, when nature in the Bohemian Forest is still demurely shrouded and delicate, I step away from the woods towards sunny pastures and meadows, where I hunt for St George's mushrooms and Scotch bonnets, while among the deciduous trees I stalk false morels and sheathed woodtufts. But after each foray, I quickly return to my companion, the path, which by now is impatiently looking out for my shoes.

April and May are merely a prelude to what will happen in the summer months. In June, once the chanterelles and bluing boletes have started, I won't deviate from my route by even one millimetre. I tread the same trail all the way through October, when I need to veer off among the deciduous trees again to find fall mushrooms, so as not to arrive at the Toadstool with my basket half empty.

Towards the end of November, I start feeling the blues. The days are getting shorter, I have to go into the woods later, and I generally get to Sušice with just a handful of dregs. To make my time spent in the forest meaningful, I try at this time of year to repay the forest for all of the gifts it has given to me over the preceding months. I stuff large garbage bags into my pockets and use them to collect plastic bottles, rum flasks and potato chip bags. Instead of a full basket of mushrooms, I arrive in Sušice with bulging black trash bags. I drag them behind me like carcasses.

In December a period of depression sets in. I subsist on canned food, compotes, boiled potatoes and rice, but even then my supplies run thin—and by March there's barely anything left to put in my mouth. I feel my body withering and growing soft from doing nothing. Often, I stand at the kitchen window and look out towards the forest. The huddled trees cling to each other, resting their arms on each other's shoulders and showing me their backs. Sometimes, just for practice, I trudge my path in the snow and stop in places where I can sense the frozen mycelium under my shoes. I end up sitting on the double stump beneath the pine where it all started. And come April, I finally reach once again for the family basket and head out to survey the terrain.

'You've been hunting mushrooms since before you were born!' Dad said to me once, pointing his finger at a photograph that still hangs between our kitchen windows—my mom is holding a basket full of mushrooms on her lap, and my dad and my brothers are smiling and pointing their index fingers at her big stomach. In the photo they look like a happy family. And if back then I hadn't been born, perhaps it could have stayed that way.

Even the earliest memory I can recall involves mushrooms. I am sitting on a wooden bench in front of the cottage in Dvorce, kicking my feet that don't yet reach the ground. All I can see of my mom is a slim torso wearing a chequered apron. Every so often a knife flashes over my head, with which Mom is cleaning the pine needles and moss off the mushrooms. 'Cleaning mushrooms is women's work,' I hear my father's words. My mother takes the big lurid bolete that I'm holding out to her from my hand and gives me a slight smile.

04

Because of my mother's death and funeral, this year I missed the start of the mushroom season. Yesterday I got a call from Krušina, the head chef at the Toadstool, and from the tone of his voice I could tell that he was a bit annoyed with me. And well he might be—last year had been a bad one for mushrooms, it hadn't rained much, so they were few and far between. Since April I'd been showing up at the restaurant with just a couple of wrinkled thimble caps and false morels. The pub was surely running low on last year's dried stock and they wanted to show off something fresh. Let's just hope—my heart skipped a beat—that in the meantime they hadn't found someone else.

In the morning I tossed down a buttered roll and set off to do reconnaissance. The dewy grass was lounging lazily in the sun. It looked as if someone had combed it in one direction. The air was pleasantly warm, the rays of the sun rubbed up against the soggy ground, but when I would stop, the cold still snapped at my ankles. I could feel a powerful force beneath the soles of my shoes that wanted to break through to the surface. I was separated from the mycelium by a layer as thin as tissue paper.

This year, the Bohemian Forest had been pummelled by heavy snowstorms right up through the middle of April. Then an abrupt thaw set in and from practically one day to the next, temperatures soared to twenty degrees. Warm days alternated with rainy ones. Conditions seemed more than promising. And indeed—just a few steps past the footbridge, I got lucky. In the pasture, nestled in the freshly grown grass, I found several pale St George's mushrooms. Not enough for a large pot of soup, but they could be stewed with meat and vegetables. Half an hour later I celebrated an even greater victory. In a well-known spot under the ash trees crouched dozens of black morels. There were so many that Krušina could make several courses out of them: morels can be baked, stuffed with meat, sautéed, and who knows what else. Right after the St George's, it's my favourite spring mushroom. Near Rajsko I added a few parachutes to the basket and even stumbled across a smattering of field mushrooms that had arranged themselves on the pasture in a fairy ring. And along the way back from Annín I found a handful of pig's ears.

When in the late afternoon I handed Krušina a full basket, he just mumbled something and took it from me, not even saying thank you. It was a good sign, silence was often an indicator of Krušina's good mood. He was pulling one mushroom after another out of the basket and turning each one over in his hand.

'Is that a Judas' ear?' he smirked, pointing at a twisted brown cap. Krušina has a passable knowledge of common mushrooms, but with the lesser-known ones he often gets them mixed up.

'Oh no, that's a Discina,' I explained, and because he kept on looking at me uncomprehendingly, I added: 'Ancillis.' Not even that helped, so I explained to him that although a Discina looked a lot like a Judas' ear, it wasn't nearly as tough, you just needed to sauté it lightly.

The Walrus just wrinkled his nose, took the mushroom in his hand and turned it from side to side. It's true that it's no beauty, but it tastes better than many other boletes.

'It's best just sautéed in butter. Or you can throw it under some meat. You'll be amazed.'

The Walrus didn't look particularly amazed, but at least he didn't just toss it into the trash. He put it back with the other mushrooms and handed the basket to his kitchen helper. Then he reached for the cash box he kept on the top shelf. Two 100-crown banknotes and one 200-crown note, not so bad.

In the seven years that I've got to know him, I've grown quite fond of this untalkative fellow. Granted, he's a bit of a grump, and prefers to use gestures rather than words, but when it comes to preparing mushrooms, he is hands down the best cook in Sušice. Although this may also be because there is only one mushroom restaurant in town.

Spending a whole day with him must be purgatory though, because he rarely says more than two words. I renamed him the Walrus because of his pointy, drooping moustache. When he's tasting a sauce, he soaks the tips of his moustache in it, which then dry up and stiffen. It's rather distasteful, so it's a good thing one can't see into the kitchen from the pub.

'Hey, whereabouts is Vobořil?' it suddenly occurred to me as I was already standing in the doorway. I couldn't remember when I had last seen the owner of the Toadstool.

But the Walrus, who by now had turned his back to me, just waved his hand.

I wasn't all that surprised, I was used to old Vobořil showing up only minimally at the Toadstool. For years now his pub has been running on autopilot, literally. During the summer months, when Sušice is overrun with tourists, eager to stuff their bellies to the point of bursting, it just manages to hold on to the brink of the precipice. But come winter, the direction in which business is going is clear: it's plunging headfirst into the abyss.

I said goodbye to the Walrus's back and marched off towards home. Along the way I stopped at the Vietnamese convenience store. I didn't linger long among the shelves, just grabbed a quarter loaf of bread, and made a beeline for the basket to the right of the counter marked 'Expired Merchandise'. I tossed some sardines, a carton of milk and a jar of pickles into my basket. I hesitated for a moment over a packaged croissant, but in the end resisted the temptation, I hadn't yet earned much this year, I'd better save my money. Lately my water pump has been giving me some trouble, it's drawing water ever more slowly, it's possible that I might have to replace it. It would be no surprise if it stopped working, I've had it for a couple of years already and bought it second hand.

Before turning towards Santos Island, I noticed next to the recycling bins a large plastic crate with discarded things. There were a few broken glasses, a flowerpot with a Ficus, a doormat and some books. Graham Greene's *The Quiet American* and a few romance novels. I hesitated briefly over Greene, but in the end put him back. I haven't read a book in years and didn't feel like starting again. Why bother trying to relate to the fates of others when I have enough trouble with my own? I rolled up the doormat, stuck it into my basket and added two scratched up glasses.

On the way home, not far from the footbridge, I spotted a thick log. I usually don't start collecting firewood until the summer, but this one was too nice to leave for someone else. Except that my hands were already full. I would go back for it sometime during the week.

As I was about to place the doormat on the doorstep, I fortunately stopped myself just in time. Winding its way up the steps from the porch was an ant highway that passed through the gap under the door and into the hallway. I ran into the kitchen for some sugar and sprinkled little piles into the grass by the porch. I moved the doormat off to the side, wiped my shoes on it, removed them in the hallway and entered the kitchen. I rinsed the glasses, put them in the cupboard and pulled a small cup off the back of the shelf. I threw in the rest of the banknotes and kept the loose change in my pocket. Around ten o'clock I went to bed with the pleasant feeling of not having disappointed. Only then did my usual nighttime ordeal begin.

05

When the doors of the psychiatric hospital in Dobřany shut behind me seven years ago, I felt stronger than I ever had before. I could do this, I was absolutely sure of it, I didn't need doctors or pills, I was perfectly fine. That very same evening I was plodding through the streets, lugging a heavy backpack, not sure where I would end up spending the night.

My resolve hadn't yet completely evaporated, smouldering inside was still the hope that I would prove to everyone, especially myself, that I really was *normal*. Once I had managed to find a place to stay, at my friend Kamila's, I set out to look for a job. A few days later I started working at the first job of my life. Considering that I hadn't finished high school, as a first job it wasn't half bad. The company hired me as an assistant, and for starters I was supposed to fix coffee, sort mail and make copies, but once I got the hang of it, HR told me there was no telling how far I could go.

I promptly trampled any prospect of advancement into the ground during my first break. I made the coffee so strong that the boss spat it out in disgust, and while I was making copies, the paper jammed so badly that they had to call in a repairman. In the days that followed, I went full steam ahead throwing sticks under my own feet. 'Look at it as an opportunity to make a completely fresh start somewhere else,' the HR director said encouragingly two weeks later, as she pressed a termination letter into my hand.

I started my second job with a packet of pills from Dr Mouchová, my psychiatrist, already in my purse, as well as the feeling that I wouldn't succeed. I wasn't about to take these downers, I assured myself, but tossed them into my bag just in case. This time the agency had found me a job as a warehouse clerk at a supply company.

'Don't worry, they're short on staff, they won't fire you just like that,' the agent tried to reassure me, but I still felt as though my chest was being laced into a corset.

Fear of failure kept me awake night after night. I came to work so sleep deprived, that I would nod off while unloading merchandise onto the shelves. As I went around with the cart, my head would sink onto the loaded crates that I was pushing ahead of me through the aisles. Then one time my supervisor found me slumped between pallets of merchandise, and she kicked me out within the hour. I tried a few more odd jobs here and there, but the outcome was always the same.

'There's nothing to be ashamed of,' Mouchová declared as she helped me fill out the social security disability application. She was right, I tried to convince myself, but even then I couldn't banish the feeling of shame. The very thing that I had fought against tooth and nail was becoming a reality: the district social security office, the medical expert, who hadn't even examined me, and finally a piece of paper stating that I was temporarily disabled and incapable of work. They put me on a partial disability pension, a measly 2,600 crowns, because I hadn't even worked a full year. I walked out of the office with a feeling of relief, shadowed by a sense of dismay at having given up.

On top of that, I increasingly had the feeling from Kamila, at whose place I was staying those days, that I was beginning to get on her nerves. She didn't tell me straight to my face but would give vent to her growing aversion in subtle ways. For example, she would often creep into my room around five o'clock in the morning, just as I was finally managing to fall asleep. 'Gee, I didn't realize you were still sleeping,' she would always say, and then slam the door hard behind her by way of apology. When she worked the night shift, she would make a point of leaving her alarm clock in her locked bedroom, which would then go on ringing until the batteries ran out. The day I found a suspicious looking hair on my toothbrush, I knew it was time to cast off.

I packed up my army duffle, pulled 500 crowns from my wallet, left them on Kamila's table and shut the door behind me. In the pocket of my jacket I had the keys to our family cottage in Dvorce. And so, after a two-hour train ride, I arrived at the scene of the crime. The last time I was here I was not quite ten years old. Now I was eighteen. Since my accident in Sušice, my family and I had never come back here again. Only Dad would stop by twice a year, to take care of any essential repairs, otherwise the little house was falling apart.

Standing in front of the green varnished door I swallowed hard several times, but the lump in my throat wouldn't go down. 'It's just for a while, a few weeks at most,' I repeated to myself as I unlocked the door. My fingers around the key were trembling so hard, it took me three tries to get the door open. For a moment I stood shuffling my feet on the threshold in front of the open door, as if I were facing a glass wall. In the entryway, my nostrils were immediately invaded by scents I knew from my childhood. The eight years that I hadn't been here vanished at once. The musty dankness in the hallway, the ashes from the stove in the kitchen, the chopped wood and blend of spices from the pantry. The kitchen clock showing half past six. I broke out in goosebumps and my throat tightened in anxiety. I almost turned on my heel and fled, but in the end common sense prevailed. Dvorce was my only option right now, otherwise I would end up on the street or back in the psych ward. I opened the kitchen windows wide and sat down on the creaky lounge chair. It took me at least an hour to breathe my way through the panic attack.

For two days I lurked about the house and sat around in the garden. On the third day, my eyes fell on my father's old hiking boots in the hallway. I put them on and wiggled my toes. They were three sizes too big, but if I tightened the laces properly, they stayed on. After that, everything went on automatic. I grabbed the basket and dishcloth, stuck a penknife in my pocket, and headed for the footbridge.

It was strange. At first, I stepped carefully, the forest seemed foreign and unfriendly. But I quickly remembered my father's path. It was as if the boots fell into the footsteps he had left behind of their own accord, as if the soil and their soles held magnets that attracted each other. Suddenly it all came flooding back, I could hear my father whispering mushroom hunting tips into my ear, in my mind I traced the route on the map with my finger, before my eyes I could see the photographs of the mushrooms in the atlas and the descriptions beside them. It was as if the period during which I hadn't gone mushroom hunting had never existed, the eight years had become mere pages of a diary that someone had ripped out.

From that day on I never wavered. In the morning I would head into the forest and in the evening return with a basket full of mushrooms that I would scramble up, mixing in an egg every other day. I used my first pension payment to buy just the barest necessities: pasta, long-life milk, bread and potatoes, and set the rest of the money aside. A couple of times I also managed to barter with the locals. For example, I traded a dozen porcini mushrooms for cheese at the local cheese shop, and another time I was able to get eggs. Once I was even lucky enough to get a whole rabbit.

No matter how much I saved, I soon realized that my meagre disability pension was not enough to live on. One day in the middle of July, I ran into old Vobořil in the woods. I remembered how my dad and I would sometimes run into him on our expeditions and would compare our harvests. Unlike my dad, Vobořil was an amateur who only recognized the basic species. One time he came to ask my father for advice. He pulled a scaly mushroom out of his basket, a shingled hedgehog, and wanted to know what to do with it. Dad gave him a full-blown lecture—class, subclass, order, family, characteristics, habitat, similarities, the whole thing took several minutes during which Vobořil nodded his head in a daze and tried to break into Dad's speech—he wasn't interested in any of that, he just wanted to know if he should add the mushroom to his scramble, bake it with a roast in the oven, or ditch it. But there was no getting around Dad. Anytime my dad sensed a chance to shine, he couldn't pass it up. Vobořil never asked Dad about mushrooms again, and when he walked past him, would lower his eyes, pick up the pace and hide his basket behind his back.

When I ran into Vobořil that day in mid-July, he didn't want to know about anything. He was sitting on a log by the side of the road, his face buried in his hands, an overturned basket by his feet from which a few gnawed red cracking boletes had spilled out.

'Girl, I'm not up to this any more,' he sighed when he noticed me, and I tried to avoid his alcoholic breath.

He was drinking already back when I used to come to Dvorce with my brothers and parents. His wild drinking sprees had become legendary. All the places where he had thrown up, what he had smashed while raging, where he had been found in the morning. Twice he went into rehab, the first time he didn't finish the treatment, the second time he returned 'completely cured', he would never touch the stuff again, he kept the Antabuse on hand just in case.

The next day they found him in the little forest grove on Santos Island, an empty vodka bottle still in his hand.

'Man, how did you manage it, aren't you on Antabuse?!'

'Willpower. It took determination. It was hard, but my willpower won out. I washed it down.'

Afterwards he tossed the Antabuse into the Otava river for the fish, it was of no use to him any more.

I sat down next to him on the knobby log and offered him some water from a plastic bottle. He just waved it away.

'Water? That's not going to do it.'

He took several deep breaths, braced his palms against the log, tried to hoist himself up on his shaky arms and slumped back down again.

I picked the mushrooms up off the ground and put them all into my basket, which I had filled halfway. Vobořil looked at it admiringly but said nothing. I thought I could lift him up by his armpits, but he sat on that log as if stuck with glue. I had to plant myself in front of him and pull him up by his arms. When I managed to get him back on his feet, he swayed and fell again. We had to repeat the whole procedure one more time. I finally succeeded in getting him into a fairly stable, upright position. When he grabbed me around the shoulders and exhaled his noxious breath at me, I wrestled for a few seconds with the thought of letting him topple back down to the ground again, but in the end I slipped both baskets onto one arm and together we hobbled down the forest path to the road, not too far from the Radešov campground. Vobořil sat down on the asphalt, leaned back against the guard rail, while I waved at passing cars.

It wasn't until it got dark that someone took pity on us. And no wonder: a half-dead, sloshed bum slumped by the road and a homely girl with greasy hair have poor prospects of getting a ride.

That night, once I'd hauled him back to his room above the pub, Vobořil said to me in a wheezing voice:

'Bring those mushrooms down to our place. I'll work out with Krušina later what we'll give you for them...'

And so began our collaboration. The very next day I went looking for mushrooms and then took them straight to the Walrus in the kitchen. He received them in silence and laid out four 100 crowns on the counter for me. From then on, that's how it went every day. And one year later, Vobořil's Sušice Tavern was renamed the Toadstool.

Meanwhile, the pub had become somewhat of a second home to me. It wasn't among the best places in Sušice, but it wasn't a complete dive either. It had its steady clientele, regulars who mixed up their card games with plates of mushroom scrambles or breaded and fried mushroom cutlets, and then every so often a more affluent clientele wandered in.

From time to time I myself like to sit down here and have one of Krušina's specialties—groats baked with mushrooms or kulajda soup.

Meanwhile, the few weeks I had originally planned to spend here turned into seven years.

06

My dad used to like to be first in everything. In school he was always team captain, and as he liked to tell us, it didn't matter whether it was dodgeball, rugby or a speech contest. He was on top of his studies as well, and received his diploma in analytical chemistry with honours. Following graduation, he quickly realized that a practice was not the right forum for him, so he remained on the faculty, where he climbed the ranks like a rooster ascending a coop ladder. Not even around the village of Dvorce did he try to hide his competitive nature. One might have been surprised that my own father, who counted himself among the city's elite, had taken a liking to such a widespread and commonplace hobby, one popular among the broadest cross sections of society, from blue-collar workers to wealthy entrepreneurs. But even in this my father had to be number one. I can't remember a time that he came home empty-handed. No matter how dry or how cold, he always filled at least the bottom of the basket.

Once the mushroom season started, we went every single weekend to our cottage in Červené Dvorce, and then we would spend our holidays there too. We always left in the early afternoon, took our place in the line of cars and set off with them as a single mass to head out of the city. I sat in the middle of the back seat, the worst place in the car, with bad views in all directions, and my knees squeezed together to keep me and my brothers from touching thighs. But on the way to Dvorce I didn't mind. I would have been happy riding flattened to the floor the whole way, just to get to our cottage. Just to be with my dad.

In the city my dad was known as an elegant gentleman. He was always clean-shaven, dressed in a tailored suit of fine material, with meticulously polished shoes. But as soon as he passed through the narrow gate in our fence, he turned into someone else. He quickly took off his jacket, slipped off his loafers and with them, the serious expression on his face. He stashed his suit in the downstairs closet and pulled on his worn corduroys and checkered flannel shirt. On his feet, he would put on a pair of once upon a time beige, leather hiking boots that had never seen a damp rag, sit down on the porch bench, cross one leg over the other and give me a wink: 'So what do you think, are they growing?'

I liked this dad much better than the polished dandy back home, who in the evenings would quiz me on my calculus. I couldn't wait to head out the next morning. For mushroom hunting, he was always accompanied by one of us three siblings. Our mom used to say that she had no interest in mushrooms, because they were hard to digest and made one sleep poorly, but the truth was that our father would never have taken her along.

'It's not a thing for women.'

One time I asked her how come I could go mushroom hunting but she couldn't, since we were both girls, to which she simply said: 'Well, that's because you're still just a kid, so it doesn't count. You're not quite a woman yet.' She gave a shrug and went into the kitchen.

Dad always told us that one had to go out to hunt mushrooms early, while they were still sleepy and slow to react, and couldn't hide themselves quickly from mushroom gatherers. He said that he wouldn't wake us, so that at least on the weekend we could sleep in, but at the same time he would be giving us a conspiratorial wink.

It was sort of our ritual. We finished dinner, played some cards or word chain games, and when our mom started hurrying us to go brush our teeth, our dad would stop her. First it was necessary to establish who would keep him company in the woods the next day.

We three queued up in front of him and he looked us up and down.

'So who . . .'

It didn't sound like a question, more like a statement, like when a nurse in a waiting room calls out: 'Next'. Early on we would still try to convince him to take all three of us, promising not to whine and to carry our own basket, but he was adamant.

'I have only two hands, my right one for the basket, my left for one of you.'

And then he held out his finger and we held our breath.

Eeny, meeny, miny, moe,
Catch a bolete by the toe.
Dapperling or false morel,
Which is edible, who can tell?
Parasol, milkcap, which will it be,
My little finger points to thee!

I followed the play of his index finger holding my breath, not letting the air out until the very last word. Whew. And then again. I noticed that the first time around, Dad usually started counting with me. Regardless of the order in which we had queued up. This was true of the next round as well, so in the end I was always the one who was left. But so what, I deserved my victory. I was the only one who spent each night in bed flipping through the atlas and committing each mushroom to memory.

Naturally this didn't escape Evžen either, because one day he interrupted our father with a rude 'Fuck this,' stared daggers at me, spun around and ran upstairs, followed by Milan, just a hair behind him, as if they were attached by a string. Our father still managed to say 'dapperling,' his face went from red to white a few times, and then he took off after the boys. I had no idea that at his age he was able to move so fast. All I could hear downstairs were muffled cries and a rhythmic thudding on the floor.

That was the end of the counting rhymes. At the same time, a process that had begun long ago reached a point of culmination. Our family began to function as two separate entities, my dad and I, and my mom with my brothers. The trio of Mom, Evžen and Milan represented the static contingent, who loitered around the cabin, hot dog stands, movie houses and the swimming pool, whereas my dad and I operated dynamically, covering a broader area. And when Dad would have to go back to Plzeň for a few days because of work, I would at least go along the fence line and make the rounds of our garden, retracing our path on a smaller scale.

We called them lazybones. What names they called us we never found out because we let them sleep in and didn't reconvene with them until afternoon tea. We all got used to it, and I think in the end it suited my brothers just fine.

Our mushroom-hunting expeditions followed the same unvarying schedule. At seven in the morning, my father would climb a few steps of the staircase leading up to us on the second floor, and would clear his throat a few times outside my door, his way of asking if I wanted to join him. I flew out of bed, wriggled into my clothes, which I had put out already the night before, and quietly snuck out of my room. I raced downstairs to brush my teeth. I wanted to have Dad all to myself. He always apologized, he hadn't wanted to get me out of bed so early, but at the same time was already handing me a roll that he had buttered.

As we stepped onto the footbridge over the river, the whole village was still asleep. Striding through the forest was just the pair of us, and I was glad that there was nobody to make fun of me or to force me to be their slave. That no one would pinch my neck from behind and hiss into my ear: 'Go on, tell Daddy, stupid cow!' Once we were on our path I never gave my brothers a second thought.

To this day, whenever I see one of them, the word *zilch* comes to my mind. And yet it's been a long time since I last heard that insult from them.

My brothers and I used to play lots of games, although it would be more accurate to say that they played them with me. Their little games in fact were a transfer of our sibling hierarchy into practice—Evžen represented the controlling element, Milan was his assistant, and my role was that of the slave and scapegoat. For example, Evžen often came up with the clever idea of playing prisoners, so Milan would dash off to fetch a rope, and would tie me to the trunk of the walnut tree in such a way that the thick trunk blocked my parents' view from the house. And then they made me eat all sorts of gunk. They would hollow out a gooseberry and stuff it with lovage, garlic and arugula, and then cram it into my mouth. Once they even slipped in a small slug, but I managed to spit it out.

Another pastime of theirs was to play slaughterhouse. For this, they took a football that they had previously tossed into a barrel to make it waterlogged, and tried to hit me with it. They had marked off a section of the garden in which I was supposed to run around and try to avoid the ball. Every time I went over the imaginary line, hid behind a tree, or fell, there was a penalty. I had to stand straight as a pole and not move while they fired away.

And their all-time favourite entertainment was to play the general and the *zilch*. They formed a party and promised me that they would induct me as well. I just needed to complete the tasks they would assign to me. Evžen drew a spiral on a piece of paper and marked several points on it. *The party path*. At the outer end of the spiral was the highest rank, that of the general, which referred to him; right below was the director, that fell to Milan and further down there were other points: secretary, orderly, minion. The last stop on the party path was the zero. Below the zero, which was the gateway to get in, was one more line made of dashes that led only as far as the threshold.

In order to get into the party, I had to move up the inside of the spiral and attain at the very least the zero level. But I kept messing up. I got as far as the quarter zero mark pretty often, even the half zero mark wasn't that much of a stretch, a few times I even got close to the three-quarter zero mark. But then I would always do something, for example laugh when I wasn't supposed to, or not say hello fast enough, and I'd plummet all the way down to the lowest level. The *zilch*. 'You know how it is, sis, rules are rules . . .'

Even though I knew I'd never reach zero, I still kept trying to convince them that I deserved to, and I would fold their laundry, wash their dishes and let them smack me with a wet towel. I did whatever they said, and would have been ready to do just about anything, in order to make it to the end of that dotted line and not be forever a *zilch*.

With my dad it was completely different. With him I could finally breathe freely. From him there was no danger to fear. On our expeditions he used to like to tell me about mushrooms—that I was likely to find a king bolete alongside the fly agarics, and that the best way to recognize a bitter bolete was by the webbing on its stipe, and like a diligent student I would repeat everything to myself as we walked along, and once we got back to the cottage I would write it all down in my notebook. Later on, once I had begun to leaf through the atlas on my own, he would quiz me, to see if I could identify mushrooms correctly. I have to say that for the most part I did well. Afterwards, my father would always stroke my hair saying: 'I knew that out of all my children you were the one cut out for mushrooms . . .'

But my favourite times were when we were silent. It felt like we were two conspirators. We always entered the forest hand in hand. At that moment we were the only two people in the world, surrounded by the still forest, full of mushrooms that were waiting for us. We had to squint against the low-lying sun that was reaching for us through the tall spruces, lapping at the moss and blueberry bushes. I remember the coarseness and warmth of his palm, the chapped skin on the pad of his thumb with which he stroked the back of my hand, my dad, who otherwise gave short shrift to everyone. These gentle caresses were meant for me alone.

I always found the first mushroom.

'It's a disgrace, I've spent my life hunting mushrooms, and a slip of a girl like you shows me up every time!' he said, pretending to be angry.

My pride even managed to muffle my guilty conscience that clawed its way to the surface now and then. 'Who are you kidding?' it would say to me. 'Why, you absolutely despise mushrooms!' It was true. I found them cold and dirty. There was nothing solid in them that one could sink one's teeth into, their shapeless, slimy substance stuck to my tongue and wouldn't go down my throat. With scrambled mushrooms, which as far as I was concerned was nothing but a heap of mushy, brown goop, it took a supreme effort for me not to make a face. And when I imagined that I might swallow a grub, I felt like vomiting.

But I got over it. Dad never noticed the expression on my face when I was flicking slugs off a mushroom cap. I never let on that for me the mushrooms weren't the goal, but merely a means to spending time with him. And this is precisely why out of the three of us he chose specifically me. Because I proved that I could maintain decorum under any circumstances. I didn't whine, I walked obediently by his side and eagerly answered his questions. I didn't let on about the slightest discomfort. I was happy to do it. I've never in my life been happier than when I was walking in the woods with my dad.

By evening my eyes were closing with exhaustion but I would bite my tongue and pinch my neck to ward off sleep. In my mind I would go over all the mushrooms we had found together, and yet at the same time I could feel something snatching at my foot and dragging me away from the pleasant memories. I was falling deeper and deeper into the hole, trying in vain to find something to grab onto.

What I wouldn't give now to be able to fall asleep as quickly as I did then. To simply close my eyes and give myself over to the darkness.

Kamila, the anorexic I got to know in the mental asylum, would laugh at me and say I was full of it.

'When you're tired, you just lie down and you go to sleep, right?' she needled me.

'What kind of nonsense are you saying?' I pretended to get mad. 'You are going to lecture me about it, you of all people? If you ate normally, you wouldn't have to stay locked up in here and be fed like a baby. You're the one who can eat whenever you want, but falling asleep is not a question of will, I can tell myself a hundred times to fall asleep, but it's of no use if my body won't listen,' I pushed back.

'Yeah well, our stupid bodies . . .' Kamila laughed.

In all fairness I have to admit she was right. It truly is stupid that my body is incapable of doing the most natural thing for it to do. To rest when it's tired. But my mind and my body haven't worked the way they should for years. In the sleep lab, where they sent me when I was at the clinic, they calculated that I needed between seven and seven and a half hours of sleep. I was supposed to come up with an evening ritual that would help me induce a feeling of sleepiness. Except for me, the evening preparations went slightly awry. Out of all those big and little bedtime rituals I created a jail, and now I can't tunnel my way out.

There is so much I need to do before going to sleep! My evening is programmed down to the smallest detail, the individual activities follow each other precisely, I never change their sequence. I eat my last meal after seven o'clock at night and then relax for a bit on the sofa in the living room. Next comes warm milk with honey, always drunk from the same cup, which I call my goodnight mug. There has to be enough milk to warm up my insides to the point of inducing sleepiness, but not so much that I would need to get up during the night to go pee. A couple of times I traded the milk for a glass of wine, as some people advise, but it doesn't work for me, alcohol makes my head buzz and then I can't fall asleep long into the night. Besides, wine is expensive. I've even tried the fly agaric, that I keep dried in a jar in the kitchen. Sometimes it works, but other times it turns into a wild ride. Sleeping pills would help me, but someone would have to prescribe them, and with my medical history no doctor would dare risk it, not even Dr Mouchová, whose treatment consists solely of prescribing medication. At the pharmacy, I used my hard-earned money to purchase a whole slew of herbal remedies: Deep Sleep Hops, a natural hypnotic and extra strong Lemon Balm. All useless.

After drinking the milk, I prepare my clothes, my basket with a dishcloth and my pocketknife for the next day. If I had a bathtub, I would fill it with hot water and add some aromatic oils, as the handbooks advise, but the house doesn't have a bathroom, so I just bathe myself with a washcloth in a basin and put a few drops of scented oil in a little lamp, or on sweltering days I'll just pour water over myself outside on the porch. After drying off I throw on pyjamas and a robe, walk out into the darkness and sit down on the bench near the house. I look around, breathe in the fresh air, while trying not to look up at the sky. I don't want to see if the moon is waxing or waning, the awareness that a full moon is approaching always unsettles me. When there is a full moon, I usually don't sleep all night. I get into bed at eleven, with a five-minute grace period.

And then inside the room, where the fresh air tickles my nose and the rustling of the forest and babbling of the brook fill my ears, a merciless duel takes place. The body wants to sleep, but the mind resists tooth and nail, sulking in a corner somewhere and refusing to be switched off. It's not about to leave the body without supervision, at the mercy of the darkness, which can do with it whatever it likes. Beneath my closed eyelids my eyes are wide open, my pupils on guard, afraid to go to sleep. Sometimes it begins to look hopeful, I feel myself slowly succumbing to sleep, but then abruptly my mind stumbles onto an unpleasant memory. In that instant sleep disappears, thousands of nagging thoughts start marching through my head like pesky insects. It feels as if I've made my bed on an anthill, it tickles, stings, itches all over. I twist in my bed, hide my head under the duvet, pull the covers right up to my chin and then kick them off again. And in the end, one final fear arises, massive and toxic as a hornet. I fear that I won't fall asleep at all again and that the entire following day I'll be lethargic and achy. My eyes will be so tired that I won't see the path clearly, let alone the mushrooms. There'll be a buzzing in my head, and I'll be hot for a minute and then freezing cold the next minute. And added to that will be an excruciating hunger that will not be appeased. This fear usually haunts me for several hours. I fall asleep long after midnight, or just before daybreak.

As for waking up, there I have no trouble. I rise exactly at seven o'clock, whether I've been up all night or managed to sleep for two or three hours. I don't need an alarm clock, instead what always awakens me is a sound forever stored in my memory. My dad clearing his throat outside my door.

07

Today in the woods of Annín I found my first bolete, and it's only May! This is very unusual for the Bohemian Forest. It was a little pine bolete that would fit into the palm of one's hand. It was hiding in the moss next to a young pine. I examined him with delight, then stroked his brown cap, tickled his chubby leg, and covered him with a bit of grass, so that nobody else would find him and the little bolete would have enough time to grow up and release its spores. I do this with every first mushroom I find.

It seemed a harbinger of an excellent year.

But no sooner had I parted with the little bolete, my good mood was dashed. My cell phone rang in my pocket. It was Evžen. During the last seven years that I have been living in Dvorce, he hasn't called me once. In fact, apart from a few curt exchanges, we have never spoken. I imagined him starting to bark at me through the telephone and stuck it back into my pocket.

I continued along my usual trajectory, but didn't come across any more mushrooms. I was in such a bad mood, that this time I bypassed the double stump on the riverbank and from Annín headed directly north, back to Sušice. My basket was half empty and I hoped I might still fill it. Perhaps in the fields I would find a few button mushrooms or sheathed woodtufts that the Walrus could toss into a soup.

Halfway between Annín and Sušice my eldest brother phoned again. That is, I assume it was him, the number that came up on the display was my mother's. I guess he really needed to talk to me. It had to be because of the inheritance, I couldn't think of any other reason. Maybe the lawyer told him he couldn't just cut me out, and he wanted to make a deal with me. But that could wait. I had no wish to completely ruin my day by having a conversation with my eldest brother.

I let the phone ring and looked at the picture of my mother that popped up on my cell. On my phone I had deliberately saved a photograph of my mother from the period *after*, when she was no longer young and beautiful. When she no longer looked like my older sister but like a wilted old matron with a sagging body.

And now suddenly that mom was looking at me from the screen. With big baby brown eyes that hadn't changed even after 30 extra kilos. She had on a big smile, maybe a bit too big. I preferred to tuck the cell phone back inside my pocket and continued on my way. Even so, it burned a hole in my pocket the whole time. *Missed call: Mom.* I imagined that it was really her calling me from beyond the grave, wanting to tell me something I had been waiting to hear for years.

The thought had me so agitated that I missed some of my spots along the Otava, and apparently missed out on some potential spoils. I only managed to add a few St George's Mushrooms and false morels, but as for button mushrooms, I didn't come across a single one, let alone any more boletes.

But the worst was yet to come. That afternoon when, with a humbled expression, I handed my basket to the Walrus, there suddenly appeared in the doorway to the restaurant a thirty-something-year-old guy with wavy hair, long in the back and nondescript in colour, wearing camouflage pants and a khaki cargo vest. With the words: 'Hi, I'm Ruda, don't you recognize me?' he held out his hand that was as clammy as a slimy spike-cap.

'Tichá, nice to meet you,' I murmured and he made a face.

'Hey, this isn't the Alcron Hotel, is it? First-name basis, OK?' and snickered.

He sized me up from top to bottom, and back up again. That's what men do, it's a gesture of superiority. A girl is supposed to lower her eyes demurely and look embarrassed. And that's exactly what I did, although I'd rather have looked him brazenly in the eye. As I looked down at the scuffed tips of my hiking boots, I tried to remember from where I knew him.

Ruda reached for the basket that I had set down in the kitchen and peered inside. He asked me if I would bring him up to speed, these were mushrooms he didn't know very well and he'd like to learn more, after all he needed to know how things worked around here, seeing as he was the new manager, and now practically the owner.

Right then I finally was able to connect his face with a specific memory. Ruda had to be the son of old Voboříl, the proprietor of the Toadstool, who apparently had been whisked off again to some rehab facility for alcoholics. Already seven years ago, when I got back from the hospital, he was saying he would turn the pub over to the kid.

I remembered how once Ruda had passed my dad and me in the woods on a stinky old Pionýr motorbike that was making an incredible racket because Ruda didn't know how to shift into a higher gear. 'That's not a hobby, that's a diagnosis,' my dad had declared, barely managing to get out of his way by leaping into the bushes.

It was clear to me that Voboříl had to send over a surrogate to keep the joint going, but I couldn't believe that of all people he would send Ruda, who didn't understand a thing about mushrooms. My dad always used to tease him, saying he couldn't tell the difference between a milkcap and a piece of horse manure.

The new manager carefully examined the contents of the basket, asking what each mushroom was good for, all the while jotting down my answers in a little notebook that he pulled out from the breast pocket of his khaki vest. Finally, he turned to me and asked how much

I expected to get for *this*. I said I would like 300 crowns, at which Ruda whistled and shook his head. No shooting from the hip like that, they'll have to be separated according to type and weighed. And what about bookkeeping, where were the income and expense ledgers? Furthermore, we'll need to keep a mushroom log, what's growing when, and plan ahead. And what did you say these weird slimy mushrooms were, sheathed woodtufts? I'm not going to get any *clients* in here with those, it's going to take something substantial, some nice boletes. I pointed out that boletes aren't in season yet, and that one can't command the forest to produce whatever strikes one's fancy, but Ruda wasn't listening, he clapped shut his notebook and tucked it back into his pocket. Over the weekend he had reviewed the pub's papers, he said in a meaningful tone, assessed its evolution over the past five years, and after careful consideration had concluded that we're just a bunch of dilettantes. But that was now going to change. What the Toadstool needs is to raise its standards, he explained to me, world-class gastronomy is going strong everywhere else, but here we're still used to the socialist order. This joint simply needs a new concept, something fresh, with its own flair. I glanced over at the Walrus, but he was studying the stains on his greasy apron.

'From now on, we're going to step it up,' Ruda added, giving a little stomp with his foot to emphasize his determination.

I stared at him, at his pompously arched eyebrows and bared teeth, then let my gaze slip down to the swanky khaki vest and protruding round belly, which looked as if it could hold a keg full of beer, and at his wavy hair, which fanned out from his neck to his shoulders.

I was beside myself with fury at what he was saying. It was true that things at the pub were going from bad to worse, but worse was still better than nothing. Old Vobořil had spent twenty-five years building this place up, and even though he was an alcoholic, who more than once had drunk through his proceeds, his pub was one of the traditional Sušice establishments, and now some arrogant fop was going to ruin it. What made me even more furious was that I'd had to meet Ruda today of all days, when the basket I had dropped off was only half full. And only of remnants.

I ended up taking home 150 crowns in coins. I didn't bother stopping at the convenience store, with such miserable earnings I couldn't even afford to. At home I grabbed an unlabelled jar of preserves from the pantry. Opening it up, I discovered that I had landed on currant jam. Over the years that it had sat in the cupboard, all of the moisture had evaporated leaving a solidified gelatinous cylinder in the middle of the jar. It took a long time of beating my fork in the mason jar to get water to recombine with the gelatine. I spread the jam on the end of a loaf of bread left over from the weekend. As I chewed on the hard crust, dark thoughts raced through my head. I was afraid that after today's fiasco Ruda would show me the door and I would lose my shabby little shack in Dvorce, which was my only real home. If I lost my position at the Toadstool, I would be hard pressed to find another restaurant that would buy so many mushrooms. I would have to start pleading with the greengrocers or maybe set up my own stand at the farmer's market, but I'm not up for that. Without the Toadstool I was sunk, and even a dimwit like Ruda could see as much. After all, I didn't know how to do anything but gather mushrooms, and even if I did, what good would it do me, I have it written at home in a drawer, black on white, that I am unable to work. Even though for some time now I've been planning to leave Dvorce, I haven't yet been ready.

Walking up the stairs I sighed out loud. I knew what was going to happen over the next few hours behind the door of my bedroom. Instead of sleeping I would be tossing and turning on the uncomfortable mattress, tormenting myself with visions of losing my job, ending up on the street, or worse—in a room with a row of beds and windows that cannot be opened.

08

In the Bohemian Forest one usually has to wait until July, sometimes even until August, for the first mushroom harvest, but this year was exceptional in many ways. Maybe the mushrooms sprouted so early thanks to the mild winter, or because of the alternating warm and rainy days this spring. Who knows. But right now, demolishing that splendour, were herds of mushroom gatherers.

Over the years that I've been encountering them, I've divided them into several categories. The most common variety of mushroom gatherer that I meet on my forays is the *wuss*. He sticks with the safe bet, which is why he generally picks only spongy mushrooms, namely boletes. Mushrooms that have a tubular hymenium, or gills, he'll leave alone, in case they are poisonous toadstools.

The second widespread group are the *patriots*. They don't gather mushrooms because they like them, but because it's the *Czech* thing to do. They go in groups, because for them picking mushrooms isn't an intimate affair, but a bolstering of the collective consciousness. They set off to hunt mushrooms with a wicker basket and a penknife in the shape of a fish, and in the evening, they order a mushroom scramble made with butter, onions and caraway seeds, eat local rye bread and drink beer.

The *hunter* is, of all the categories, the most like me. He sets off to hunt early in the morning and he doesn't care whether he gathers mushrooms in a canvas bag or in a basket, that's not what it's all about. For a hunter, it's all about trophies. When an amateur looks into his basket, he is unable to name a single mushroom. Meanwhile I know perfectly well whether he has managed to snag an Old Man of the Woods, an apricot bolete or a golden waxcap.

The final category is represented by the *rednecks*, the mushroom riffraff. Twice a year, the redneck grabs a plastic bag and heads into the nearest forest. As a rule he doesn't bring a knife, he simply rips the mushrooms out of the earth, twists off the end of the foot with the soil, and wipes his dirty hands on his fatigues. And usually, he'll toss the mushroom straight into the plastic bag, whether there are slugs on it, pine needles, or whatever else, it gets eaten, it's nature. He doesn't care if the mushroom is wormy, gnawed or mouldy. He calls all brown mushrooms porcinis or ceps and all the pinkish ones blushers.

No matter to what extent the individual categories might differ, they have one thing in common. They are insatiable. Their feet hurt, they've consumed their snacks long before noon, they've guzzled every plastic bottle down to the last drop, and their basket is overflowing, but they keep on combing the trail with their eyes, ducking every now and then into the woods. Just one more mushroom, the very last one!

Like my father, I too considered all mushroom hunters to be a scourge.

And suddenly, I had this self-proclaimed mushroom hunter on my back. He tried to keep up with me, mopping his sweaty forehead and every few steps letting loose a mild expletive. The flip-flops on his bare feet were slapping against his sweaty heels, the collapsible canvas basket with its metal handle rustled against the branches and tall grass. Every other minute Ruda would have to stop, bend down and swat a mosquito that had bitten his bare calves. Damn pest! Aside from that he kept pulling out his cell phone, into which he would always type something, and then take a picture of the mushroom, and finally tuck the phone back into the small pocket of his khaki vest. He lingered over each mushroom, asking questions like a little kid. Things like, can one dry a parasol!

'Ruda, do you want me to take the photo for you?'

'No, I have to do this myself.'

And I, practically doing it in my pants, pitiful suck-up, nodded with a smile as if I understood. As we walked, I even held back twigs to keep them from scraping his calves: 'Pay attention over here, Ruda!' and I'd pretend not to see mushrooms over which I practically tripped. I had to endure his breathing down my neck and the way he kept slowing me down with his cell phone.

Not far from Hartmanice, I began to get suspicious. Was he texting someone? Was he sending out selfies of himself with the mushrooms? Was he recording what I was saying about the mushrooms? At my favourite mushroom-gathering spot, near the double stump on the piney slope, I nonchalantly stepped back and glanced over Ruda's shoulder. I froze and caught my breath.

Ruda was saving the GPS coordinates of the locations where we had found the most mushrooms. All my years of work could amount to nothing! All my hiding places would be revealed to the world at large!

He looked back over his shoulder and gave me a wink.

The idea had come to him still back at home, but now, along the way, he had thought it through down to the minutest detail. On the top floor of the pub, where his father had lived, there would be a flat for tourists from the city, whom I would guide through the woods and teach them how to forage for mushrooms. I have the know-how and he has the organizational talent. We'll turn mushroom hunting into an interactive game. After all, these days mushrooms are totally *in*, today everyone wants to eat local, natural food, it's simply a goldmine.

'But I don't even know how . . .' I protested timidly.

Except that Ruda was so hyped up by the idea that he wasn't listening to me at all. He grabbed me by the shoulders and looked me right in the eye. He was standing so close to me that I had to lean back. 'It's going to be a blast,' he grinned at me encouragingly. A fortune, he was going to make a bloody fortune! And now, I'd better head on home, the sooner he starts the better. He'll post the photos on Facebook and send out a *mushroom alert!*

09

As long as I can remember, everyone complimented my dad on having picked such a pretty wife. Mother was very short in stature, I caught up to her by the time I was not quite twelve years old, so with her petite and slim figure she looked like a schoolgirl. Her eyes were large, her lips full and her bleached yellow hair always shiny and perfectly done. Once I heard two of Dad's faculty colleagues, whom he had invited over for dinner, talking about her. They were standing in the great room, each with a glass of white wine, observing with pleasure, Mom in the kitchen in her tight white blouse, as she stacked the dirty dishes into the dishwasher. She looks like a *little girl*, commented one, while the other one licked his lips. Dad must have heard them too, because he quickly went over to Mom, hugged her from behind and then gently caressed her breasts. I clearly saw the palm of his hand slide along Mom's stomach all the way down, to *that place* one doesn't touch, and then he patted her bottom. Mother lowered her eyes and blushed. Today, I could no longer say with certainty that it was out of modesty.

In fact, Dad's colleagues had it wrong. Mother was no innocent *little girl*. Behind her childish appearance there was cold calculation. It was the most salient point on her professional CV. Mom had only a high-school diploma in home economics, and in her entire life had worked for just two years as an assistant waitress in a restaurant in

Bratislava. And that was also where our father found her, when instead of a beef carpaccio she served him halušky with brynza cheese and then with an 'L' so soft that it would melt in one's mouth, asked him please not to tell her boss, that she was already in hot water. In her shallow beseeching eyes, father found what he had long been looking for. Back at the faculty he quickly put in for another business trip to Slovakia, and as soon as he stepped off the train he headed straight for that restaurant. On his third visit to Bratislava, he brought her home. 'I like to bring a prize back from every business trip,' he used to say with a laugh and Mom would always give him a gentle smack on the back. 'A calumet from Mexico, a Persian rug from Iran, and from Slovakia, Magdaléna!' They were married less than a year later, little Evžen already hiding under Mom's loose dress. And when little Evžen grew up enough for Mom to have to start looking around for a job, her stomach swelled up again. And after Milan, I joined the family. Once again, we were two years apart. Mom was relieved, after two sons finally a girl, whom she could dress up however she liked. After that, all she had to do was keep fanning the little flame under our problems—Evžen's asthma, Milan's dyslexia and my shyness—and no one asked her about a job any more. Nor did she have any intention of going to look for one. Any employment that she could find given her education and experience would appear ridiculous beside a dean and later a vice-rector.

Her job description became taking care of the children, our father and the house. And above all, herself. Her body flexed muscles, fasted, lifted weights, vibrated on a platform, stretched, sunbathed, absorbed moisturizing creams and underwent detox. And so it stayed young, pretty and toned. Rouge on her cheeks, straw-yellow hair, cut in a bob with a long strand tucked behind her ear, and an above-the-knee dress with an empire waist, that was mom's girlish dress code, her work uniform. She was perfectly groomed under all circumstances. Even in her first picture with me, which is tucked along with the other photos behind the cupboard glass. She is sitting up in the hospital bed leaning back against the pillow and smiling into the lens. If it wasn't for the small bundle in her arms, no one would believe that she had just spent several hours in childbirth. Her hair is perfectly styled, and if one looks closely, one can see that she is wearing mascara on her eyelashes. All that can be seen of me in that picture, on the other hand, is a little bit of my ear and one tiny hand. The rest is wrapped up in swaddling clothes.

I was proud of my mom. I was never embarrassed when she held my hand on the way to school, I liked her short wide skirt and her shiny hair falling over one eye. She looked nothing at all like the other moms whose breasts, when they would pick up my classmates after school, would be bouncing around in bulging bras, and when they would squat down in the locker room to tie their shoes, their enormous buttocks would spill out of their pants. Then there were the others, on whom you could see, outlined under their canvas pants, tendons like branching pipes, and whose dry skin around their eyes creased into unattractive folds. When my mom walked past them, slight, slender and supple, without a single wrinkle on her face, they frowned in anger. But my mother never even deigned to look at their frowning faces. Her smooth complexion deflected all of the contemptuous stares. As if it were made of porcelain. We would always leave the locker room as a pair, hand in hand, but when in the hallway I had to let go to zip up my jacket, my mom stuck her hand in her pocket and continued on without even looking back at me. I then had to catch up to her and wheedle my way back into her palm.

Mom carried out all the tasks that were expected of her. She cooked a fresh meal every day, Friday morning she vacuumed and mopped the floors, Monday she took me to my flute lesson, Wednesday she took Milan to ping-pong, and Evžen to football practice the next day. She made sure that Milan never forgot his homework and that Evžen wouldn't stay up watching TV late into the night. Before we left for school, she always made sure my shirt was properly tucked in so that I wouldn't catch a chill in my kidneys. But I always had the feeling that her mind was somewhere else. She basically did everything that was needed, except it always seemed half-hearted, as if her thoughts had wandered off to some faraway place, and she was present only in her body.

'What happened in school today?' she asked me every afternoon, and I would answer her. She would nod along, tapping her long, polished nails on the kitchen countertop and keeping her face turned towards the window. My first two years in school I didn't pay much attention, but gradually her absent-mindedness began to annoy me. I would tell her nonsense: 'For lunch today we had moles with plums,' and 'Today in art class Janička's head fell off,' and she would just smile: 'That must have been nice,' she said. 'That's very good.'

It was the same with everything, Mom always had one foot in the house and the other somewhere up in the clouds.

And so, it went on until the moment that her ethereal body materialized to the point of falling out of the sky and hitting the ground hard. A few days after the New Year, mother slipped clumsily on the stairs that she herself had waxed earlier and fractured her femoral neck. An accident that happens mostly to pensioners. We went to visit her in the hospital, Dad brought her an enormous bouquet. Mom looked tired, but she was as well groomed as ever—her hair was freshly washed, her face powdered, the ribbon on her nightgown meticulously tied, and the duvet on her bed as smooth as a sheet of paper. But she was in a bad mood because she couldn't move properly, and she was also a bit angry about how Dad had dressed us—it was January and we had neither hats nor scarves. On top of it, Milan's pants were completely soiled because outside he had fallen into the slush.

After three weeks they finally let her go home. With our help she hobbled from the car into the house. Already in the doorway our laziness hit her smack in the nose, during the entire time nobody had vacuumed, done the washing, or aired out the house. After all, it wasn't a man's job, said Dad, and I was still too little to do it.

On the threshold of the kitchen Mom gasped. On the counter were stacks of Styrofoam boxes from ready-made food, the embroidered tablecloth that her mother had given her as part of her dowry was strewn with pizza crusts, the floor was covered with sticky stains and dust bunnies had accumulated in the corners.

'The main thing now is for you to rest,' said Dad grabbing her around the shoulders. 'All of this will wait.'

I noticed that Mom clenched one of her fists and narrowed her eyes. She tapped the toe of her healthy foot on the floor, but then relaxed her fist, lifted the corners of her mouth into a smile and hobbled over to the sofa in the living room. She tapped out her anger on the parquet floor with her elbow crutches. She collapsed on the sofa and asked us for some tea. Black tea with lemon and one, or just this once, two cubes of sugar.

She hoped that she would heal quickly so that she could put the house back in order. But her leg wasn't healing well, her joint developed an infection and she had to go back into the hospital. During the two weeks she was there, we went to visit Mom in the hospital only once. This time without a bouquet of roses. Dad spoke at length with the doctor, rubbing his moustache and furrowing his brow, while Mom looked much more wilted than last time, her hair dishevelled and her face oily. She didn't even try to smile. The conversation lagged, which is why we quickly excused ourselves from the visit and headed back home.

When our mom came home for the second time, she was still having a hard time moving around. She was embarrassed to be limping on her right foot like an old lady and to be needing to use crutches to support herself. Dad told her that he was sure it would get better soon, because after all she was still young and in no time would be as pretty and agile as before, and then they would go out together and see people again, but he didn't take her into his arms as much or caress her breasts as he had done before.

Mother spent most of the day in a horizontal position. She lay on the sofa and stuffed herself. Maybe she was making up for all those years of starving herself to keep her figure. Over the course of a few months, she gorged herself on all the things she had denied herself over the past fifteen years. And suddenly, this cute little girl with a freckled nose who had been Dad's crown jewel began to transform into an overripe, overweight matron. Her lithe youthful body began to swell, billowing out on the sofa and spilling over the edge of the upholstery. It was as if a portrait of a Renaissance beauty had been retouched by a drunken Baroque painter. As soon as I close my eyes, I can see her ample figure on the sofa by the television, an already bitten bun in one hand, and resting on her stomach another whole roll, she would always butter two at a time so that she wouldn't have to get up. Every other moment she would reach with her free hand for the mug that she had ready on the table. A medicinal herbal tea, she told us, good for the joints, but the herbs in it were scant, and she poured hot water over the tea bag only halfway, and filled up the rest with rum or Becherovka.

Even our household began little by little to change. In the pantry, the rye flour, unhulled lentils and unsulfured dried apricots were replaced by bags of chips, cinnamon cornflakes and spreadable chocolate. Groceries were randomly stashed away, cartons and cans were falling all over, piling up on the floor were boxes, jars of preserves and wine bottles, as if we were preparing for a war. When opening the overflowing refrigerator, I perfected a special trick—each time, I would instinctively extend my foot towards the fridge, so that I could deflect any potentially falling object with my instep. To get at my yogurt, I first had to pull out sticks of butter, pudding desserts and fatty cheeses, and then put them all back in.

Our once-hardworking mom now spent entire days in front of the television, watching endless soap operas. Even later, after her femoral neck had healed to the point that she no longer needed crutches to walk, she would spend up to several hours a day lying down on the sofa. She would watch the infomercials and started to order exercise equipment, weight-loss products and slimming underwear, in which she looked like a sausage being strangled by a bandage. And then she would eat out of desperation because none of that stuff worked.

That's how it was when Dad was away. In his absence, she would give free rein to the tacit defiance stored up over the years. She gave herself fully over to her gluttony, stuffing every last crevice in her already very bloated body.

As the hour of Dad's return home would approach, however, she would brush the crumbs off her chest, wipe her greasy lips with a napkin and hobble off to the kitchen to clean up any plates and leftovers. Her emancipation was limited to the times when our father was away. Huffing and puffing she swept the floor, ran a rag over the sticky spots on the counter and hid the mug of medicinal tea in the pantry. At the squeak of the gate, she straightened up her back, sucked in her stomach and stretched her lips into a smile. Punctually at seven, she served dinner on the table, same as always, as if nothing in the family had changed, and during our evening ritual we experienced a temporary whiff of normalcy.

Even Dad eased up for a moment, he took his place at the head of the table, let himself be served the soup, sniffed and tasted. After a few spoonfuls, he started to frown again. I saw him keeping an eye on my mother, the greasy soup glistening in the corners of her mouth. She had served herself just enough to cover the bottom of her dish in a show of goodwill, but we all knew that once the table was cleared, back in the kitchen she would scrape and finish any leftovers from our plates as if that didn't count.

I watched my father as he listened to her chewing and swallowing. It seemed to me that with every slurp she stabbed him in the back. Out of the corner of his eye he noted how she had dribbled down her chin and tried to dry it with her napkin.

'I chilled a Pilsner for you,' Mother tried to dilute the aspic-like atmosphere.

But she couldn't get Dad to soften up. Every other minute he would drop a comment about lard, hogs and fattening, while my brothers and I sat in silence staring at our plates and inhaling our soup so that we could get this over with quickly and go hide in our rooms. Our throats were burning, but it wasn't because of the pepper in the soup.

'Go easy on the food,' Dad muttered through his teeth, while Mom just kept smiling, although she gave a little start as though she had sat down on the tip of a larding needle.

'For our main course we're having duck with cabbage and dumplings,' she went on, still trying to butter up Dad. Except Dad couldn't last until the main course, he never ate the Hungarian goulash, the marinated sirloin with cream sauce, or even the stuffed potato dumplings. Before we had a chance to finish, he threw his spoon into the bowl, splashing the soup all over, swiftly stood up, and retreated to his study, slamming the door so hard that we jumped in fright.

'Milan darling, the elbow doesn't belong on the table,' Mom went on smiling and darling Milan drew back his hand so fast, he practically knocked his plate to the floor.

The nightly fights, the slamming doors and all the other sounds that to a child mean the end of the world, I took in through my bedroom door that wouldn't close properly. Mostly it was my dad who did the shouting, Mom spoke in a muffled voice and then sobbed out loud.

But the next day in the morning we all assembled for breakfast, good and proper, and Mom piled buttered bread or plum buns onto our plates. Both she and Dad wore starched smiles, as if everything was in the most perfect order, and we knew better than to ask. We all sat obediently in our chairs, and the buns in our hands blocked our view of Mom's eyes, swollen with crying, that she tried in vain to conceal with powder and mascara.

As time went on, it became unbearable. We three preferred to stay out after school to avoid the stifling atmosphere at home. Even Dad would come home from work later and later, usually already after dark. There were no more dinners around the oval table with napkins beside the silverware.

In those days, my dad would often come at night to visit me in my room. He would sit beside the bed, put his hand on my foot or on my side, and remain silent. The soft light from the street filtered into the room through the curtain, and I could see his tall silhouette settled in my little armchair, he was still slim, but with age he had acquired a little potbelly that clashed with his otherwise slender figure. It looked as though he was hiding a ball under his shirt. I couldn't see his features, they were submerged in the shadows, but according to how he turned his head, the beams from the headlights of the cars passing through the street would fall on different parts of his face. This is how I've kept him in my memory to this day. If I were to reconstruct an identity sketch of him, I would be able to accurately describe his eyes, nose, mouth and chin. I know that his hairline was receding and that his fair, thinning hair stood up on the crown of his head, but I wouldn't be able to turn that cubist image into a coherent portrait. For me my father will forever remain a figure partially shrouded in shadow, crisscrossed by narrow strips of light.

Back then I wanted to say something encouraging to him, but my words got stuck in my throat every time. One time in bed when I was again pondering how I could break the silence, I got up and hugged him. At first Dad resisted, but then he drew me close and buried his face in my hair. I was overwhelmed by an intense feeling of pity and compassion. At the same time, I felt a blast of fear. Dad was holding me so tightly, I could barely breathe. I was afraid he would crush me, I tried to wriggle free of his grip, but at the same time I didn't want to let him go, so as not to hurt him. Finally, he let go of me and left. I climbed back into bed and in my mind I berated my mother for how she had transformed my dad. For what she had done to our family.

I could swear that nobody ever said the word out loud, but even so it was constantly in the air. *Divorce*. Each of us dealt with that nonexistent ubiquitous word in our own way. Evžen tried to rise above it. He would saunter through the living room with his hands in his pockets while softly whistling. 'So, any more yowling today?' he would ask Milan, coming home late from practice. The word 'yowling' was a technical term in our family. Because in fact, there was yowling almost every day. Then when Milan would rattle off the insults our father had hurled at our mother that day, Evžen would snicker. If I hadn't once accidentally caught him in the attic, I might even have believed the expression on his face. After yet another messed-up Sunday lunch, I had gone up to the attic. I needed a moment alone. It was the very first time I had been brave enough to go up to the attic by myself. But I wasn't the only one who had wanted to hole up somewhere that afternoon. Evžen was sitting all the way in the back corner, his elbows on his knees, his forehead resting against his thighs. 'What are you staring at, you cow? Beat it!' he barked at me, but by then I had already noticed his reddened eyes in the semi-darkness. Besides sadness, they burned with hatred. For the fact that I had seen him like this.

Milan dealt with the situation the best of all. He relished the fact that the strict regime at home had become relaxed. He slacked off at school and on the guitar, and secretly snuck coins from a drawer in the kitchen. And when our father would lock himself in his study while our mother ran crying into her bedroom, he would put his feet up on the low marble table in the living room, set his plate down on the leather sofa, and turn on the television.

I focused all of my negative emotions on that matron, the one who had swallowed our mother. Wasn't she the one to blame for all our problems? I was angry with her and did all kinds of things to her out of spite. When we were outside, I would run away from her past the corner of the block, and would laugh at her for the way she waddled down the street like a duck, trying to find me. I poured vinegar into her bottle of sweet syrup, soaked a bottle of wine in the toilet, and spat into the apricot preserves. I switched around her channels and then, through the glass door to the living room, watched with glee as she furiously pressed the remote and cursed. I dumped baking powder into the bag of peanuts she kept hidden under the cushion on the sofa. And then by evening I always regretted it.

But what troubled me most of all was the fear that because of the disagreements between my parents we wouldn't go to Dvorce.

10

It was a beautiful sunny weekend at the start of the summer holiday. My fourth-grade report card was in my room, tucked in the drawer of my writing desk in a folder that nobody had opened. I had packed already the night before.

Saturday morning I was awakened by the purr of an engine. From the window I could see the car, which Dad had pulled out of the garage onto the driveway and into which he had started to load the luggage. All excited, I ran down the stairs. Less than an hour later we were on our way, heading to Sušice.

Sunday morning looked promising, and I was practically breathless with joy when around seven I heard my father's cough behind my door. I shot out of bed like an arrow, I didn't even have to get dressed, after all I'd been expecting Dad for a good hour.

At the end of the village we held hands and stepped into the forest. We walked along our usual path, passing the same trees, treading the same moss, and stopping in the same places. We were doing exactly the same things as on any other mushroom hunting day, and yet everything was completely different. Dad strode briskly, I could barely keep up with him. He pulled me by the hand, deeper and deeper into the forest, as if our path was a direct line to a precise point. He passed by all of our stopping spots. I tried, as best as I could, to ask him about the various mushrooms, but it was useless, his eyes were fixed directly in front of him, he never made a sound. He didn't even notice a pair of nice bluing boletes growing right next to the trail.

Midway through our course, there weren't even a dozen mushrooms in our basket yet. And then in the woods by Annín I saw a nest of lurid boletes. I broke away from my dad's grip and started picking one after another. Hopefully they would make him happy, they were fresh and not nibbled. Carefully, just the way Dad taught me, I cut off the dirty tip of each stem, cleaned the pine needles off the caps and turned to put them into Dad's basket.

In that instant I froze. I looked all around—no one in sight. I looked around again and stood up on my tiptoes so I could see better. He might have just bent down for a mushroom or was standing just behind the trunk of a tree. I called out to my dad several times. Nothing.

There was no doubt, Dad had abandoned me. He had left me completely alone in the middle of the forest. He had led me deep into the wilderness and deserted me there. And yet he knew full well that I struggled to find my way in the forest, just a few steps off the trail and I was lost. I set off in the direction that I thought was the right one. At first, I walked very slowly, looking around attentively so that I wouldn't accidentally miss him, but my heart kept pounding harder, I sped up, and finally broke into a run. Dad was still nowhere in sight. The lurid boletes tumbled out of my hand at the first root over which I tripped, but I left them there and hurried on.

I tried to orient myself according to the sun. I could feel it beating down on my back through the trees, but when moments later I stumbled across the spilled lurid boletes, I realized that I was going around in a circle.

My feet hurt from the long trek and my calves were scraped up by the blackberries. I squatted down and burst into tears.

I must have been crouching there for about half an hour before I managed to calm myself. I sat down on the moss and wiped away the tears with the back of my hand. Then I lay on my back and fixed my eyes on the sky above my head. The sight was reassuring. The blue sky flashing through the branches of the spruces. The hushed rustle of the trees. And in that stillness I suddenly heard something familiar. It was really true! I heard water! Somewhere down below a river was burbling, it had to be the Otava. If I followed the current, it would take me all the way back home! Maybe Dad was waiting for me there—lost in thought as he was, he must have walked on and then hadn't been able to find me, of course, how could I even have imagined that he would leave me here. Maybe he thought I went back home. By now, they were bound to be looking for me.

Full of hope, I made my way down the slope. My sore feet, that a moment ago had almost given out on me, obediently started to move again. My scratched calves and the blisters on my feet were hurting, but the pain was much duller than before, and the prospect of getting home made it bearable. Before I reached the riverbed, however, I stopped short. Something wasn't right. There was someone sitting on the double stump on the bank beneath the tall pines.

It had to be Dad, he was wearing Dad's clothes, but still I hesitated. The person on the stump seemed a complete stranger to me. He was as bent as the pine tree above him, his elbow propped on his thigh, his head resting on his fist. He sat still as a statue and his eyes were fixed on me. He was looking at me in a completely different way than he ever had before. He was staring at me as if I was someone he was seeing for the first time in his life.

I wanted to call out to him, to reassure myself that it was really him, but I couldn't get out even a peep. I was frightened by his sad look. Something must have happened to him, maybe he got hurt in the woods. I wanted to go to him, but my body wouldn't listen, it resisted like an animal that had caught wind of a dangerous beast of prey. I couldn't pry my feet away from where I stood.

Finally I managed to force myself to move, slowly approached my dad, and after a moment's hesitation, hugged him. I felt as if I was embracing a cold stone. But then the boulder moved and grabbed me around the shoulders. Dad pulled me down to the stump, drew me close and buried his face into my hair.

And finally my father, Prof. Ing. Evžen Tichý, PhD, the dean of faculty—with whom people had to book appointments weeks in advance and then sat in the secretary's office, knees clamped together, wiping their sweaty palms on their trousers—broke into loud sobs.

It made me feel anxious. I didn't know him like this. His embrace was suffocating me, I could barely breathe, but I didn't want to wrench myself out of his arms, so as not to disappoint him.

Then I looked into his basket and I knew nothing would ever be the same again.

11

There are only a few. The deadly skullcap, fool's webcap, deadly fibrecap, fool's mushroom, spring destroying angel. And the queen of them all: the death cap. It is the cause of the highest number of deaths by poisoning in our country each year. She prefers deciduous forests, but from time to time won't disdain a forest of pines. Loathing solitude, she surrounds herself with ladies in waiting from the same lineage. She is said to be very tasty, more delicious than any other mushroom. In fact, it is said that on their deathbeds, many have claimed never to have eaten a tastier mushroom scramble in their lives.

Except for two snakes, it is nature's most poisonous creation, not even the cobra is more pernicious. With the exception of rabbits, its poison is lethal to all other species of mammals. After two or three days of diarrhoea and vomiting, relief sets in, but that's merely the toadstool granting its victim a brief respite. While the sick person rejoices in his recovery, his liver and kidneys are turning to mush. Soon after, the poisoned person falls asleep, never to awaken again.

No other mushroom leaves me so unsettled. When I come across it, I set down my basket and crouch down beside it. Sometimes I feel the urge to pick it and place it in my basket among the other mushrooms. To bring it all the way home, slice it up and add it to my scramble. So far, though, I've held myself back every time. I just stare at it with respect.

Just like the time I saw it in Dad's basket. We returned from the piney hill, once more holding hands. He was gripping my palm so tightly that I fought the temptation to wrench myself free, although at the same time I was afraid to let go of him. In the meantime, I kept on peeking into the basket he carried in his other hand. The toadstool was rolling around on the bottom among a few other specimens we had found that day.

At home Dad wordlessly set the basket down in the hallway and shut himself in the bedroom. Mom was sitting with my two brothers outside on the porch playing cards, and called out for me to join them. I wasn't in the mood for playing; I grabbed the basket and went into the kitchen. I had to keep staring at the mushroom, I couldn't understand what it was supposed to mean. How could Dad make such a mistake? After all, he was *the best mushroom gatherer in the world!* Maybe I was simply wrong, I tried to convince myself, and to make sure, pulled the mushroom atlas off the shelf.

I grabbed the mushroom and examined it carefully in my hand. The whitish cap tended towards olive green, a shade not seen on any other brittlegill. With my finger I lifted the rim of its cap to make sure that the gills underneath were indeed deathly white, as I expected. Had they been brownish, it could have been a button mushroom. The final irrefutable proof of Dad's mistake was the ring and chalice of death on the tip of its foot.

At that very moment I heard a door behind me creak on its hinges. I jumped and tossed the mushroom back into the basket.

It was Dad. Without even looking at me, he picked up a cutting board and started to take one mushroom after another out of the basket. He cut them into cubes that he tossed into a plastic bowl. First, he would carefully run the knife over each cap to clean off the last remnants of pine needles and dirt. He did this with the toadstool as well. He showed no hesitation at all and cut it up into the same neat little cubes as the other mushrooms. As if with that penknife, knocking sharply against the cutting board, he was chopping off time. I was incapable of uttering a single word and just stood there obtusely, trying to make sense of this enigma.

Dad finished cutting up the mushrooms and left the bowl with them standing on the countertop. There were just about enough mushrooms to make a scramble for one person. He finely chopped the onion and threw it into a small saucepan with butter. He broke several eggs into a cup and beat them. Beside them he placed a small bag of ground caraway seeds.

I forced my petrified body to move. I gently took the wooden cooking spoon out of his hand and with my hip nudged him away from the stove. He didn't protest. He stood by the stove a little longer, observing as I poured the mushrooms from the bowl onto the glossy onions. I added some water, sprinkled the caraway seeds, and covered the pot with a lid. Dad nodded, as if to indicate that I had done it right, and then turned and left the kitchen. I removed the lid, stirred the contents and knocked the wooden spoon as loudly as possible against the side of the pot. As soon as I heard the bedroom door slam, I turned up the gas.

Later, when my mom burst into the kitchen, she threw up her hands and started to berate me: 'That pot is going to have to be thrown out, there's no way to clean it, you really are a klutz, what an idea, to leave the cooking to a little girl,' she railed as she tried to scrape the burnt mushrooms from the saucepan that she had thrust into the sink. Dad also peeked out of the bedroom. He continued to say nothing, but I had a feeling that I saw the hint of a smile flicker across his face.

For dinner our mother served us bread with apple compote. 'I can't whip something up at the last minute just like that...' The compote was already several years old, only vaguely reminiscent of apples, more like a brown overcooked mush. I wouldn't have been at all surprised if my mother had scraped off a layer of mould from the top first. The spoon slowly sank into that sloppy mush, the taste of which, no matter how hard one tried, had nothing in common with apples. Meanwhile I was keeping an eye on Dad, who was sprawled on the chaise, his face turned towards the television. The evening news had just come on but his eyes were fixed elsewhere and he couldn't have seen any of it at all.

Maybe it was just a test, I thought. Dad had tried to give me a sign and I had deciphered it. I was proud of myself for having succeeded. For having proved to him that I wasn't a zilch, but a true mushroom gatherer, who wouldn't be fooled just like that.

12

I hate when I have to deviate from my path for whatever reason. Like today, for instance.

Ruda unearthed from somewhere an old, yellowed cookbook that had been his father's, and wrote up a list of what mushrooms I should pick. He said he needed to know in advance what would be cooked and when. This business of cooking according to whatever I happened to find had no prospects. Soon it would be summer, so we had to collect as many spring mushrooms as possible while they were still growing. Take a morel: it would be a shame not to have them on the menu. Up to now we've never had any morel specialties, we've just added them to soups, and that seems a shame. Krušina can make us a ragout, a soup and a cream sauce, and on the menu, we'll put Czech truffles, hahaha. Krušina and I tried to object that the very essence of the Toadstool was that customers came in out of curiosity to see what would be on offer that day, and that in general, mushrooms did not grow on command. So far this hadn't been a good year for morels and besides, it was probably too late for them by now. Lately it had been pretty warm, spring mushrooms were almost gone, it was looking more like boletes, we should focus on those. I even pointed with my finger to the page with the morel recipes. 'April and May,' it stated in black on white. But it was pointless.

For this reason, just past Dvorce, I took a little detour into an orchard and studied the grass. Once with my dad we had found some here. Morels, in fact, are partial to broadleaf forests, gardens, parks and meadows, they have no time for conifers.

Do I really need this? I thought to myself as I slogged through the tall wet grass, the legs of my pants soaked up to my knees. And right away I had to answer my own question truthfully: yes. Without the Toadstool, I don't know what I would do.

When I don't have Ruda in his khaki vest breathing down my neck, I'm quite happy to go looking for morels. I like their peculiarly wrinkled egg-shaped hat, which looks like a honeycomb growing out of a fat white stem. Inside they are hollow, which for edible mushrooms is not at all common, so they can be prepared stuffed—with meat or even with other mushrooms, such as wrinkled thimble caps.

I roamed around for a whole hour, and as expected, didn't find a single wrinkly little head. On the other hand, I did almost trip over someone's feet in the grass. They were sticking out of a small bush in the apple orchard. At first, various spine-chilling scenarios flashed through my mind, but in the end, I figured out what was going on here. On the feet were beaten-up blue sneakers with bright green shoelaces, triple knotted, the ends of the laces equal in length. It could only be Vojta. It was the last weekend in June and he had come home for the holidays. He must have had another argument with his mother and had gone outside to sleep.

I tried to make as much noise as possible, I stepped on twigs and made my feet rustle in the grass. Finally the shoes withdrew into the bush. It took Vojta a little bit longer before he picked himself up off the ground.

He was scratching his dishevelled fair hair and seemed to be in a quandary.

'What're you doing here?' I asked.

'I couldn't stay at home, my mom cleaned up my room,' he said by way of explanation, but didn't look me in the eye.

I wasn't at all surprised. Vojta is a very peculiar case. He works in the depository of a library in Prague, and in the summer, when the library operates on reduced hours, he comes home to his mother. To stay in the same house with Vojta for two months must be purgatory. As the start of the holidays approaches, his mother, instead of a greeting, cheerfully announces to everyone who passes by: 'Vojta is coming!' She throws up her hands and gives a big smile. By late August, I see her instead pacing up and down the pavement from one end of the village to the other, muttering disjointed phrases to her shoes: 'It's unbearable!' and 'Am I supposed to be a saint or what?' After Vojta leaves again, though, it only takes her a few days to recover. By mid-September I start to meet her in the woods. She treads Vojta's favourite paths all the way to Hartmanice, her head bowed and her back hunched. She looks neither to the left nor to the right, just down at the tips of her shoes.

At times I too find myself at a loss when it comes to Vojta's behaviour, but gradually I've come to realize that Vojta can't help it. I could understand how he must have felt when, after several months, he arrived back at his mother's, and she in the meantime had 'tidied up' his room. Maybe she had rearranged his clothing by type—not by colour, as he does. Or reordered his books, which Vojta had organized in a way that no one but he understood. In any case, she had introduced such chaos into his system that Vojta couldn't bear it and had to clear his head outdoors.

'What're you doing here? This isn't your route,' he asked me.

'I have an assignment from the Toadstool. I have to gather morels, the new manager's idea,' I explained with a sigh. 'I'm having a lousy day,' I added.

'Come on,' he said and without hesitation turned around and strode away. I set off after him, but could barely keep up, I was so tired from my sleepless night. We walked out of the glade and headed for a nearby coniferous wood. I felt a twinge of doubt, wondering if Vojta had made a mistake—morels can't abide conifers—but I was curious about what he wanted to show me.

We traipsed through the tall wet grass, skirting a young grove. Through the silence we could hear the shrill, piercing sound of a circular saw coming from the nearby cottage colony. Vojta led me to a fence, behind which stood an uninhabited, dilapidated trailer. He drew aside the torn mesh and motioned with his hand for me to follow him. Walking through the tall grass he reached the corner of the garden and pointed with his finger in front of him: 'Right here.'

I didn't know what he was trying to show me. Before us was just uncut grass full of weeds and bits of bark. I bent down just to be sure, but there was no sign of any mushrooms anywhere.

I turned and gave Vojta a questioning look.

'So this is where the morels grow. Especially in late April. Try it next year.'

I sighed in disappointment, but immediately regretted it because it obviously upset Vojta. He lowered his eyes and started rubbing his temple.

'Thanks, Vojta, I'll come back next spring,' I said and forced myself to smile. 'Any other tips?'

Vojta gave it some thought. It took an eternity for him to begin.

'Yesterday I took a walk on Santos Island. I found velvet boletes there under the pines.'

'Isn't it too early for them yet?'

'It's the heat,' he shrugged his shoulders. 'Just past the Luh Colony. Do you remember how much your dad used to like them?'

I nodded and bit my lip. We stood there for a moment in silence.

'Great, so, thanks for the tip. I'd better be going, or I'll show up at the Toadstool empty-handed.'

I found my way back to my path and thought for a moment whether I should head over to Santos Island, as Vojta had suggested, or continue south. In the end I headed as usual towards Krušec. The velvet bolete doesn't taste that interesting, it would be a shame to turn back for it. It's not suitable for breading, not especially good for drying, either, maybe just good to put in a cream sauce... I stopped in midstride. From my memory, I fished out the page in the atlas describing the velvet bolete. But of course, now I knew how to fulfil Ruda's assignment. I spun on my heel and headed back towards Sušice.

In front of the Luh Colony, I veered off towards the pine forest. It wasn't long before I discovered the first yellowish cap. I cut off the mycelium and looked at the stipe from below. It wasn't a smooth cut, there was a small hollow in the foot. The white flesh was slowly turning blue. The cap was a bit rough to the touch. I placed the velvet bolete in the basket and looked around for others. In less than two hours I had found at least thirty of them.

I set off with the basket towards town. It was early afternoon, the heat was stifling. The Otava riverbed by Santos Island was strewn with towels on which people lounged in bright bathing suits. On the benches near the snack bar, they were sipping beer and cocktails, while the loudspeakers blared upbeat music. All of these people were just the advance guard of the army that would invade the area in July. In the beginning of the summer, on Santos, it's impossible to move. I passed by the island and its enticements and continued along the river.

When one hour later at the Toadstool I handed Ruda the basket, which, as always, I had covered demurely with a dishcloth, I noticed a hint of suspicion and doubt in his eyes. He pulled back the cloth and frowned. To be extra certain, he glanced at the mushroom atlas still lying open beside the stove to confirm that I really hadn't brought him morels. I had the feeling that in his expression

I detected a trace of malicious glee. As if he was glad that I hadn't fulfilled the assignment.

He shook his head at me in silence.

'You're right,' I said, 'They are not morels. But you can easily pass them off as such.'

Ruda raised his eyebrows perplexed.

'If you dry them,' I continued, 'And then soak them for a few hours and cook them in a cream sauce, very few people will be able to tell them apart from morels. So you can go right ahead and add those Czech truffles to the menu. If you like, I can bring more of them, you can pop them into the dehydrator and sell them right through the winter.'

Ruda turned to the Walrus: 'Is that so?'

He nodded. 'Yeah, yeah, Sisi's right, they say that's how they do it in Switzerland, it's their specialty.'

'Hmmm,' grunted Ruda. 'We'll try it,' he conceded.

He didn't look thrilled, but in the end handed me three 100-crown bills.

By four o'clock I was already unlocking the door of the shack in Dvorce, I don't think I had ever returned so early from a scouting mission. I decided to lie down and make up for the sleepless night.

But no such luck. As I was setting the empty basket down on the table, I noticed the blinking cell phone. Three missed calls. Plus a text message written in all caps: SIS, CALL ME, IT'S IMPORTANT!!!

I hit the green button under the display with my thumb. But before I heard it ring, I hit the red one. Milan was certainly not calling me to chit chat. To ask how I was doing and did I want to come down and visit him. That he could have done long ago. Before our mom died. This had to be about the inheritance. Evžen had put him up to it.

I was in no mood to discuss anything with my brothers. I threw the cell into the drawer of the table where I stash useless things. Documents for the house, telephone bills and unopened packets of risperidone. Let the battery drain in there.

13

My little cabin certainly doesn't rank among the most beautiful homes in Dvorce. In fact, if someone were to call it the ugliest house in the village, I couldn't blame them. You see, it's really not much more than a dilapidated old shack that the weeds in the garden have already set their sights on.

It wasn't always like this. My current dwelling was once a well-kept country cottage, where the walls were repainted every three years, the porch was swept at least once a day, and where the grass in the garden was kept short even in the hardest to reach corners. My grandfather went so far as to call it the 'summer residence,' which sounded like a joke, although nobody dared to laugh. The villa in Plzeň was supposed to go to my father, and the car and the cottage in Dvorce to Aunt Věrka, his sister, so it had been decided in the family a long time ago. But in the end my dad walked away with everything.

As for Aunt Věrka, I never saw her myself, but she must have been an oddball, a crazy woman, at least that's what our dad, speaking in a half-whisper, always claimed. Supposedly, she left home the day of her eighteenth birthday. Her mother, my grandmother, brought home a birthday cake that afternoon and when she went up to find her in her room, discovered that not only was her daughter missing, but so were all of her books and clothes. She had left a note saying she was going to study in Brno. After that she returned to the house only rarely to see her mother, and always only in the morning when her father, my grandpa, wasn't at home. And then she moved to Germany, 'to concoct callus ointments for the Krauts,' as Grandpa disdainfully would proclaim when he was still alive, and she had stopped coming home altogether.

The cottage in Dvorce eventually went to my dad, who took meticulous care of it. It then also became our cottage, where we spent summer holidays and weekends in the spring and fall. After my tenth birthday, however, it remained abandoned for a long time, the walls became damp and cracked, and over the last seven years, since I've been living here, the cracks in the walls have widened.

Today the cottage, due to the overgrown hedge, is practically invisible from the street. The bushes have spread out laterally as well, so to pass through the gate I have to go sideways while ducking under the branches in order to get through at all. The thorns of the roses try to rip off my shirt and pants. Each time I have to extract their spines from my trousers, I vow to cut them back once and for all, but I never do.

The shack sits in the left half of the unkempt garden, and the surrounding vegetation is encroaching on it as well. The once ochre facade is covered with ivy, the branches of the walnut and the linden trees rub against the windows and stroke the sheet metal roof. One day, nature will swallow up my shack completely.

In order to get to the paved doorstep, I have to go around the shack. To access the front door, painted green, one ascends four well-worn steps. Just beyond the door is a miniature hallway and the toilet, a dry one of course, but with a view of the surrounding countryside as compensation. Next is a second hallway with a pantry, where I keep potatoes, spices and various canned goods. Lined up on the shelves are compotes and preserves still made by my mother. I don't have much of a sweet tooth, which is why I generally open them in winter, when my supplies are running low. I'm careful to proceed from the oldest to the younger ones, last winter I polished off several jars of vintage apricot jam.

The door to the left of the pantry leads into the bedroom that my mother and father used to occupy. I don't go in there, the door has been closed for years.

To the right of the pantry is a small kitchen and a living room, all in one. In the middle stands a rickety oak table and five chairs. Against the wall next to the door is a classic white sideboard with a miniature countertop, but the small workspace for preparing food doesn't bother me because I hardly cook. The stove with the gas cylinder has two burners, but one would certainly be enough for me, I don't need more than one pot to heat up water for frankfurters. In the corner under the lattice window is a cot with a cotton flannel sleeping bag that serves as a couch. Dad used to lie on it when we would come back from our mushroom hunting expeditions, but now I use it when I listen to the radio. The television on the small table in front of the cot hasn't worked in ages. In the winter, when the cottage soaks up the frost through its weathered chinks like a sponge, and spends the next few months sniffling and coughing, the cot becomes my bed as well. The kitchen, in fact, is the only room that can be heated. The stove is small, it can only take little pieces of firewood. In the evening I always stoke it to make it red hot and then lie sweating on the cot, and by morning the cold settles in my feet and before long spreads throughout my body.

The upper floor is actually just a simple attic that my grandfather converted into two separate rooms. On the right was the room that I first shared with my brothers, but because I complained bitterly that I didn't want to be in the same room with them, they moved me to the one on the left, separating me from their games of generals and zilches at least for the night.

As a young girl I could walk around the room fully upright, but now I have to duck down in order not to hit my head against the low ceiling. It's a modest little room with a plain wooden bed under a single dormer window and a row of cabinets arranged along the sloping wall. Next to the wardrobe on the opposite wall are boxes of old junk, that for some time now I have been meaning to throw away. The room is practically unchanged from how it was. Only the contents of the cabinets have changed, the girlish skirts and blouses have been replaced by cotton twill pants and flannel shirts. I left the walls white, without a single picture on them. I know, however, that beneath the bed there is still the little suitcase in which I used to hide my treasures. Toy cars, Čtyřlístek comics, pebbles, Kinder egg surprises, yogurt labels and the notebooks in which I wrote down which mushrooms I had found.

There is no bathroom in the shack, from spring to autumn I make do with a bucket of water with which I rinse myself on the porch. In the winter I heat up water to put in a basin, or I go to bed unwashed, the extra warm clothes can hide a thing or two.

The shack is a bit like a dollhouse. Since I moved in almost nothing in the entire cottage has been altered, I keep it in its original state. Mother's lace curtains, which have since turned yellow and can no longer be washed, hang on the windows, old, cracked dishes still sit in the cupboards and nailed to the walls are pictures of our family with cobwebs at the corners. Sometimes I feel as if I'm visiting a folk museum. It's as if I were living in the past, in every corner, in every drawer, memories lurk. They take me back to the time when I was nine years old and found the toadstool in my dad's basket.

14

That night I couldn't fall asleep. Perhaps for the first time in my life. It must already have been late, because despite the solstice, it had been dark for a while, and I was still staring up at the pale ceiling. Under the baked roof, the room had heated up, but the cool air had begun to creep in through the open window. Outside, the first summer storm was brewing, the nearby forest rustled. The wind billowed the curtains and across the walls roamed shadows cast by the branches of our walnut tree, whose talons were rapping at my window.

After some two or three hours, the play of light and shadow on the ceiling finally began to have the desired effect. Slowly my eyes began to grow heavy, my arms and legs grew numb. But suddenly something snapped me out of my sleep. I heard someone cough. It sounded familiar. But all around it was still dark.

That was the first time he came to my room.

My childhood ended that night. Never again did I pull out my little suitcase with its treasures from under my bed. For fifteen long years now it has been gathering dust.

15

Last night I dreamt that I was standing in a river and the icy water was reaching up to my knees. When I woke up, I discovered that I was not so far removed from reality. I touched my feet. They were wet, my toes were completely numb with cold, the skin on the pads all wrinkly. I looked around sleepily for a moment and then my eyes wandered to the ceiling. I saw an enormous drop, it was slowly swelling at the centre of a giant stain, then broke loose and splattered on my comforter. Immediately I felt a twinge in my lower belly. All I needed was to get a chill in my bladder again or, even worse, a kidney infection. I forced myself to get up, pulled on thick socks, ran to grab the basin and moved the bed.

Outside it was still drizzling, but it was clear that the shower would soon pass. I looked out of the dormer window but couldn't see anything on the roof. I needed to go into my brothers' room to look from their window, which faced the other side. Just shy of the ridge I spotted a loose sheet of metal. And on the horizon beyond Sušice more dark clouds were gathering.

I ran downstairs and grabbed my cell phone. Ignoring the missed calls and texts from my brothers, I punched in Krušina's number. I couldn't go to the Toadstool today, this was a priority, if I didn't fix the roof at least temporarily, it would be a disaster. Besides, after such a downpour there was no point in going out to gather mushrooms, they would all be soggy. Hopefully the Walrus would find a sensible way to explain this to Ruda.

I didn't have that long a ladder, one that would reach all the way to the roof, and besides, I would have no idea what to do with the leak. I would need to get dressed and go a few doors down to see Zatloukal, he was the local do-it-yourself expert. When anyone around here needed to fix something on their house, they preferred to go to him than to call a company. I remember one time he secured a loose gutter for us.

I pulled on my pants and my shirt and took the porcelain cup with the lid out of the cupboard. I laid out the banknotes and coins on the table and started to count—2,124 crowns, not much, plus I had to put aside another 300 because I needed to replace the gas cylinder. But hopefully it would be enough, if not, I still had some cash in an old tea tin in the drawer of the kitchen table. Now and then, if I have any money left over, I put some in there. Sometimes I imagine that I've saved up a fortune by now, but most likely we're talking about a few thousand crowns, if not just a few hundred, and mostly in coins. In all the years that I've lived here, I haven't needed to use the money from that tin, and I hope today I won't need to either.

I put on my rubber boots, pulled the hood of my jacket over my head, and set off for Zatloukal's cabin. Few would recognize in it the ordinary concrete block structure that the original owner built here in the 1970s. From a distance it looked like a traditional log cabin. To the grey cube, Zatloukal had added a steeply sloped shingle roof, and had clad all of the walls in dark stained wood siding. To the white-painted shutters he had added marigolds in the windows. But on closer inspection, the mica plaster showed through the fake timbering and through the windows one could see an orange kitchen counter with black trim.

It took a long time before Zatloukal answered the door. After ringing the doorbell several times, I heard a sound, the varnished door creaked, and an unshaven man came hobbling out.

Zatloukal was wearing an old pair of boxers and a shapeless undershirt from which protruded a hefty paunch.

In our family this would have been utterly unthinkable. Anything that had to do with nudity and sex was totally taboo, after all we're not savages running around in banana-leaf skirts, was the refrain. When a love scene would appear in a movie, our mom would spring up from the sofa like a jack-in-the-box, grab the remote and switch the channel. The three of us would pretend to be annoyed, but in reality, we were glad, to watch a sex scene with our parents, even if it was only acted, would have been agony.

I don't even remember ever seeing my parents undressed. In our villa in Plzeň we had two separate bathrooms, one for us and one for our parents, so that we wouldn't accidentally catch each other with nothing on. Even at the swimming pool everyone changed in their own cubicle, and we never went into the sauna together. At the beach, if we walked past a woman who was sunbathing without the top part of her bathing suit, our mom never failed to drop a stinging comment. *Shameless hussy.*

Zatloukal briefly stroked the comb-over on his head, hooked his thumb into the elastic of his shorts and after a significant pause, launched into a litany. Hadn't anyone told me that he doesn't do this any longer, I should get out and see people sometimes, I know nothing about my own neighbours, he's long retired and needs his peace and quiet, what nerve, and I didn't even have a proper ladder, next I'd be asking to borrow his, and anyway, how big is the hole?

As the two of us carried his ladder down the street, he was still swearing. Luckily, in the meantime the rain had stopped, and the greyish clouds had been lanced by the rays of the sun. Hopefully the metal sheet on the roof would dry out quickly and be possible to fix.

Zatloukal climbed up to the next-to-last rung of the ladder, leaned over the roof, and wedged his paunch under the eave. For a while he went on banging away up there, and I had all I could do to hold the ladder steady.

It's not going to be a picnic, there's a big gap along the ridge, Zatloukal's headless body hollered at me, it can't be reattached by hand, it's going to take plastic cement, he'd pop over to Sušice and pick some up.

I could leave him the key, he'd have a look from the inside too, by tonight it would be fixed. Best thing for me to do is to take off and let him do it, he doesn't like people gawking at him while he's working.

Now what? It was just before noon, the storm clouds had retreated somewhere towards Budějovice. I put on my shoes, grabbed the basket, tucked the penknife into my pocket and set off on my daily pilgrimage.

The forest resembled an impressionist painting. The colours were blurred, the puddles along the trail reflected the sky through the branches. No bright colours anywhere, only muted greens, blues and greys. Just outside Dvorce, I met Vojta. He was returning from the excursion he makes almost every day. He was soaking wet, he must not have found a place to shelter from the rain. His damp hair was even kinkier than usual. We greeted each other with a single word and then went our separate ways.

Right by Nuzerov my mood lifted a bit, under a pine tree I found a few nice boletes that hadn't even been nibbled by slugs yet. Not even later did my luck desert me.

By early evening, when I walked into the square in Sušice, my wicker basket was full to the brim. From beneath the checkered dishcloth emanated the scent of about two dozen assorted mushrooms, one orange birch bolete, a bunch of smallish blushers and several parasols. There were also a few button mushrooms that didn't fit into the basket, which I carried in a canvas bag in my left hand.

The Walrus would be pleased and hopefully that dolt Ruda would appreciate it too. With the prospect of a good profit, all excited, I sprinted up the steps to the back door of the Toadstool. I knocked on the door to the kitchen, but no one came. From inside I could hear sizzling and bubbling. I carefully opened the door and looked around—not a soul. The kitchen smelled of braised meat and fresh vegetables.

I set the basket on the countertop and froze. On the cutting board, on top of the stainless-steel countertop, was a sliced bay bolete. Where had it come from? On exceptional occasions, it happened that Krušina now and then had to buy additional mushrooms elsewhere. Except these weren't mushrooms from the supplier, who dropped them off in a small wooden crate stamped with a company logo. On the stainless-steel surface sat a wicker basket, just slightly smaller than mine. Dapperlings, blushers, except for a few scaber stalks, exactly the same, except that the mushrooms were covered with pine needles, the stipes dirty with soil, the caps not cleaned off, and one mushroom even had a slug peeping out of it. I broke off a piece of the red cracking bolete's cap—it was worm-eaten.

Somewhere a door slammed, I returned the mushroom to the basket and turned around as if nothing had happened.

'Not bad. These pinkish ones, you didn't need to bring in so many, we have plenty from another source. What's this orange one, some kind of a russula? Oh right, an orange birch bolete, you said?' he asked with an innocent air. To confuse a gilled mushroom with a boletinoid one, that's already an art, I winced inwardly. Before I had a chance to ask where the mushrooms in the foreign basket had come from, Ruda interrupted me.

'How about real boletes, have any of those? So that the Walrus can finally make a proper scramble, and not always have to use those red cracked ones.'

I wanted to object that something like a real bolete doesn't exist. That several different kinds are considered to be real, like for instance the king bolete, summer bolete and *Citrinus boletus*, although these are no more real than any other bolete. And that while a king bolete is a beautiful mushroom, it doesn't do much for a scramble. It's better to dry it or add it to something, whereas the considerably uglier red cracking bolete, for example, will give a scramble a much richer flavour. But instead, I just repeated: 'Yeah, yeah, OK.'

'And on top of that, bring in some chanterelles. We're getting lots of Krauts these days, they go after those like a duck on a June bug. A Bavarian *knödel* with chanterelle cream sauce and freshly chopped parsley, with a nice Black and Tan—that'll get 'em. It'll take at least half a basket, OK? Otherwise I'll need to buy them from a supplier, and that'll cost me a fortune. Here's three hundred for today, well, all right, make it four, here. See ya tomorrow . . . .' He didn't wait for an answer and was already pushing me out of the kitchen.

'Oh yeah, and with those shroomer tourists, hopefully something will work out soon. No bookings so far, but a few curious emails have come in. I'll keep you posted, stay tuned.'

I reached the square beside myself with fury. Why hadn't I been able to ask him where the basket came from? Why hadn't I pushed back that in the Bohemian Forest chanterelles are in scant supply? And back home my mood certainly didn't improve.

'That roof of yours is a ticking time bomb. I had to make another trip with the car to get more putty and rust inhibitor. It's temporarily patched up and varnished, for the summer it'll hold. I don't want anything for the labour, I'm not about to ruin you—I did it for your dad, I always liked him. Just give me 2,000 crowns to cover gas and supplies. But by next winter you're going to have to invest another five or ten into it, you'll need to replace a few metal sheets, and eventually you're not going to get away without putting on a whole new roof, unless you plan to open a public swimming pool in your house.'

But the worst was yet to come.

'And sometime around two, a fancy black car pulled up and this slick dandy dude got out. Wanted to know where you were. He hung around here for over three hours and then took his leave. He left his number for you and said it was urgent. He looked familiar to me, could it have been your brother, the cuter one? You know, it's been years since I last saw him, I hardly remember him.'

Gee, I thought to myself, the brothers aren't giving up easily. At the right time, I'll have to call Milan.

I gave a vague answer and emptied some coins and banknotes into Zatloukal's hand. He had to cup his hands, as if he were about to scoop some water from a spring. I removed a 20-crown coin and two 2-crown pieces from his hands and added another 200-crown banknote from my back pocket on top. Now it was finally an even two thousand. Zatloukal raised his eyebrows but didn't protest.

Around seven o'clock the sky to the north clouded over again and before long another downpour began. If it keeps up like this, Ruda can say goodbye to his chanterelles. And Zatloukal's prophecy about a swimming pool in the shack will come true. I haven't had this bad a day in a long time.

As usual I managed to fall asleep only as day was breaking. At seven, right on the dot, I opened my eyes and gazed up at the wet stain on the ceiling. Swirling in my head were echoes from my dream. Sometimes I'm amazed at how much dreaming I manage to do in barely three or four hours of sleep. Every night I walk through our villa in Bezovka. The entire house is empty and still. I walk into each room and look around. I open the window, sit down at the table, caress the countertop with the palm of my hand. I recall all the sounds that are associated with that house. And finally, I arrive in Dvorce, fifteen years back, and in my dream relive it again, everything that took place fifteen years ago in my bed. I am not quite ten years old. The branch of the walnut tree is knocking on the windowpane.

By the curtain a moth is beating its wings. The swollen heart trying to burst through my chest. The throbbing in my ears pounding against the pillow. My forehead is beaded with a cold sweat.

The short sleep didn't bring me any relief. Upon waking my eyes were burning and somewhere behind them I felt pressure. I got up, walked out to the porch, and scooped up some cold water that I splashed onto my face until the throbbing behind my eyes stopped.

16

When I walked into the kitchen at the Toadstool the next day, the Walrus was standing with his back to me, stirring some soup in a pot. He didn't even notice that I had come in. I looked around the room to see if another mysterious basket might be lying around.

The Walrus tapped his wooden cooking spoon against the side of the pot, covered it, turned around and startled at the sight of me.

'Hey, Sisi, on the early side today, aren't you?' he asked, pointing the wooden spoon at me.

'Good afternoon,' I greeted him and held out my hand with the basket. The Walrus rested the wooden spoon across the lid of the pot, took the basket from me with both hands and set it down on the stainless-steel surface. He pulled out one mushroom after another and turned each one over carefully in his hand. It wasn't like this before, normally he would have simply emptied the mushrooms into a shallow basket, taken a quick look at them, at most asked about certain ones and how to prepare them, and would have paid me.

'It's pretty slim pickings today,' he grumbled.

I shrugged my shoulders. After yesterday's rain lots of mushrooms got mouldy and new ones hadn't sprung up yet. I'd had to resort to gathering underground mushrooms as well, or my basket would have been half empty.

I cleared my throat.

'So how much do you think you'd be willing to give me for them?'

'Girl, girl,' he shook his head, 'You're going to have to wait for Ruda. It seems that everything has to go through him now. I have no more authority around here any more,' he waved his hand that was still holding the larch bolete that he had picked up earlier.

I shuffled my feet uncertainly.

'And when will he be back?'

'What do I know, he went to buy something. He keeps trying to figure out where to get our groceries. He's researching suppliers and looking for new ones.'

'And—' I got stuck right at the beginning of the sentence. 'And where did the mushrooms from yesterday come from?'

The Walrus heaved a sigh.

'Well, exactly. Ruda tried to make a deal with some local old geezer. He kept insisting what a great mycologist he was, and in the end, he brought back mushrooms that were all wormy and rotten. There was even a toadstool. I managed to convince Ruda to forget about him. But he keeps probing, to see if there are any others with whom he could give it a try. He seems to think that if there's competition, it improves performance, or something like that. And today he was going on about giving imported mushrooms a try. Somewhere from Eastern Europe. Because I guess we don't have enough growing in our own backyard.'

He rolled his eyes and shook his head. My throat tightened. I sighed and set off for home.

Along the way I stopped at the convenience store and with the bit of change left over in my pocket, bought myself dinner—three discounted doughnuts from yesterday. As I was fishing for coins in my pocket, the Vietnamese cashier looked up from his cell phone and waved his hand: 'OK, OK.' For a moment I pretended that I couldn't accept such a generous offer, but then I forced myself to smile and walked out.

I took a bite of the first coated doughnut and headed home along the river. At the weir in front of Santos Island, I noticed, sitting on the stone steps going down to the water, there was Vojta. He waved and moved over a bit to make room for me. I wasn't in the mood for his company, in fact I really would have preferred to be on my own, but I didn't want to offend him.

I sat down beside him and put my basket under my feet. I leaned my elbows on my knees and rested my head in my hands. The sun was warming my back, but it wasn't so hot as to make me regret that I wasn't sitting in the shade.

Vojta was balancing an open box with a snack on his knees. He had placed two smaller boxes inside. In one was an apple cut up into crescents, and in the other a piece of bread folded over in half with ham and butter. I noticed that he had trimmed the ham along the crust, to make sure it didn't stick out anywhere.

An old recollection tied to this place surfaced in my memory. I was still wearing swimming wings, so I must have been at most six years old. A little way from us, a boy was having a tantrum because his mother, under the blazing sun, had tried to put a baseball cap on him. He threw himself down on the grass, kicking, even banging his head on the ground. Obviously, there was nothing all that strange about it, children do such things, but at the time Vojta had already been in school for a couple of years.

'Good Lord,' whispered my mother, who was lying on the towel next to me and watching the whole spectacle through her round sunglasses. 'Can't she take him aside?'

In the end his mother did in fact grab him by the elbow and using all of her strength, had dragged him away.

The Vojta sitting next to me now in no way resembled that enraged little boy. He seemed perfectly calm. Each time he would take a bite of his sandwich, he would wash it down with some kefir set on a nearby stone, and then wipe his lips with a napkin. Not a single crumb would fall. He gave the impression of being engaged in some highly sophisticated activity, so intense seemed his concentration.

It made me wonder how such a person had managed to get out of Dvorce. How had he been able to leave his home, where his devoted mother took care of him, and graduate from a special high school in Budějovice? I imagined him wandering through the dormitory corridors, meticulously organizing the clothes in his closet, arranging his books and then looking for the cafeteria. With his eating habits, how could he even have ingested anything there? And what was more, he now had a job in Prague.

I pulled the bag of stale doughnuts out of the basket. The whole package was sticky with powdered sugar that had melted in the heat.

'Thanks for those velvet boletes,' I said after I finished the first doughnut.

He nodded.

'If you have any other tips, I'd be grateful, what I really need right now are chanterelles.'

He nodded again, slowly finished chewing, and opened his mouth to answer me, but suddenly stopped and turned to the left. A dog was approaching us. It was a Labrador puppy that had just gone swimming in the Otava, the water was dripping from its fur. Vojta grew visibly nervous. He put the bread back into the box and gripped his knees with his hands, his chest touching the box. The dog ran up to us, stopped, and shook. Vojta leapt up in fright, the box fell to the ground and the sandwich fell out onto the steps.

'Ben, leave it, yuck,' came a woman's voice from somewhere behind us.

The dog ran off, but Vojta kept looking in its direction until it completely disappeared from view. Then he looked down at the spilled snack. He gave such a woeful sigh, as if someone he knew had just died. He squeamishly picked up the sandwich with two fingers and put it back into the smaller box, which he set inside the larger one next to the apples and then snapped them both shut. Had it been me, I would have eaten the dusty sandwich with no problem.

'If you'd like, I can give you a doughnut,' I offered, but the sticky sugar clearly didn't appeal to him.

'Tomorrow at seven fifteen I'm heading out to go mushroom hunting. Want to come?'

And again, he just nodded.

17

The first morning was the strangest of all. I woke up a bit later than usual and cautiously went downstairs. Everyone was already sitting at the table. I sat down and whispered good morning. My parents mumbled something in reply. I looked around the room. On the table there was an old red-and-white chequered tablecloth, and in the middle a tray with buttered bread. My mother set me a plate and poured me hot cocoa from a teapot. My eyes travelled around the space. The left window shutter with a crack, the vase of strawflowers on the sill. Between the windows, the wall clock that had stopped at half past six years ago. The cream-coloured cupboard, the chipped dishes on the shelves, the humming refrigerator, the trunk of the walnut tree outside the window. It was the same as always, everything seemed to be totally normal, except that it wasn't at all. The image before my eyes spun and I had to grab onto the edge of the table with both hands to keep from falling to the floor. 'What the heck?' asked Evžen, who had just kicked me in the shin for practice and was surprised that I didn't tell on him. But it hadn't hurt at all, it was as though my skin was cushioned in a layer of foam. He kicked me again for good measure, but I couldn't behave according to the usual rules. My eyes wandered to my dad. He was sitting at the head of the table but his face was turned to the side, his legs were crossed, and the newspaper was spread across his lap. He had slipped the coffee cup onto his right index finger and from time to time took a sip. He didn't look at me at all. He didn't seem to be aware of my presence. This sometimes also happened when he was deeply absorbed in reading.

This morning he hadn't cleared his throat outside my door. But not even that was strange, we usually didn't go mushroom hunting two days in a row.

Yet something did strike me. His icy calm. During the preceding months the household had been fraught with his nervousness—that is if he came to the table at all. And suddenly there he sat, sipping coffee and reading the paper. He was serenity personified. As if at long last he had found some relief, as if after a strenuous day at work he had finally been able to relax. His sense of calm had spread even to the other family members, to Mom, Milan and Evžen. Suddenly we again resembled what we once had been. We were again a family. It was obvious that Mom also felt a weight had fallen off her shoulders, no one grimaced at what she said, no one chided her for getting up from the table every other minute to sneak a bite of the slab of bread with jam that she kept on the sideboard. Even my brothers had evidently heaved a big sigh of relief, they were kicking each other under the table and exchanging gestures. And no one reprimanded them.

I was the only one spoiling their idyll. No one suspected what price I'd had to pay to keep the family peace.

We finished eating, the boys went outside with Dad, I helped Mom clear the table.

'Are you all right?' she asked me, as with trembling hands I piled the dishes into the sink. 'You're looking a bit pale.'

I shrugged my shoulders and went out into the garden instead. By the porch, I almost tripped over my dad. He was crouched down with the lawnmower in front of him and was tinkering with it. I held my breath.

'What are you doing, Dad?' My voice sounded as if it belonged to someone else.

'I'm trying to replace the V-belt,' he replied, without turning towards me.

I shuffled my feet. I took a deep breath and asked again.

'What are you doing, Dad?'

Dad dropped the mower, clenched his jaw, turned his face towards me but his gaze stopped somewhere around my knees.

'Are you deaf?' he barked. 'I'm replacing the belt.'

No, I wasn't deaf. But right then I wanted to be. To be deaf, blind and numb to feeling anything at all. I moved a little farther away and sat down on the bench under the window.

My mother looked out from the kitchen to the porch: 'Today we could go blueberry picking,' she said. 'Zatloukal stopped by last night with some wood and said that behind the pine grove they're already growing.'

Dad nodded in agreement and the boys, who were sitting in the hammock and playing with their Game Boys, looked annoyed as if on cue.

'I'll make blueberry dumplings,' added Mom.

It occurred to me that maybe I had dreamt the whole thing. From time to time I would have bad dreams, and often for that reason I had to sleep with my little light on. It must have been a nightmare, it was the only logical explanation. But it remained before my eyes.

I went back into the kitchen and took a bite of the bread with jam. The soft morsels descended into me, I washed them down with lukewarm cocoa and my stomach filled with gravel. Something had to be done, but what? What can be done in a situation such as this?

Zatloukal was right, the bushes were loaded with dark blueberries. It had been a warm spring and early summer, and the blueberries were unusually big, black and juicy. With some, it was enough to touch them and they burst immediately, staining the fingers with thick dark juice.

As usual, we organized a picking competition. I took a plastic cup from my mom and went over to a bush that seemed to me to be the heaviest with berries. No sooner had I crouched down among the blueberry bushes, the strange unfamiliar feeling came flooding back over me. Once again, I felt like a spectator, who from somewhere high above was following what was happening down below on earth. I was observing myself picking berries off the bush. I was holding the cup between my knees, picking with both hands, index fingers and thumbs extended, letting one berry after another slip into my cupped palms. Same as always. When both of my hands were full, I tipped the berries into the cup and went right back to picking. Unlike my brothers, I didn't give in to the temptation of now and then popping a blueberry into my mouth. I picked quickly but not hastily, in a steady rhythm, like a machine. I carried out every activity as usual, yet I should have been desperately screaming and hurling myself against a tree. Grabbing a sharp rock and slashing my wrists with it. Stabbing my carotid artery with a stick, or bringing it down on my father's back.

And suddenly I felt a violent jolt. It gave my other me, the one looking down from above, renewed hope. What if? Could I run over to my mother and blurt out to her what had happened last night?

But instead I just swatted a mosquito that had bitten me on the thigh. I straightened the cup between my knees and went back to picking. There I was, squatting down again, careful not to tip over my cup. As soon as the cup was full, woosh went the blueberries into Mom's container. Not a single blueberry was allowed to go to waste. I wanted to pick the most blueberries of all so that I could be the first to go for seconds of the dumplings with blueberry sauce. As always. I tried to do everything the way I had always done it before, to make things go back to normal.

I won the contest. I ate twelve dumplings, and that evening my stomach felt as heavy as if it were full of rocks.

But not even my stomach ache could save me.

18

Tonight, a thunderstorm swept through the village. It cleared the air. The sky continued to be overcast, but the grey clouds broke apart revealing pale blue patches that were mirrored between them. The fresh breeze made the fine hairs on my arms stand on end. Around seven in the morning, the forest was still chilly. My fingers were so numb that every other minute I had to check with my eyes to make sure I was still carrying the basket.

'You're wearing two different socks,' Vojta said to me instead of good morning.

I instinctively curled up my toes. He was right. Not having slept, I was so brain dead that I hadn't managed to get dressed properly. I unrolled the legs of my pants all the way down to my shoes so that Vojta wouldn't be disturbed by the sight.

At first, we walked in silence, pushing aside the wet grass with our feet. As I, in my well-worn leather hiking boots, was enjoying the last few moments of feeling dry, Vojta's sneakers became completely waterlogged almost immediately. He didn't seem to mind at all. As long as they were tied properly.

I thought hard about what we would say to each other the whole time. I remembered how roughly two years ago I had helped his mother bring in crates of apples from the garden. I carried them all the way into the kitchen, and then as I was putting on my shoes on my way out, I couldn't help but glance at the bookcase in the room right next to the front door.

They say one can gage a person's character by looking at their bookshelf. I am sure my parents' library in Plzeň would keep an entire psychology department busy. But in this case, I couldn't figure out the logic according to which the books were arranged. A pop-up version of *The Three Little Pigs* stood alongside Kant's *Critique of Pure Reason*, next came *The Magic of Photography* and *The Art of Meditation*. So it went on, Foucault snuggled with *The Princess with the Golden Locket*, *The Morning of the Magicians* leaned against a Czech–Finnish dictionary, *The Good Soldier Švejk* sidled up to *The Poem of Hashish*.

It seemed as though Vojta had tossed the books on the shelf in no particular order, but I knew him too well for that, there had to be an ingenious system behind it.

'How do you actually sort your books?'

I immediately regretted asking him. Vojta stopped, turned the basket in his hand, looked directly into my eyes and let loose. It was as if after long and steady rains a dam had burst.

For a good hour he explained to me the way in which books are numbered. The ISBN is no random figure, it encompasses plenty of information—such as the publisher and the year of publication—and he pulls these numbers apart, recalculates them and reconfigures them. It's an entirely new approach to sorting books, the genre and author are of no interest, it's all about the numbers and algorithms. Maybe one day in the library where he works, he would be able to implement his new cataloguing system.

I didn't understand a word he said, math has never been my thing.

Vojta had a strange mechanical way of speaking, the syllables would fly out of his mouth at regular intervals, a bit like fingers tapping on a keyboard. My brothers called him the robot.

By the time we passed Vatětice, the whole right side of my body was tingling, pummelled by the needles of his incomprehensible syllables, with not a single mushroom in my basket.

'Vojta, will you help me with those chanterelles?' I managed to slip into a tiny pause, as he was taking a breath.

He stopped and tousled the twisted wires on his head.

'With the chanterelles? I don't think sooo...' he shook his head in surprise, as if hearing about them for the very first time.

'Look,' he crouched down after a moment. 'Stagshorns...' With his outstretched index finger, he touched the jagged orange tips.

'Vojta...' I sighed, about to ask him again to help me, but I never finished my sentence. Behind the spruce tree beside us, something was peeping out.

It was yellow-orange, just slightly paler than Vojta's Stagshorns. Of course! A chanterelle! With a whole family behind her! So my chatty companion had been of some use to me after all. I left him with his Stagshorns and advanced towards my prey. There were five fine common chanterelles. I scoured the area and found a few more king and pine boletes, a bunch of sooty heads and two young parasols.

And then again, the torrent of numbers, plus and minus signs, multiplied, divided, it set my head spinning.

As we approached Hartmanice, he finally started to run out of words. For a few minutes he went totally quiet. He stopped at a tourist sign and remained silent.

'I need to go to Hartmanice.'

'Why?' I asked, surprised.

'I have to return the same way.'

'But this way is much nicer...' I countered.

Vojta just shrugged.

We exchanged apologetic smiles and each went our separate way. Vojta headed south and I, as always, to the east. In the clearing I turned back again to look at him. He walked with his head down, the basket bumping in a steady rhythm against his striped suede leggings. Suddenly I felt sorry that I hadn't thanked him.

Near Annín I managed to add a few more pale chanterelles, and to those a few summer ceps, three parasols, a handful of blewits and even three tawny milkcaps. The mushrooms were spilling out of the overflowing basket, I picked out a few of the finest specimens and put them in a canvas bag. In the afternoon I would take them to Zatloukal.

As I walked along the Otava, I picked up the pace.

At the Toadstool, the Walrus, without a greeting, waved me in the direction of Ruda's office. I turned and cast a furtive glance around the kitchen. There was no sign of the other basket, but on his chopping board the Walrus had already started cutting a small heap of brownish mushrooms. They might have been button mushrooms, but I couldn't be sure.

I sighed and knocked on the plywood door. No one answered so I went right in. Ruda was sprawled in the office chair by the desk, his legs spread wide, his hands on the armrests, his head leaning back against the leather-covered headrest. His mouth was wide open and he was making horrifying sounds. I was overcome with a wave of anger. Such injustice, that at three o'clock in the afternoon someone can just kick back in a chair and fall asleep like a log, whereas I have to go through a series of rituals that usually don't even work. I looked over to see if there might be a dead fly on the windowsill that I could drop into his open trap. But by then he was already blinking in my direction: 'What? What is it? . . . Oh, it's you . . .'

He put five 100-crown notes on the table, more than any other previous time. I rolled my eyes at him, as if to say he had gone nuts. The expression that appeared on his face filled me with a powerful sense of alarm. He grinned from ear to ear, patted me on the shoulder and fired away: 'So, tomorrow morning at half past seven in the square. They'll be really nice folks, you'll see.'

19

I spotted them immediately. They were standing by the fountain, looking around with curiosity. Dad, mom, sonny boy. They were all dressed in turquoise, yellow and salmon-coloured outdoor clothing, with even brighter zippers to make sure they wouldn't get cold in the woods in the middle of July. On their legs they wore lightweight nylon pants with zip-off bottoms, in case instead it got very hot. On their feet they wore Gore-Tex hiking boots because one never knows if one is going to step into a puddle. I'd bet my life that each of them was wearing athletic underwear.

The mom and dad were testily snapping at each other, the sharp words slapping even the boy, who was sitting a short way off on a low step, playing with his Swiss Army Knife. He was pulling out one accessory after another—the can opener, the nail file, the corkscrew—flipping them open, polishing them and snapping them shut, over and over. He could have been twelve or thirteen years old and looked like a total geek, who had just stood up from his computer. He was skinny, his chest was sunken, and he was wearing square, self-tinting glasses.

'I told you so, you never . . .' the mom stopped in mid-sentence as I walked up to them. Her gaze flicked towards me for a split second and then landed back on the dad's flushed face.

'You couldn't care less what I think.'

I continued to stand there, not moving from my spot. The mom turned back to me again and frowned.

'What would you like?' she asked, her eyebrows almost touching in her scowling face. Then her eyes fell on my basket. 'Oh, is that you? Mrs Tichá?'

'Yes, good morning.'

She rubbed her chin and scratched her head. Her short hair was teased and brushed back, as if it had been hit by a gust of air, she resembled some kind of a dinosaur. Was there no kind-hearted soul among her friends who would tell her how dreadful such a thing looked?

'Excuse me for being so surprised. Mr Vobořil praised you to high heaven, saying what a great expert you were, a master in the field...'

'My wife must have thought,' the dad interjected, 'It would be some antiquated dame waiting for us here, and not a young chick like you,' he smiled at me and heartily shook my hand. The mom glowered at him. Then she looked over my washed-out flannel shirt, dropped her gaze once again to my basket, from which broken reeds were sticking out, and stopped at my shabby boots of an indistinct colour.

'My name is Šindelářová,' she held out her hand with its meticulously manicured nails. I imagined their sharp points digging into the cap of a mushroom. 'Call me Irča, and this is my husband Jirka, and our son's name is Toník.'

'Pleasure,' I attempted a smile. 'I understand that you would like to go by car?'

They both nodded as if on command.

'Our car is right behind the office. You see, it's because last week Toník was at his grandmother's house, and she made him scrambled mushrooms all the time. So Irča and I had this idea...'

'You had this idea...' Irča interrupted him.

'We had this idea,' Jirka repeated with a particular emphasis on the first word, 'That we would give mushroom hunting a try with him. Except I haven't been mushroom hunting since I was a kid, and my wife was already born in the city, so we really don't know a thing about it,' he explained.

'And then we happened to come across Mr Vobořil's website.'

We stopped at a black SUV. The kind of a car one buys if one is planning to have a large family. Jirka sat down behind the steering wheel and motioned for me to sit beside him.

'Where to?' he asked, GPS in hand, once everybody was in and the leather seats had stopped squeaking beneath them.

I suggested Dolní Staňkov. At home I had given it quite a bit of thought. I couldn't take them on my route, that was obvious, it was bad enough that a few weeks ago it had already been desecrated by Ruda. But at the same time I wasn't about to go too far afield.

'I'll tell you how to go,' I said, but Jirka was already punching our destination into the navigator. With his eyes fixed on the display, he put the car in gear, started the engine, the car died and the mother gave an ostentatious sigh.

I tried to concentrate on the road. I had never gone mushroom hunting by car. It was a novelty for me to observe the countryside through the car window, as if I were watching a movie. The spruce trees in the forest sadly hung their branches low, turning their pointed tops away from me. I felt like a traitor.

We left the car by the boom gate. Baskets in hand, we entered among the spruces. We stopped at a little clearing by the stream, all three glanced over at me, as if to ask: now what?

I have to confess that I had a bit of the jitters. I didn't know how to begin, I was sweating like a pupil called up to the blackboard, even though I had convinced myself in advance that it would be a piece of cake. It was clear to me that I couldn't just drag them around the forest in silence, they certainly hadn't paid for that. I was hoping that some mushroom would soon save me, but as luck would have it, there wasn't a decent one to be found.

And so, I took it from the top. I started by saying that a mushroom is a peculiar organism. It is neither a plant nor an animal, it represents its own specific and distinctive kingdom. There are tens of thousands of different varieties in the world, but most of them are invisible to the naked eye, they can only be perceived under a microscope. Yet at the same time there is a fungus that is the largest living organism in the world, it is found in North America and grows over an area larger than a thousand football fields! One single mushroom!

I got a bit fired up, strode on at too brisk a pace and looked only under my feet. I completely forgot about the tourists. I turned around to find that I had lost my audience. Jirka and Irča were still stuck at the edge of the clearing in a heated discussion about something. Their voices reached us through the sparse spruces, sounding like the barking of guard dogs.

Toník sat down on a stump a few steps behind me, his gaze fixed on the moss, trying with his thumb to pry loose a reed from the handle of his basket. The sports clothes hung on his rickety frame like on a scarecrow. His back was hunched under an invisible weight. He looked like a foot soldier who had accidentally strayed into enemy territory. It wouldn't have surprised me had this been his very first time in a forest. I felt a bit sorry for him, but wasn't sure how to strike up a conversation.

'Have you ever found a mushroom?' I finally blurted out after a while.

Tonda nodded awkwardly.

'Last week I brought my grandma a puffball,' he answered. His voice was soft and high pitched, but it was already showing signs of breaking. 'She made schnitzels, and told my folks how clever I was, and since then they won't shut up about it.'

The voices of the parents not too far from us grew louder.

'I couldn't give a shit about some damned mushrooms,' Jirka was shouting.

'And I could give even less of a shit,' retorted Irča. Look at that, so there was something they could agree on after all.

Through the trees came the sound of snapping twigs, the slam of a car door and the sputter of an engine. And after that, just the sound of spinning wheels. I looked over at Tonda in embarrassment.

'A while ago Dad got himself a new secretary. Ever since, this is how it's been at home,' he stated.

Jirka strolled over to us. He fished a cigarette out of his pocket, blew a puff of smoke our way and his gaze wandered over to Tonda's empty basket.

'So, how's it going, are they growing?' he asked as if nothing had happened. 'Tonda, what do you say we meet back here in an hour? I'm not feeling up to much today. You don't mind, Tonda, do you?' Without waiting for an answer, he sat down on a moss-covered rock, his back to us.

I looked over at Tonda, again with embarrassment. He shrugged his shoulders, turned, and started walking in the direction that we had originally set out.

Together Tonda and I made our way up a gentle hill. I stayed about three steps behind him and sized up his physique. His figure actually wasn't all that bad. He was slight, perhaps even too skinny, but with a symmetrical body. His dark hair curled into ringlets, which from time to time he would tuck behind his ear. I noticed that he had lovely long, slim fingers. If he shaped up a bit, one day he'd have the girls eating out of his hand. But that would be a few years down the line, his voice hadn't even started to change yet.

He had no idea that I was studying him from head to foot. He seemed very vulnerable to me in his obliviousness. We arrived without speaking at an impenetrable wood of unpruned young spruce trees.

He turned and looked at me with his innocent eyes that behind the thick lenses of his glasses appeared even larger: 'Which way now?'

I motioned with my basket towards a group of pines on the right. I caught up with him and walked along beside him, my eyes fixed under my feet.

Soon we came across the first viable mushroom. That is to say Tonda did. It was a matte bolete, a small one, but nice and fresh. The first bolete of his life.

Parting the grass, we found a few more. I was a bit concerned seeing how clumsily he was handling the knife, I didn't want to return him to Jirka without fingers, but after a few tentative attempts he successfully managed to cut off the dirty end of the stipe and clean off the cap. His initiation was progressing very satisfactorily.

In fact, he really wasn't that hopeless a case. He recognized a parasol, a red cracking bolete and even a slippery jack. In the end we had the best time of all on the russula slope in the beech woods. I advised Tonda on how best to gather them. If an inexperienced mushroom gatherer isn't sure whether or not it is truly a russula, he or she must cut off a piece of its stipe with a pocketknife. If the stipe doesn't fray and nothing flows out of it, it must be a russula. And how to distinguish the edible ones from the inedible ones? I had my own rule, namely that the uglier the colour of a russula, the greater the likelihood that it will be edible. Naturally this doesn't work one hundred per cent of the time, not by a long shot, but it can offer a clue. The best way to recognize an edible russula, however, is simply to bite into it. If it doesn't burn your tongue or leave a bitter aftertaste, whoosh, right into the basket. And if one were to make a mistake after all, there's no cause for alarm, no russula is terribly toxic, one would at most throw up a few times or ruin one's mushroom scramble. And only a total dilettante could mistake an amanita for a russula.

We found masses of them. Charcoal burners, flirts, olive brittlegills and russula mustelina, also known as the russet brittlegill. When we got back to the mossy rock after about an hour, Tonda's eyes were shining. He truly had found most of the mushrooms himself.

Jirka in the meantime had managed to smoke half a pack of cigarettes. There were cigarette butts lying all around him.

There was nothing to be done, Irča was sulking in the car in some unknown place, so we had to get back to Sušice on our own. Jirka's bad mood radiated towards us like an aura. After every few steps he would stop, place his hands on his hips and with a loud sigh, arch his back. Maybe right then he was realizing that the neon-yellow jacket, designed for outdoor activity, was no substitute for flabby muscles. It took us an hour and a half to arrive at the Toadstool.

Tonda had carried the heavy basket the whole way himself, when I offered to help, he flatly refused. At the Toadstool we sent Jirka off to the taproom and went into the kitchen. I discreetly scoured the kitchen with my eyes, but this time didn't see any mushrooms that were not mine.

We laid out the mushrooms on the cutting board and finished cleaning them off ourselves. I set a few brittlegills aside and then Tonda and I cut up the rest of the mushrooms into cubes. The Walrus whipped them up into a scramble for us.

The brittlegills I didn't entrust to the cook. I melted the butter in the frying pan and tossed in the caps without their stipes and the gills facing up. After a while, the caps started to turn up at the sides and a little lagoon formed in the centre of each mushroom. I scooped up the juice with a spoon and let Tonda taste. He was elated.

Tonda and I joined Jirka in the restaurant and brought the Walrus's scramble and our russulas sautéed with butter over to the table. I bit off some dry bread and washed it down with water from the tap, keeping an eye all the while on the kitchen door that was ajar. No other mushroom gatherer showed up in the kitchen in the meantime.

One hour later, I reluctantly returned Tonda to Jirka. He waved goodbye, then pulled out his Swiss Army Knife and went back to examining all of its functions, one after the other.

20

The Walrus stood with his back to the door, bending over the printed menu for the day. I peeked over his shoulder. He was running his finger over the lines, muttering something to himself in a low voice. He greeted me with a barely perceptible nod.

'What's a portobello burger?' I asked.

'Another Ruda idea. A plain old brown mushroom grilled and served on a roll,' he shook his head and made a face.

'Is he even here?' I asked him in a half whisper.

'What do you think?,' he waved his hand. 'He's back there philosophizing again,' he added, pointing a finger towards Ruda's office.

'And what about the other mushroom gatherers, did he find anyone?' I asked him quietly and looked around the room, to see if I might spot any more foreign mushrooms.

'Nothing as of now, but he keeps on talking about other suppliers. He discovered a bag of frozen mushrooms in the Russian deli and now we're supposed to try those too. But that's only over my dead body, cooking with frozen mushrooms at the height of the season!' he spat symbolically.

I sighed, thanked him and left the kitchen to go down the hallway. I knocked on the half-open door of Ruda's office and stepped inside, basket in hand.

The entire office had been transformed into a jumble of cardboard, Styrofoam, bubble wrap, screws and curse words. Ruda was kneeling on the floor, trying to bolt a wooden shelf to a metal bar, but the piece of wood kept slipping out of his hand. I squatted down next to him and held the shelf in place.

In a few minutes the rack was finished. We sat beside each other on the floor, hands propped on our knees, and gazed up at the assembled shelving as if it were an altar. Neither of us said anything and I, in that unexpected double silence, suddenly realized that I could hear Ruda's breathing.

I stood up.

'Things went well with that family. So I've come up with a new plan,' Ruda told me, once he too had stood up. 'Now I know how to get this joint back on its feet.'

He rested the palms of his hands on the table behind him, took a breath and dumped an avalanche of ideas on me.

'The other day was just the beginning. A trial run. We'll test out a few more elements and then we'll go big time. And I even came up with some accompanying accessories. Check this out!'

He leapt up and shoved a piece of paper under my nose with some doodles and tons of numbers.

'That's the starter pack,' he explained. 'Penknife, canvas tote, map. Before I send the mushroom hunting tourists out to you, I'll cash in on them already here. The more expensive version includes a wicker basket and a mushroom atlas, that will be the deluxe pack. And I've got other ideas taking shape in my head. I'll sell dried mushrooms, pickled mushrooms, cookbooks, calendars, whatever you can think of. In short, I'll be offering the ultimate mushroom service, an authentic experience with all the trimmings.'

I made a supreme effort to wrap my head around the idea of this megalomaniac from Sušice forcing penknives and chequered tea towels on people without sneering in derision.

When it came time to say goodbye, Ruda paid me for two days since he hadn't been at the pub the day before. I headed home with seven 100-crown bills. There was a bonus for guiding tourists. I felt as though I had a million bucks in my pocket.

Ruda must have infected me with his megalomania, because before I got to the end of the square, I found myself turning around and walking back a few steps. In the electronics shop window, a cylindrical white object with a red 'sale' sticker on it caught my eye. A dehydrator for 999 Czech crowns. It occurred to me that when I had some money left over, I could buy the device and start selling mushrooms on the side. First, I would try it in Dvorce, and if it went well, I would look around for other markets.

By the time I got home, my crazy plan had begun to seem pretty realistic to me. But first I would try my hand at growing them. I went past the shack and continued a few more houses down to Zatloukal's. It didn't take much to convince him to go and get me what I needed. He handed me a full bag of soil and I handed him 200 crowns. I dragged the bag all the way to the pantry and raked through the substrate. It smelled promising. On my fingers there was a residue of oily clay.

I walked out onto the porch and soaked my dirty hands in the rainwater collected in a tin barrel. I remembered there was a time when I would take forever to wash them. I was literally obsessed with hygiene. Not that I had a phobia about germs attacking me in public places. I wasn't squeamish about using the bathroom at school or eating in the cafeteria. I didn't carry hand sanitizer around and I didn't insist on antibacterial soap. I had the feeling that the dirt was inside my body. Oozing from my pores. I constantly felt that I was unclean, and no sooner did a drop of sweat break out anywhere, my entire body began to itch. I was afraid that everyone around me couldn't help but see it and smell it. For this reason, I got up early every morning so that I could take a long shower, and in the evening, I would wait until everyone was asleep, so that no one would disturb me while I was washing myself. Most of the time, I would rinse off when I got home from school too. And when I was in school or elsewhere, I would at least focus on my hands. I was capable of washing them as many as thirty times a day, scrubbing them with soap, working a special brush between my fingers and underneath my nails so that not a speck of dirt would be left on me. And sometimes I would repeat the whole process a second time.

After the graduation ball my obsession with hygiene ended overnight. Now I don't bother with washing at all because I know there's no point. As a result of picking slimy mushrooms, a thin brownish film has formed on my hands. Not even the most vigorous scrubbing can wash it off.

21

Today I took the day off from the Toadstool. I was due to make another trip to Plzeň, which I have to do regularly every three months.

I stood inside the compartment, one knee resting on the seat, looking out through the open window. My otherwise limp hair was blowing in the wind. The countryside beyond the window started to disappear behind the first tall buildings. Soon I saw a tram passing by. The train veered left and screeched to a stop. I got off and ran down the steps to the street. I had plenty of time but not much cash, so I proceeded to the polyclinic on foot.

I stepped inside the six-storey prefab building with the sign Bory Polyclinic. I passed by the lift and made for the stairs. I climbed each step a bit more slowly than the previous one, although by now I was a good ten minutes late. I sat down on the leatherette chair beside the door to the doctor's office and waited obediently for the nurse to invite me in.

Mouchová, in her office chair, turned from her computer and looked at me. 'Miss Tichá, you must be even thinner than you were last time . . .' she shook her head in disbelief. 'Have a seat.'

'You're a rare case,' she added. 'Others on risperidone gain weight, but you stay as thin as a rail. How do you do it?' she smiled at me. As always, I had the feeling that concealed behind her smile there was an air of suspicion, which is why I got all bristly inside.

'You know, it's just genes, in our family everyone's skinny,' I said and then lowered my eyes because I was ashamed to be lying to her. She was right in that my skinny body was, compared to other patients with the same diagnosis, rather an exception. The thing is, I feed it very little, just enough to keep it from becoming too emaciated, because as an anorexic I would attract excessive attention. But my lifestyle isn't the main reason for my thinness. Each time I dutifully pick up the box of antipsychotics at the pharmacy, I take it home and stash it away in the drawer. I just pop a few tablets before my office visit in case the doctor decides she wants to do a blood test. They don't cause me to gain any weight, but afterwards I always feel sluggish and practically lifeless.

'You're simply lucky,' Mouchová said, ending the discussion as she turned to her computer. She opened the file with my name on it and then came the typical set of questions. How do I feel? Any changes since my last visit? Anxiety? Mood swings? In exactly the same order as last time.

I answered the same way I did at every other visit. If it were up to me, I would put my responses in writing and just reconfirm them to her every three months by text message.

Mouchová finished typing my responses into the computer and pulled a prescription pad out of the drawer. Now she'll just prescribe a new package of tablets for me and I'll be able to go home.

Instead, she tapped her fingers on the tabletop and looked at my medical record again. She scrolled down with the mouse and examined the notes in my file.

'It's already been two years since your last episode,' she stated, having reviewed the previous entries. 'Excellent. And since then no changes... So we're going to start once again to wean you off the drug.'

My heart skipped a beat.

'Really?'

She nodded.

'I... The last time it didn't go so well.'

'I understand your concerns,' she intertwined her fingers on the table. 'But you're not suffering from any serious manifestations of the disease, in fact, you're doing very well,' she continued to speak to the computer and not to me. 'There is no reason not to give it a try. I suggest we proceed with more caution than last time. I'll go slower on cutting back the doses. We'll see how it goes.'

She clicked her ballpoint pen and started to fill out the prescription.

'But what... What about my pension?'

'Don't worry. For the time being you're certainly not going to lose it. If all goes well, I'll lower the dose again at your next visit. For a few more months, you'll definitely need to continue taking the medication.'

'And then?'

Mouchová pushed her glasses down towards the tip of her nose, looked at me and furrowed her eyebrows so she could focus on me.

'You are twenty-five years old. You are a young woman who has a future. It would be a shame to be dependent on drugs forever. Besides, like any drug, risperidone has a number of side effects that are not insignificant. We'll see each other in three months, should you experience difficulties of any kind, come back immediately.'

'But... but...' I couldn't come up with any argument for her to keep me on the same dose.

'Don't worry, you'll manage,' she gave me a wink.

There was nothing to do, she was adamant. I sighed and reached for the script, said goodbye and slowly dragged myself back into the hallway. Outside, the bright sunlight forced me to look down. With my eyes glued to the tips of my shoes, I made my way back to the train.

Every time I am on my way back from the Bory Polyclinic, I veer away from the main street and turn towards the Bezovka quarter. I walk through the quiet streets, passing one First Republic villa after the next. Close to ours, I stop. I have a spot picked out at the intersection under a tree. I stand right up against the trunk, so that I'm completely hidden in its shadow and gaze into our windows. As if I could see anything through the heavy curtains. I imagine that I go inside, take off my shoes in the hallway, walk through the living room and the kitchen and then make my way up the stairs to my bedroom. Once I've gone through every room in my mind, I continue to the train station.

Today I did the exact same thing. I stopped in front of a villa that hasn't been my home in a long time. It looked empty. There was no car parked out front and nothing moved behind the windows. And then... instead of turning as I always did to go back to the main street, I moved towards the house. Before I had a chance to think it over. Evžen hadn't yet managed to get the gate fixed, so all it took was to press my knee under the handle and give a gentle push. Once again, I was standing in front of the dark inlaid door. My knees were shaking. My stomach was in knots. I pulled the keys out of my pocket. The key slipped inside the lock but wouldn't turn. I pulled it out and slipped the set back into my pocket. I felt like a thief.

From the street came the sound of a car passing by. The engine stopped and I could hear a door open. I bolted down the three steps, yanked at the gate, didn't bother closing it behind me, ran into the street and continued to the main street, never turning back. And so, I never did find out if it was Evžen or a perfect stranger.

On the way to the train station, it still occurred to me that I might as well give Milan a call. I would stop by and ask him why he had called me. But when I felt around my pockets, I realized that I had left my cell phone at home.

At the train station, I took the key that no longer fit into any lock off the keyring and tossed it into the garbage. Then I got on the train.

22

Every night I stiffened in bed as if I were lying in a coffin. I would observe the free world beyond the window like a cutout, the moon in the sky, beginning to wax, growing full, then waning, the stars, sparkling for a moment before being obscured by floating clouds, and the branches of the walnut tree. I never managed to fall asleep before he came. And afterwards, for many long hours, I would lie there like a rotting corpse in a grave. And then finally, even I could fall asleep. But it didn't go well.

They started to call me Sleeping Beauty. I would nod off in the morning over my cup of tea, they would find me curled up in the corner of the garden next to the raspberries, my eyes would be closing as I brushed my teeth. Playing canasta, every so often I would hit my forehead on the table, the cards spilling out of my hand onto the floor, and once I even crashed during a game of table tennis. One time my mom found me tied to the tree, folded over down to my knees, held up only by the sturdy rope. On an excursion to Kašperské Hory on the main square, I fell out of the car onto my father's feet, having fallen asleep leaning against the door. And on one of the mushroom hunting expeditions with my dad, in which I now participated only reluctantly, I dozed off on some moss. In short, I could fall asleep anytime and anywhere, except for at night in my own bed.

'What's the matter with our Sisi?' my mother asked shaking her head, and I wanted in the worst way possible to spill everything out to her, but I couldn't, I found it impossible to describe the foul-smelling sludge inside me with words. I tried to say something, but the words caught in my throat, so I just stood there in front of her gasping like a carp that has swum up to a hole chopped into the ice. And she never asked any more questions, and after a while turned away and went back to her business. Ever since we arrived in Dvorce, she had changed. She was no longer the beleaguered mother, but was once again our dreamy old mom. Albeit in a foreign, pudgy body. Everyone else also seemed as if transformed. Our parents weren't snapping at each other. My brothers weren't holing themselves away any more than usual. They had become a functional family. Only I remained on the sidelines.

The boys made fun of my ability to fall asleep at any time of the day. Upon my head laying on the table they piled whatever they could find: a dishcloth, a piece of bread spread with honey, a tower made out of matchboxes, dirty socks. Somewhere I still have a saved photograph—still life with me and some rotten summer apples.

But their stupid games didn't bother me as much any more. I would have given anything to be with them. I would have eaten that slug stuffed into the gooseberry, remained forever a zilch, folded their laundry into a perfect stack.

'Could you sleep in my room tonight?'

I noticed Milan turn up the corner of his mouth in a sneer.

'It's here. It's back. The shadow,' I added.

It must have been a good five years since we last slept in the same bed together. Back then, when our mom would read to us in the evening, I would slip under his comforter and he wouldn't protest. Maybe in his own way he was glad, because he too was afraid of the ghost that was terrorizing us then. We called it the shadow, it was a faceless monster that would lie in wait under the bed or behind a curtain. Once the light was off, it would spread out all over the little room, then lie on top of a child and smother it. And so, we would hold hands and face that phantasm together under one blanket. Sometimes we fell asleep before our mom had finished reading the fairy tale. When I was five, our mom put an end to our evening visits. Climbing into an older brother's bed wasn't appropriate for such a big girl.

My voice must have sounded so urgent that he cautiously nodded.

'All right,' he said hesitantly. 'I'll wait . . .'

He didn't finish his sentence. Our older brother's face appeared in the window. Milan jerked away the hand that I was holding in mine.

'Yeah right, your feet stink,' he brushed me off and walked out of the kitchen into the garden.

It wasn't until the afternoon that I managed to catch him alone again. Only after our mom had assigned us our chores did I know where to find him. While Evžen grappled with mowing the lawn, I set aside my hoe and walked back from the dug-up flowerbed to the cottage. Milan lay sprawled in bed upstairs, listening to music.

I pulled one of the earbuds from his ear and grabbed his wrist. Startled, he jerked his head and squinted at me.

'Milan, will you come?'

He looked into my eyes and was silent for a long time. 'All right,' he finally squeezed my hand. 'After Evžen is asleep, I'll come to you. But not a word in front of our brother. And now get off my case already.' Then he closed his eyes and stuck the earbud back into his ear.

Shortly after sunset, Milan truly did come. He sat down in the little armchair that he pulled up to the bed and held my hand. I fell asleep almost instantly.

When I woke up in the middle of the night, I was no longer holding the soft hand that loved to avoid doing work. Gripping my palm was a large adult paw. I could feel the roughened pad of a thumb stroking my wrist.

The next morning, I glimpsed Milan through the kitchen window, sitting on the porch bench. Before I had a chance to say anything to him, he got up and ran away, looking down. We never spoke about it again. Even during the days that followed he avoided me.

And so every night I would go to bed alone. As if I were lying down inside a coffin. I remember the clammy fear that would cling to me at night and that I couldn't rid myself of even during the day.

I learnt to turn off my body. It became just a shell that weighed me down. If I tried very hard, I could step out of it for a moment. It became an inert piece of flesh, its eyes closed, lips pressed together, its limbs like rags. It was buried deep in the ground and I floated above it. Had I been able to, I never would have returned to it.

But these moments of freedom were only fleeting, soon my body would pull me back down and fasten the shackles.

Until one time, in the middle of the night, someone attempted to liberate me from the grave. At first, I thought I was mistaken, but then it happened again. Discreet but distinct knocks. Three of them. As if my heart had stopped and someone had begun to pump my chest. My father stiffened in fright. Those three dull knocks on the door returned me to my body. Someone wanted to save me.

23

The banging on the door would have woken the dead. I delayed for another moment, but had long suspected whom I would find standing behind the front door. I should have called him. It was just past six o'clock, he must have got up around four in the morning.

I went into the hallway. The door was in danger of popping off its hinges, it was shaking so hard under the blows.

I opened the door just as Milan was getting ready to strike again. He froze before me, his fist raised like a communist revolutionary on a poster. A look of surprise flashed across his face, perhaps not even he had expected he might succeed this time. He relaxed his fist and ran his fingers through his gelled hair. He looked as always casually elegant, on his face a manicured stubble that went well with his black biker jacket and worn jeans. Peeking out behind him was a shiny car, once again different from the last time.

'Ciao, sis!' he blurted out and spread his arms to give me a hug. I backed away from him into the hallway and he immediately took advantage of the opportunity and slipped inside the door after me, keeping his hand on my shoulder. All with a friendly smile, as always. It was typical of him. A smile on his face, a dagger in his hand, with which he was about to stab me in the back. Not even I had changed, I was still instinctively cowering, as if I was afraid a blow was going to come down from somewhere.

For a long time, Milan had been the black sheep of the family. He didn't make it into the gymnasium and it was only thanks to our dad's good connections that he was able to get into a business academy. There, he flailed around like a fish out of water, took a bunch of makeup exams and had to repeat one year. He managed to graduate by the skin of his teeth and, just to avoid having to get a job, enrolled at a private university for which our father had to pay. He didn't attend lectures, slept through seminars and took all his exams on make-up dates. For the second semester he only showed up in class during the first few weeks, and finally stopped going altogether. Not even the offer of a large donation to the school, one that even the biggest slackers managed to complete, helped. He was kicked out after just one year of study.

Our parents then paid for various language courses in Great Britain and Malta. 'Milan is studying in London,' they would say, but one day even that came to an end.

Once, when I was visiting my mother in the hospital, in the hallway, he gave me a brief overview of what he did for a living. He had got into selling cars by accident, through a friend. At first he worked with him, bringing in totalled cars from Germany, getting the worst defects fixed, the undercarriages straightened out, and then selling them to fools who fell for his suave attitude. Then he took it up a notch. Take a car that's gone through five owners, been in three accidents, lose the registration, roll back the odometer, polish up the hood and bingo: you've got a pristine luxury vehicle that's only been preowned once. A model in near-mint condition. He just needed to sell one or two a month, and he was all set.

From a lazy, clumsy kid he had transformed into a dashing, well-heeled young man with a respectable home on the outskirts of Plzeň, an adorable little dog and a cuddly girlfriend. When things began to go well for him, it seems our parents breathed a sigh of relief. Now the owner of a car dealership, as he referred to his business, he had suddenly become acceptable to our parents. Even without a college education.

Milan looked around the hallway a bit awkwardly, as if it was his first time here. I realized that from the time of my accident, fifteen years ago, he really hadn't been here even once. That in the meantime, the shack had become an entirely foreign home to him.

'So, how have you settled in here?' he boomed after peering into the kitchen. Not waiting for an answer, he stepped across the threshold, but the too-low doorframe, that intercepted his forehead, knocked him back into the hallway for a moment. He managed not to curse. Then he shook his head in surprise. 'Wow, in all these years it seems as if nothing has changed in here,' he marvelled. 'Mind if I take a look upstairs?'

This time he ducked in the doorway at the right moment and proceeded up the stairs expertly stooped, so as not to bang his head against the ceiling. He opened the door to the room that he had once shared with Evžen. He advanced to the wardrobe and ran his hand over it. Then he tapped on the little table beside his bed. Except for the old mattresses, there was nothing left on the beds, my brothers' blankets came in handy in the winter when the shack got cold, so I had moved them down to the kitchen. Something in the corner of the room behind the door caught his eye. He bent down and pulled out his dusty old toy police car. He blew on it and turned it over several times in the palm of his hand, as if wondering what to do with it. Finally he tossed it on the bed. He walked out of the room and proceeded to mine. He glanced at my unmade bed and froze. He swallowed hard, then turned around and descended the stairs in silence.

Without being invited, he sat down at the table and placed his hands on the tabletop on which the paint was peeling. I offered him a cup of tea. One by one I opened every single cupboard door before I finally found something I could serve him. Chocolate wreath cookies that I had bought last winter after the sell-by date had already expired. Why am I making such a fuss over him? I reproached myself silently. Out of the corner of my eye, I could see him snooping around the room with his gaze.

'Hey, you've still got my mug,' he said, pointing his finger at the glass door of the cupboard. 'The one with the squirrel.'

'But that one was Evžen's.'

'Really? Oh well, OK,' he shrugged, sipped his tea, and bit into a cookie.

'I brought some papers with me,' he added after a moment, with his mouth full. 'But that'll wait, I thought we might go out hunting for some mushrooms, huh? They're growing, I hear.' He gave me a wink and smiled. He knew just how to get me.

The morning was still chilly, but the blue sky promised fine weather. In front of the shack Milan automatically made for the car, but then, like it or not, he had to follow me on foot.

Along the way he whistled, one hand stuck in his pocket, in the other a cigarette. We didn't speak, maybe he didn't know how to begin, and neither did I.

I led him along my route. We stopped at the usual spots. With Milan, there was no reason to hide them, he posed absolutely no threat. At least not in this regard. Mushrooms were of no interest to him, not one bit.

In fact, like me, he didn't even care for mushroom dishes. Unlike me, however, he didn't pretend. Once in a while he would have a few bites of blushers or parasols sautéed in butter, but a mushroom scramble, most of the time he wouldn't even touch it.

Today, though, he was making a real effort. With his leather loafers, he determinedly parted the grass under his feet, peered under every fir tree, ran his hand over the blades of grass, trod carefully on the moss. After an hour he celebrated his first success. Not far from the patch of matte boletes he found a giant bolete. It was so big that it would have been enough for a decent mushroom scramble. It had a splendid sturdy stipe covered with a meshlike pattern, a smooth, pale brown cap and white sponge-like pores with pinkish tubes. A bona fide bitter bolete. It had hidden beneath a smallish pine tree and was gloating at the idea of ruining some amateur mushroom gatherer's scramble and mushroom cutlets.

'Look, it's not even wormy,' Milan proudly showed me the stem, from which he had torn off the tip. Obviously he was right, worms usually steer clear of bitter mushrooms.

Milan mustered the sweetest facial expression of which he was capable.

'So you see, sis, I'm not totally out of practice, you don't have a big king bolete like this one in your basket yet.'

I looked at Milan as one looks at a foolish pupil, took a few steps and bent down, not far from him, towards a little group of young king boletes. Milan, arching an eyebrow, went on turning the mushroom over in his hands for a bit longer, and in the end flung it against a tree. The cap split in two and the bulbous white stem smashed against the trunk.

We continued further south. Milan was still tentatively peering into the grass, but no longer with the same zeal. Just before Krušec he plunked himself down on a pile of logs by the side of the road.

'I can't go on ...'

I sat down beside him and set my basket on the ground. We sat there like that for a while, staring down at our shoes. Then suddenly he grabbed my hand. His palm was warm and soft. I pulled away from him and slipped my hand into my pocket. He shrugged and lit a cigarette.

'You probably know why I'm here, sis, right?'

I remained silent.

'The estate has to be settled. We wrote up a contract with the lawyer for the division of the inheritance. Evžen and I have been trying to track you down for weeks, but you, nothing, so our brother had the lawyer draw it up without you. I left it on the table for you.'

Milan took a drag on his cigarette and ran his fingers through his hair.

'You didn't make out so badly, when you figure . . .' he cleared his throat, 'Well, considering all the circumstances.'

I looked at my shabby hiking boots, ragged jeans and dirty hands. I thought about the small stove in the kitchen that stayed hot for just a few hours, and the hose I use to draw water from the well to the kitchen when the pump happens to be working, and the basin, in which I wash first myself and then reuse the same water for my laundry. He was right. Things could always be worse.

Milan dropped his cigarette butt on the ground and crushed it with his heel. He wiped his palms on his thighs and awkwardly stood up.

'I'm going to have to head back, they're bringing me some new cars today.'

'Yeah, and I've got to get going too, I'm barely a third of the way.'

Milan smiled at me and patted me on the shoulder. Then he pulled me close and hugged me.

'I'll be back later for the contract,' he whispered into my ear, as if someone could overhear us, 'Don't worry, it's not as bad as you think. In the end you'll pocket some of the inheritance too, not the house, obviously, but if you sign, you'll get the cottage and some moolah too.'

'I'll think about it,' I mumbled.

He pushed me away and asked: 'What was that?'

'I said I'll think about it.'

He looked me straight in the eye and frowned a little, as if I had a screw loose.

'Don't dilly-dally too long with that signature. Evžen's on the warpath, he's ready to take it to court. I've been trying to talk him out of it, but you know how he is. The electricity and other payments are still coming out of the family account, and Evžen wants to shut it down. See that you don't end up without a pot to piss in, he's capable of taking even your shack away from you. He's trying to figure out with the lawyers if he can disinherit you. You know what I mean, you didn't come by to see the parents much these last couple of years. I know, I get it, but who's going to testify to that? Not Evžen, that's for sure. And what's my word against his? Considering what happened to Dad, after ... Well, you know. I'm talking to you like a brother.'

I remained silent.

'What about the meds, you taking them?' he asked after a while.

I nodded. You bet I'm taking them. Every three months I pick them up at the pharmacy, scoop them into a plastic bag and take them home. What I do with them after that is nobody's business. At first, I used to burn the pills that I popped out of the packaging, or I'd bury them in the garden, but after a while I got tired of it. Now I simply stash the unopened boxes in the drawer of the table.

'Most of all, don't go doing any stupid stuff like that time in Sušice, you know what I mean, there's a solution to everything, sis,' he went on to add, by way of goodbye, before turning back. It seemed that he was being serious.

I followed him with my eyes until he disappeared in the forest and then continued on my way.

That evening I moved around the folder like a bomb squad expert circling a live grenade. I dreaded reading what Evžen had prepared for me. Finally, I sat down at the table and dove into the contract.

Milan was right. It wasn't as terrible as I expected. According to the contract I could continue to use the cottage for an indefinite period of time, during which all expenses for electricity and utilities would be paid for out of the family account, as had been the case up to now.

Furthermore, Evžen agreed to pay me the sum of 5,000 crowns per month as reimbursement for expenses related to the upkeep of the cottage.

Inwardly I felt a sense of relief and gratitude. It would make up for my disability pension, which I was evidently about to lose, and beyond that I would have about 2,000 extra left over. There was nothing to ponder. My portion of the inheritance was obviously not advantageous, the assets that would go to both of my brothers were greater by several multiples. But I wasn't about to get into a legal battle with Evžen. I had neither the nerves nor the money for that. And all three of us knew it.

I opened the drawer in the table to pull out a pen. As I was closing it, I noticed a square tin box that was peeking out from underneath the packets of meds. I tapped on it with the knuckle of my index finger. There was a hollow sound.

When I moved in here seven years ago, I thought it would be just for a short time. For only a few weeks, at the most months, before I found myself something decent. Back then in the pantry I had discovered the tin with the expired tea. I emptied it into a flower bed and after the first payment from Vobořil, I put some of the money away in it. I did this every time I earned something. With a few crowns I bought myself something to eat, some of the money, designated for essential short-term expenses, I hid in a cup in the cupboard, but most of it I deposited into the tea tin. Over the years the proportions slowly began to reverse. I had to invest more and more into minor repairs and essential purchases and there was scarcely any money left over for long-term savings. This year I had opened it only three times.

I picked up the tea tin and shook it. A barely audible rattling was heard inside.

I set it on the table beside the papers from Evžen and went out into the garden. I walked back and forth, from fence to fence, reflecting.

Lately there had been so many changes in my life. In May my mother died. With that, yet another thread tying me to my family had broken. My job at the Toadstool was by no means as secure as it used to be. Ruda was totally unpredictable. On any given day he was capable of telling me that he had found a replacement. And to make things worse, there was that business with Mouchová. Unless I started faking psychological problems again, I would lose my disability pension within a few months.

But looming over all of these problems was a question that was much more obtrusive: why had Evžen tied the 5,000 crowns he wanted to give me to the use of the cottage? Why wouldn't he pay me that sum no matter what? Why did it matter so much to him that I stay here?

I didn't have to think too hard about the answer. My oldest brother fears that the 'disgrace of the family' might return to Plzeň. Evžen is afraid of me. Perhaps for the first time in my life I possessed a very effective weapon against him. That feeling began to give me confidence. With every step I felt stronger. I sat down on the root of the walnut tree, leaned back against the gnarled trunk and looked at the shack. It suddenly appeared to me to be even smaller and more rundown than it actually was.

Perhaps my fate isn't sealed once and for all. Maybe there exists an alternative to life in Dvorce.

By the time I sat back down at the kitchen table, it was already dark outside. All around there was silence, only occasionally disrupted by the sound of a passing car.

I returned the pen to the drawer and opened the tea tin. I tossed in 7 crowns that I had fished out of my pocket. I closed it again, tapped on its tin lid and held it between my two palms. And then I silently made a promise to that tea tin that I would go back to my original plan. I would move far away. Ideally still this year. Before I failed to pass Ruda's selection process to be court mushroom gatherer at the Toadstool. Before the roof of my shack caved in. I will not let myself be condemned to a miserable existence by signing that contract. I can do better than to spend the rest of my life in Červené Dvorce.

When I picked up the folder with the contract to put it, unsigned, into the drawer, I noticed that something fell out of it.

A letter with my name on it. I recognized beyond the shadow of a doubt my mother's handwriting.

24

Although my mother was rather self-absorbed and only half-paid any attention to me, there were occasional bright spots. I have preserved several memories in which she stepped out of her dream world and actually saw me. Those few moments seemed to me like the smooth stones in a river that one could skip across to reach the other bank.

I used to love it when she cut my hair. It has always been very fine, rather like the grown-out fur of a mouse. Apparently, no one else in the family had such bad hair, perhaps only Aunt Věrka, whom no one had seen for decades now. The colour was nothing to write home about either. Neither fair nor dark, 'No one could mix a colour like that,' a hairdresser once told me, and it occurred to me that she had to be right, because no one would want to replicate such a dull brownish-grey shade. Right after being washed, my hair would go limp and get greasy, no haircut ever held its shape for more than a few days.

My mother, whose golden hair was, by contrast, very thick, got upset with the hairdresser. 'You look like a plucked chicken,' she said to me once, as we walked out of the beauty parlour into the street. Back home she resolutely slapped the table and fetched the scissors from her sewing kit.

'It needs to be shorter in the back,' she explained. 'The bangs, too.'

From that day on she cut my hair. She would sit me down in the bathroom on the piano stool, swivel it as high as it would go, throw a plastic tablecloth over me, knot it behind my neck and start to cut. I always watched her in the mirror, she would bend over me, comb my hair carefully, so as not to pull out a single hair of the fine fuzz on my head, and cut slowly, strand by strand, looking at me from such a close distance that she must have seen even the tiniest freckle on my face. She concentrated on every hair, biting her lip, narrowing her eyes, and furrowing her otherwise smooth forehead. She had completely forgotten about her mask, discarded the mannered smile, here and there tossed out a word in Slovak or just hummed, *To ta hel'pa* and *Čobogaj, něbogaj . . .* , and it didn't bother her in the least that she was singing completely out of tune. At the end she would stand behind me, hold a strand of my hair in each hand against my cheeks, and check the mirror to make sure the ends were even. Our faces were very close, her golden hair and my mousy hair touching, and we would look at our double reflection together, and sometimes exchange smiles.

Other times I managed to bring my mother down from the clouds and back to earth when I was sick. From an early age I suffered from bladder and kidney problems. It always came on abruptly, all I needed was to catch a cold and suddenly I would spike a fever and an invisible hand would clamp down on my lower belly. One time my parents even had to come and collect me from a school camping trip. I had tried to prop myself up on my elbows following the afternoon nap, but my arms gave way and I fell back on the cot, shivering with cold. I vaguely remember my mother running over, taking me from the teacher's arms and carrying me to the car, which Dad was driving. Afterwards, there was just the white hospital room. And my mom beside me, holding my hand. She looked like the Virgin Mary I had seen in a painting in the church, where our mother would sometimes take us on Sundays.

It was February, the paediatric hospital was packed to bursting, and they didn't have an extra bed for my mom. She could be glad that they had at least provided her with an uncomfortable low-backed hospital chair, which she had pulled up beside my bed and in which she sat day and night.

I heard the doctor try to persuade her to go home and get some sleep, but my mom refused, she wasn't about to leave her only little girl in the hospital alone.

Every time I would turn around, she was sitting on the hard chair beside me, stroking my hand during the procedures, wiping my forehead that was sweaty with fever, supporting my head and holding the cup of water up to my parched lips. She partially took over the nurse's duties, administering cold water compresses, taking my temperature and bringing me the bedpan.

Not having slept for several days she must really have looked awful, because I remember that during one visit even my dad suggested that he would spell her for one night so that she could get some rest.

'I can't abandon her. She's still so little,' she had flatly refused.

It was this phrase I was reminded of that night when I heard the sounds behind the door. Three taps on the door and the room was flooded with light. In the doorway stood a massive silhouette. There was no doubt to whom it belonged.

It was as if my mother had thrown open the lid of the coffin in which I had been buried alive. The light spilling in from the hallway washed away the dank stench of the stone crypt. My mother had come to rescue her daughter.

I felt my father stiffen in fear. Both of our hearts were pounding wildly.

She stared at us. She must have seen us the moment she opened the door, because the light from the stairway reached all the way to my bed. The shadow of her figure fell across my face. I couldn't see her face against the light, but I sensed that she was in shock. I could see her hand on the door handle trembling.

My mother took a step towards us. I could feel my father's nails dig into my flesh. The sharp pain filled me with hope. My nightmare was ending!

I smiled at my mother's darkened face.

I can't abandon her. She's still so little . . .

And then . . . Then something unfathomable happened. My mother did something that was utterly absurd. She froze mid-step and whispered: 'Excuse me.' For a moment she shuffled uneasily on her feet, then turned on her heel and shut the door behind her.

For a while we didn't move. Two skeletons rotting in the earth.

And then I could feel my father's claws slowly beginning to loosen. There was no longer a need to hold on to me so tightly to keep me from escaping. A new wall had gone up around the prison, one that blotted out my view completely.

I could feel the smile on his face. He had won. Definitively. There was no way I could scale a wall that high.

The sharp pain subsided and my entire body went numb again. The massive slab of stone had returned to its place. I was back in the tomb. Around me an impenetrable, foul-smelling darkness, beneath my feet the cold, rotting earth.

After my father left me, I lay in bed for a long time without moving. I couldn't understand what had happened. It made no sense at all.

25

This past week didn't go so well. No matter how hard I tried, I arrived at the Toadstool each day with my basket half-empty. The first time Ruda glossed over it, the second time he looked into my eyes with reproach and pointedly arched his eyebrows, and on the third day he let slip his first harsh word. I thought of Vojta. He hadn't particularly proved himself on our chanterelle hunting expedition, but at least he had brought me luck, something I could really use right now. If I'm going to achieve my goal, I'm going to have to add something to the tea tin again.

I got up extra early in the morning so as not to miss him. Even before I got to the gate, I spotted his slim, tall figure at the end of the street. His fluorescent shoelaces were visible even from such a distance. He must have been up for at least an hour already, as he was on his way back from Sušice with a bag of groceries.

When I asked him if he would join me, he looked at me in alarm.

'At least as far as the intersection, and then you can decide . . .' I blurted out, trying to convince him. I couldn't force him to accompany me all the way to Sušice. We were both attached to our respective routes, perhaps even more than to the mushrooms. He nodded hesitantly.

Walking south we came across just a handful of remnants. Closer to Hartmanice, where our paths usually diverged, Vojta abruptly stopped short and glanced into the basket. Then he became agitated and began nervously to look around. For a moment he stepped off to the side and took refuge under a massive tree. I didn't know what to do. I was afraid that Vojta might be having one of his episodes. I checked to make sure I had my cell phone in my pocket so that I could call his mother.

'I'll come with you,' came a muffled voice from behind the tree. Then Vojta re-emerged onto the path, wiped his sweaty hands on his pants and headed east.

I set off after him and accidentally kicked over a saffron milkcap. A little bit further I spotted at least ten more. As I gathered them up, a slew of unintelligible words rained down on me from above. My companion was babbling away to himself.

'So what are your favourite books to read?' I interrupted his monologue to distract him.

Vojta was visibly taken aback. That, after all, was hardly the point. He was able to sort the books by colour, letters in the title, name of the author, year or place of publication and the ISBN, but as far as what was written inside, that wasn't his thing.

'I don't read books. I mean, except for the first and last pages and page 48.'

'Why specifically page 48?'

'Every book has a page 48. Otherwise it's not a book, but a booklet or a pamphlet, and I'm not interested in those. I like that number. You have to divide it four times before you get a prime number. I don't like prime numbers,' he replied without hesitation.

In the meantime, Vojta's magical powers must have expired, because we didn't find the next mushroom until just past Kundratice. A matte bolete that fit into the palm of one's hand, normally I would have left it there, but I couldn't afford to do that today. The matte bolete likes to hide in the moss, to be swathed in blades of forest grass, it allows fallen leaves to cover its cap and snuggles up to tree roots of the same colour. But not even the best camouflage can fool me. These attempts at disguise are as futile as my mother's attempts to hide the rolls on her stomach with body shaping underwear.

We knelt down and carefully drew apart the blades of grass around us. It was just as I had expected. There was an entire little family hiding among the leaves. One by one we carefully scooped the matte boletes out of the moist earth. There were about a dozen of them, we filled the bottom of the basket, but no great shakes. And then on to the Annín woods, where we added two Lexies, seven pine boletes, one chestnut bolete and two brittlegills, practically nothing.

It was only when we reached the pasture beyond Annín that fortune smiled on us. Near the cow pasture in the grass, we found a small cluster of common inkcaps and a few shaggy manes. We took only the young ones, the larger dark ones aren't very tasty, they blacken and dissolve quickly. But when they are young they taste delicious. We collected exactly thirty-five of them.

It restored my morale. The Walrus knows how to prepare an excellent cream sauce with the inky caps and a goulash. I was glad that for the first time in a while, things had gone well again and the Toadstool would be able to make a good showing with dishes that hadn't been on the menu in some time.

When we walked into the restaurant's kitchen, Ruda was just in the middle of explaining something at length to the Walrus. He was waving his hand back and forth, but because he was smaller in stature, he looked like a student chiding a teacher. The Walrus remained stubbornly silent. All that was left of his full lips was a thin line. The door creaked and Ruda turned towards us. At the sight of Vojta, who remained standing on the threshold, he raised his eyebrows inquisitively.

'Who's this guy you've brought with you?'

Vojta straightened up, dropped his arms alongside his body and said: 'My name is Měšťan. Vojtěch Měšťan.'

'Aren't you a charmer,' Ruda chuckled. Then he clicked his heels, drew himself up, saluted and barked: 'Vobořil. Ruda.' He swung his right hand and extended it to Vojta, who, however, continued to let his own hang limp. Ruda made a face. It looked to me like a meeting of two force fields, where the point of collision had set sparks flying.

'And what's this supposed to be?' Ruda turned back towards me. 'A Coprinus, you say? And where did you say you nabbed these? Some dung heap?' he asked sniffing the mushroom with affected disgust. 'And what am I supposed to put on the menu? Dung soup? Dung stew?' he was fuming.

It occurred to me that I was right not to grab the three stinkhorn eggs that were peeking out at me from a thicket just outside of Sušice. With those, Ruda in his frenzy might have booted me right out the door. But I wasn't going to let anyone touch my Coprinus. Like a proper attorney, I presented my client in the best possible light. I described him as one of our finest mushrooms. A gourmet delicacy. I assured Ruda that we found our Coprinus mushrooms in the grass and that there was no dung in the vicinity. It can happen with mushrooms, that their name often doesn't correspond with their habitat. For example take the oak bolete, one usually finds it under pines. But Ruda once again showed himself to be a real dolt.

'I asked you for ceps and chanterelles, those really fly, and as for these stinking dung mushrooms, you can stuff 'em.'

I shuffled my feet nervously and looked at Krušina, full of hope. 'Mr Krušina, go on, you have to admit, last year your inky cap mushroom sauce was a big hit.'

But the Walrus didn't even bother to look up from the pot of soup.

'You see ...' grimaced Ruda.

I got so angry, I felt like flinging the inky dung caps right at him, so that he would realize that they don't have even the slightest odour, but fortunately good sense prevailed. I just had to hold out for a couple of more weeks, at the most months and I'd never see him again.

Ruda stood in front of me, holding out his hand with my basket. I could see the Walrus in the rear part of the kitchen, his back was to me and he was stirring an enormous pot with a long, wooden cooking spoon, tasting from it with loud slurps every minute, without adjusting the salt or adding any spices. That was typical of him, he was not one for confrontations, he preferred to huddle in some corner and then curse quietly to himself in the evening. The assistant cook saw fit to disappear into the storeroom.

'Dung caps! You've really managed to muck things up. Don't ever show up here with something like that again!' Ruda shoved the basket into my hand.

I obediently took it back and aimed for the door. I would make another run into the woods and hopefully by evening would bring back a better catch. I saw Vojta standing in the doorway. 'Come on,' I hissed in his direction.

But Vojta didn't budge.

'Mister Vobořil,' he suddenly let loose, 'You are wrong, Coprinus, or inky caps, and the Greek *koprinos*, of dung, are not at all the same thing. The Coprinus, or inky cap, can grow in the vicinity of cow dung, but it can just as easily be found in the grass. I can assure you that these ones never touched any cow excrement. Here, have a sniff,' he reached into the basket and held a mushroom under Ruda's nose. The latter took a step backwards, gritted his teeth and narrowed his eyes.

'Go into the woods and come back with chanterelles,' he said through his clenched teeth while continuing to look at Vojta. Suddenly I felt defiance rise up in me. Before I managed to change my mind, I blurted: 'No, I'm not going. Here are the inky caps. Take them or leave them.'

'I'm not interested in any inky caps. I'm telling you, I want chanterelles. And ceps, blushers, and Perlpilzes,' Ruda retorted, his voice cracking.

'Mister Vobořil,' Vojta interjected again, 'Once more I must point out to you that you are wrong. A blusher and a Perlpilz are the same mushroom. The *amanita rubescens*. You can recognize it by the pinkish cap and shredded ring . . .'

Ruda clenched his fists and let out a prolonged, unintelligible sound.

Lying on the table beside him were a ladle, a potato masher, a knife-sharpener and a wooden whisk beater. I concluded that all four instruments could serve as weapons, so I motioned to Vojta that it was time to leave.

'Come on, now . . .'

As we walked towards the square, I struggled with various emotions within me. Anger, that I hadn't controlled myself and hadn't promised Ruda to bring him different mushrooms. Fear, that I would lose my income and not be able to save up enough money to get out of here. Gratitude towards Vojta. But at the same time the seed of something completely new had started to germinate within me. It was the same feeling as when my brothers had once locked me in the dark cellar with the rumbling boiler and I managed to climb out through the narrow basement window and escape. I felt pride. I was proud of myself for having stood up to him. For not having been frightened and for having shown him that with me he couldn't get away with just anything. Suddenly I could breathe more freely. I peeled my eyes away from the dirty street and looked straight ahead of me.

'I could go for an ice cream,' Vojta remarked as we were approaching the bridge over the Otava. It was obvious that the scene in the kitchen had left him unfazed.

'I'm not much for sweets,' I lied, because I didn't have a penny on me, and then watched as Vojta ordered two scoops of the most toxic looking colours. Pistachio and Smurf.

We got to the river and went down the steps to the weir. We sat down on the stone bank, Vojta tucking himself into a cross-legged position, while I took off my shoes and savoured the icy caress of the river water on my feet.

I propped myself back on my arms and looked around. It was Saturday, a hot and sunny day. Couples and small groups strolled up and down along the riverbank, a few teenagers were crossing the weir, some toddlers wearing colourful swimming wings were playing in the water near us with watering cans and sand moulds while their mothers scampered around them like circus dogs.

One little girl in a blue bathing suit decorated with pink fish and a white sun hat tied under her chin had let go of her plastic toy boat and it had drifted two metres away. The little girl set off bravely after it, cautiously advancing into the water as her chubby legs wobbled. Would she make it or not, I asked myself, because the stones in the Otava tend to be quite slippery. My guess was that she wouldn't, and I had to smile as I saw my prediction come true. The little girl did manage to take a second and third step, but as she reached for the toy boat, her legs gave way and she plopped down in the water.

'Up, Libuškaaa...' her mother exclaimed in irritation.

Before she could burst into tears, her mother had already swooped in, pulled her out of the water, which barely reached her ankles, and plunked her down on the shore. Falling into the water even earned her a light spanking.

She was a mom like any other, one who at the playground doesn't let little Libuška out of her sight, who runs after her and when she stumbles, catches her before she can fall on her knees. Safety, this is the word parents swear by. Because, in fact, evil in some form is lurking everywhere—around every corner there might be a dog that bites children, outside every store a paedophile lies in wait. Some fifty-year-old with gelled hair slicked back, a gold chain around his neck and a hairy chest below, a gourd-shaped belly bulging out of his tight T-shirt. He offers children candy and entices them with promises of furry puppies, or invites them home to watch movies or play video games.

It is the job of mothers to eliminate every risk and potential danger, so that the child does not come to harm. Only back at home, behind a security door with three locks on it, in a flat where every sharp corner has been taped with rubber foam and every outlet plugged with a safety cap, can mothers, exhausted after a full day of minding and haggling, sit down on the sofa with a glass of wine and *finally* catch their breath. What goes on at night behind the closed door of their child's room is no longer their concern.

Vojta in the meantime finished his ice cream and swallowed the tip of his cone. I pulled my feet out of the river, put on my socks and slipped on my shoes. I was glad that we were finally going. In the hot sun, the headache caused by my insomnia had got worse. My temples felt as though they were in a vice.

By the time we got back to Dvorce it was already after three. A short distance from Vojta's cabin I offered him to come over for a visit to my place. We could cook the mushrooms together and eat them for dinner. Fortunately, I had a few eggs left in the fridge from last week and I had bought milk and bread the day before. What else could we do with the mushrooms? Most of them were not good for drying and needed to be eaten as soon as possible. There was no way I could eat them all and Vojta's mother wasn't particularly fond of mushrooms, nor for that matter of me, or of anyone else who was Vojta's friend.

Vojta timidly nodded and followed me. I held aside the shrubbery that had encroached on the garden gate from all sides, and let him in. He walked up the cracked walkway on his tiptoes, to avoid stepping on the lines.

I offered him some tea and poured myself a cup too. Vojta took a few sips and examined the kitchen.

'The last time I was here was fifteen years ago. Do you remember? Your dad was loaning me the atlas. It reminds me of the archive at work where they keep old editions. Almost nothing ever changes there, either,' he declared.

His eyes continued to wander around the room and he noticed the envelope with my initials on it that I had tucked behind the glass door of the cupboard.

'You have a letter from your mom.'

'How can you tell?'

'I know her handwriting. I just told you, I've been here before.'

He picked up the letter and caressed the envelope.

'Are you afraid to open it?'

I shook my head, stood up, snatched the envelope and stashed it in the drawer of the table. I slammed it shut quickly, so that Vojta wouldn't catch a glimpse of the packets of medicine.

I reached instead for two cutting boards and two knives.

'Let's get to it.'

We separated and divided the mushrooms in the basket into two halves. We set aside the boletes for the time being, in the evening I would cut them into thin slices and lay them out on the mesh stretched over a frame that my dad had once built. Vojta began to cut the inky caps into strips. He cut the caps into cubes of equal size and the stems into rounds, tossing everything into a cast-iron bowl. In the meantime, I sautéed the onion in butter, whisked up a few eggs in a dish and ran out to the garden for a bit of curly parsley that miraculously had survived in the weed-infested flowerbed. I added the inky caps to the pan, poured over the eggs, added a bit of milk, and finally sprinkled parsley over the mixture.

We brought the plates with the food out to the porch. We sat down next to each other on the wooden bench, but Vojta abruptly jumped up again, placed both plates on the bench and turned the wooden table ninety degrees. Now nothing wobbled any more. The plates on the peeling wood looked sad and lonely. I ran into the kitchen to fetch the checkered tablecloth and set the table. Then I filled a jug with water and picked a few chrysanthemums and lilies to put in it, these being the only ornamental flowers that had survived in the garden. I ran back into the kitchen and brought out two glasses of milk. Vojta in the meantime had positioned the improvised vase in the exact centre and had placed the plates and silverware at either end of the table. The sight of the table warmed my heart. Now everything was perfect. It had been a long time since my table had been so splendidly set.

I thought I would have to force myself to eat, but the festive atmosphere had its effect. We ate in silence, observing the walnut tree that was swaying its massive branches in the wind. With our spoons we scooped up the mush from the deep dishes, took bites of bread, and washed it down with milk. Had our plates been full of a mushroom scramble, no doubt we would have been making loud chewing noises as we ate, but with inky caps there was no such danger. Besides, Vojta, as he chewed, swallowed and drank, made no sound whatsoever, all one could hear was the spoon clinking against the plate.

We hadn't yet finished when we heard a commotion behind the house. Someone was rattling the handle of the gate like a madman. I thought I had best get up and go around to the front of the house.

Through the overgrown hedge I couldn't see the face of the figure standing out on the road. But the khaki cargo vest and hairy calves immediately gave away who it was.

I slipped the wire loop, hidden behind the tendril of a rose and serving as a latch, off the gatepost and bent down so that Ruda could see me.

'I figured I'd come see where you live,' he announced but stopped short midstride, because the thorns were trying to scalp his curly mop of hair.

He didn't wait for me to invite him in, although by now I was used to this kind of behaviour, and made his way around the back of the house to the porch, a six-pack of beer swinging from his left hand.

'Well hello, Mr Měšťan, I never would have expected to find you here,' said Ruda when he caught sight of my guest on the porch, and turned to give me a meaningful wink.

Then he looked at our splendidly set table and remarked: 'Looks like a great party!'

I wasn't particularly happy about Ruda's visit, but my good manners dictated that I invite him to join us at the table.

'Mister Vobořil, you'd better not sit there, you're overweight and that stool could collapse under you,' Vojta warned him in a good-natured way as Ruda prepared to descend on my seat. Ruda stopped in mid-motion, his backside momentarily hovered in the air, then he cleared his throat, straightened up and finally sat down on the bench alongside the wall. He hadn't flinched at all at Vojta's comment which made me deduce that he needed something from me. I brought him a plate of sautéed mushroom mush from the kitchen, set it down before him and handed him a spoon. My mother would have been pleased with me.

Ruda took a bite, rolled the morsel around in his mouth and swallowed it. He didn't look disgusted, on the contrary, he seemed to like it.

'That's the stinking dung mushroom, as you referred to it today,' Vojta pointed out without a trace of malice, at which Ruda just shook his head and went on eating by the spoonful.

'Nice place you've got here,' he remarked, after he was done eating and looked around. The porch was all broken up, with grass and weeds sprouting up through the cracks. The garden was overgrown, the grass yellow after several days of no rain and the fence sagging and full of gaps.

'What do you need, Ruda?'

'Well . . .' he clucked his tongue, 'I've got some more tourists who signed up for tomorrow. Austrians. I would take them into the woods myself, but you know how my German is,' he explained.

'But you have other mushroom gatherers besides me, right?'

Ruda just laughed and gave a barely perceptible shake of his head.

'So, are you in?'

I remained silent and Ruda must have interpreted this to mean yes.

'Tomorrow at nine, just like last time,' he said with a smile.

'Tomorrow I already have plans with Vojta,' I announced and Vojta looked up from his plate at me in surprise, because it wasn't true.

Ruda glanced over at Vojta and rubbed his chin. 'For all I care, he can join you, what's one oddball more or less,' he added and burst out laughing, as if he had cracked a good joke.

He pulled a beer out of the case, popped it open on the edge of the table and drank.

'Won't you have some?' he pushed the opened bottle towards me.

'No, I don't drink.'

'Actually, I don't either,' he rejoined. 'But today I'm making an exception. You see, it's an anniversary . . .' he said with an air of mystery.

I noticed that Vojta had begun to fidget nervously.

'You shouldn't drink that beer,' he said in a half-whisper.

'A beer or two in the afternoon isn't going to hurt me,' Ruda snapped back at him.

Vojta raised himself slightly from the bench, wanting to add something, but I shook my head for him not to do it, I couldn't let this opportunity slip by.

Ruda finished a second bottle and set it on the table.

'You,' he looked at me, 'Come to think of it, I don't even know your name.'

'Sisi.'

'What?'

'Sisi.'

He opened another bottle and drank.

'That sounds like a name for a cat. So what does it actually mean? Sylva? Sandra? Simona? Or . . . like the empress?'

'No.'

'Whatever, it doesn't really matter, it's none of my business, plain Sisi . . .' he made a gesture with his hand.

By the time he knocked back the third beer, his eyes had glazed over a bit with a moist film. He belched loudly several times and then finally got up to leave.

'So tomorrow, same as last time. Vojta can come along, why not, but I'm only paying you,' he specified and gave me another wink. In the scant hour that he had spent at my place, this was at least the fifth time. It almost looked as if he had developed a tic in his right eye. 'And those dung mushrooms weren't at all bad. If you ever bring them again, I'll pay you the same as I would for chanterelles. Krušina will figure out something to do with them.'

He held out his hand to me and smiled again, this time it seemed quite sincere.

'So what anniversary is it?' I asked because the thought had been niggling at my mind.

'Ah well, it's a bit complicated . . .' he grimaced and waved his hand. And after climbing through the gate, he turned back one more time and ducked down under the bush, to be able to see me.

'Listen, are you and Vojta . . . ?'

'All right, Ruda, take care, you'd better be going, it looks like rain.'

'Sure thing, yup, it's going to rain, hee hee, I'm off . . .' he was all smiles.

If it had been possible, I would have slammed the gate behind him. Suddenly I wasn't the least bit sorry that I had behaved so basely and hadn't told him that inky caps, which we had also sliced and added to the medley, contain a substance that works like Antabuse. I actually regretted that he hadn't drunk the whole six-pack; just three pints would at most clean out his insides.

I went back to Vojta and spent another hour with him in silence. It wasn't unpleasant.

Vojta got up shortly before sunset. In the meantime, on the horizon, massive white clouds had come up over the mountains. The breeze had subsided. Tomorrow it would be hot again.

Vojta didn't bother to say goodbye. Besides, we would be seeing each other in a couple of hours. I thought to myself, that's exactly what I like about Vojta. I'm almost completely unaware of his presence. Except for when he's spouting numbers and equations, he seems to me somehow ethereal, like a pleasant thought lounging in my head. It's as though his body doesn't exist at all, he gives off no odour, and when he walks through the woods, he doesn't snap a single twig or trample the grass. When I'm walking with him, I'm barely aware of him and yet I don't feel alone.

I opened the three remaining bottles and poured the beer into the cast-iron basin. Better that the slugs stop grazing on my overgrown currant bushes and drown in beer instead. And the 18 crowns I will get for the bottles, those aren't to be sneezed at either.

As I stored the casserole with the leftover mush in the pantry, I peeked at the bag of substrate that Zatloukal brought me, all the way in the back corner. Little white heads were already peeping through the sackcloth. I picked a few, deposited them into a paper bag and brought them over to Zatloukal as a thank you for having purchased the substrate for me. He was surprised, but thanked me politely. And then he asked me if I had managed to set aside anything to repair the roof. I felt my heart skip a beat, but then I said: 'I won't be needing it.'

'What are you, nuts?' he shot back. 'With that leaky roof, your house will be gone in less than a year.'

But I just shrugged.

26

I have get away from here. From here, from Dvorce. I'll get dressed and I'll run away, I'll run further and further, far away from this hell. Such thoughts went through my mind as I descended the stairs the next morning down to the kitchen. It was still early, but my mom must have been at the stove for several hours already. Yesterday's dishes were washed and dried, the tablecloth shaken out, the floor swept. The room smelled of Sunday cake.

She was standing with her back to me, bending over the oven with a cooking mitt on her right hand.

'Good morning, mama,' I greeted her. I said it so quietly that for a moment even I paused, wondering if she had heard me, but she startled in fright. And yet she didn't turn around.

'It needs a few more minutes,' she muttered to herself.

She walked over to the sink, picked up a sponge and started wiping away stains and smudges on the stainless steel that were long gone.

'Mama . . .' I whispered from the doorway.

She winced.

'I found a few more strawberries in the garden, practically a miracle, since it's already the end of July. I know you like them in your sponge cake.'

She shifted back to the stove and peered inside through the searing glass. She pulled on the mitt and pulled out the red-hot baking sheet.

'Now it's just right,' she said smelling the cake. She placed the baking sheet on the cutting board by the cupboard and moved back to the sink again.

I stared at her as if frozen.

'Mama...' I tried again.

She slipped off the mitt and once again picked up the steel wool.

'Mama, look at me,' I said and as I did, my voice broke.

Mom finished buffing the sink and picked up a knife, to slice the cake. Her hair covered her face but even so I noticed the dark circles under her eyes. She was gripping the handle of the knife so hard, her knuckles had gone white.

I stepped up to her and grabbed her sleeve.

'Mama, you were there, you saw it...'

She turned away from me.

'What are you talking about, I saw nothing at all!' she hissed through clenched teeth, her eyes fixed on the hand in which she was gripping the knife.

I continued to hold on to her sleeve. She tried to pull her arm away and free herself, but jerked it so clumsily that she ended up swinging the knife at me. The tip of the blade narrowly missed my cheek. For a split second our eyes met. In her face, a fierce battle was raging. Her bloodshot eyes glistened with tears, but her lips were tightly pressed together, full of fury. One of the two adversaries clearly had the upper hand. I am certain that at that moment, she came within a hair's breadth of stabbing me.

'Nothing! Do you understand me? I saw nothing!'

She looked away and plunged the blade into the cake.

'It's a good thing you got up early. You can have the end,' she pronounced in a voice that sounded straight out of a fairy tale. 'If you want, I'll cut you the other end too. Be careful not to burn your tongue, the cake is still hot.'

I stared at her massive back. Somewhere deep beneath the thick layer of fat, she had to be there. My mother, who not for anything in the world would leave me alone in a strange white room.

I can't abandon her. She's still so little . . .

I ran out of the house. I wanted to keep on running, further and further away from that hellhole, until I fell to the ground with exhaustion. Instead, I hid under the mulberry tree in the corner of the garden and beneath its dense, drooping branches, from which only my feet protruded, I burst into tears. I sat there for several hours, until my mother called us for lunch. And then I dried my tears with the back of my hand and went to join them in the kitchen.

On that day, I swear I hated my mother even more than I hated my father.

To this day I can't reconcile these two versions of my mother. It's as if they were two completely different people. My mother, who had almost died of exhaustion from taking care of me when I was sick. And that other person who, at the darkest moment of my life, had abandoned me.

27

Judging by the looks on the faces of the Austrian couple, the mushroom-hunting expedition was a success. The lady was even ready to hug us goodbye, but we both managed to avoid it. 'Gutes Team', the Austrians called after us as they left the Toadstool, wildly waving their little bags of dried mushrooms that the Walrus had given them for their journey. After all, they had purchased the deluxe pack.

I went back inside the restaurant and asked about Ruda. It would be nice to be able to add something to the tea tin. But the Walrus just waved his hand. Ruda had called him that morning to say he wasn't feeling well.

'He must've got himself sloshed somewhere yesterday ...' I couldn't refrain from commenting.

'Ruda?' the Walrus said in surprise. 'You crazy? He won't even touch the stuff.'

I laughed and shook my head. If only he knew what had happened yesterday.

'He said you should pass by tomorrow for the money,' he added. 'Thank God I'm getting a break from him today, I've had it up to my eyeballs with his blabbering already. Knucklehead that he is.'

Obviously, there was nothing more to say to that, so I just shrugged my shoulders.

'I've got something else to do today,' I said to Vojta when we arrived at the spot where the street funnels into the square. 'It's going to be a while, so you'd better take off, we'll see each other tomorrow, huh?'

'And where are you going?' asked Vojta without batting an eyelash.

'I have to go to the library,' I foolishly confided to him out on the street.

'Then I'll come with you,' he replied, his eyes lighting up.

Along the way he asked me what I was going to do there. Without further hesitation, I told him everything. That things at the Toadstool could go any which way, so I was looking for work. And also, that I wanted to leave Sušice. Not to go back to Plzeň, but that I was considering České Budějovice. I had been there a few times with my parents, and it was just the city for me—not as big as Plzeň, so not as easy to get lost in, but big enough for me to be able to find work and accommodations there.

'Are you coming in, too?'

But Vojta was already reaching for the handle of the glass door. He walked right over to the first bookcase and started examining the spines of the books.

The library had been renovated since my last visit. Everything was new, neat and sterile. I asked the lady behind the counter if I could use the internet.

The librarian promptly handed me a piece of paper with the Wi-Fi password on it, but when she saw the push-button cell phone that I pulled out of my pocket, all she said was 'Oh' and motioned with her hand to a nearby table.

The last time I went online was two years ago. At the time I was exploring various websites where people with the same diagnosis as mine described how they struggled with their illness. I was looking up withdrawal symptoms after going off antipsychotics. Fortunately, most of them were easy to simulate. Sweating, vomiting, anxiety, dizziness—thanks to my sleepless nights I had plenty of experience with all of that.

I opened a job search portal and typed in České Budějovice. There were plenty of offers. Only later did I realize that I had forgotten to check off the box indicating the level of education. The number of offers suddenly jumped down to only seven. Today, evidently, even a cleaning lady needs to have a high-school diploma. But three offers looked promising. Two grocery stockrooms and one office supply warehouse.

My old email address had been annulled, so I set up a new one. By the time I was sending out the third email, the librarian was already jangling her keys.

Still ahead of Vojta and me was the trek back home across the island in the Otava. We passed the last of the daring swimmers at the weir and cut through the drunks at a wedding reception on Santos. As always, we walked in such a way as to maintain sufficient distance between us. As if an invisible person were walking in the middle. Beyond the island, a drunken old geezer in shorts and rubber clogs joined us. 'Go on and give 'er a kiss, ya coward!' he shouted at Vojta, at which we both picked up the pace as if on cue.

I accompanied Vojta home and returned to the shack. I fell into bed fully dressed, and barely managed to turn out the light.

28

Only the next morning, when I was awakened by the chirping of birds, did I realize that I hadn't taken my warm milk with honey in the evening, hadn't sat outside in the garden and hadn't even lit my aromatic lamp. In fact, I hadn't even remembered that I was supposed to go to the bathroom before going to sleep so that I wouldn't feel pressure in my bladder. I hadn't performed a single one of my bedtime rituals and yet I had slept nine hours straight. And moreover, I realized with a sense of relief, I hadn't dreamt a thing.

Something of the pleasant feelings from the previous day still lingered within me. I stretched out my arms, closed my eyes and immersed myself into yesterday's afterglow. Pleasant memories were lapping at my ears, beneath my closed eyelids Vojta came into my thoughts.

I opened my eyes and leaped out of bed. I could put it off no longer, the constant uncertainty weighed on me like a massive boulder. I hurried down the stairs into the kitchen and quickly opened the table drawer. I wanted no time to rethink it.

I ran my fingertips over the envelope. It was almost silky smooth, beneath the thin, sleek surface I could feel the cursive letters etched into the paper. My mother's handwriting. When was the last time I had received a note from her? Maybe in elementary school, when I was on a school camping trip. It was hard to say how old the letter was. Maybe it had been waiting for me for years. Or maybe it was more recent, written just before she died. Either way, it had to be something that couldn't be dealt with so easily by phone. An apology or an explanation, that's all I could think of.

Suddenly I wasn't sure if I was ready to open the envelope. I held it in my hand a moment longer, caressing its creases and turning it this way and that.

In the end, I reopened the drawer and tossed it back in. Not yet.

I went to make myself some tea and to butter a piece of bread. I placed the plate and the cup on the table directly above the drawer. I tried not to think about the letter, but still I kept sensing it.

And then suddenly something possessed me and I opened the drawer abruptly, grabbed the letter and tore open the envelope. A piece of white paper covered with writing in a blue pen fell at my feet.

I leaned over to retrieve it, sat down, and started to read. I raised my eyebrows, puzzled.

Spicy saffron milk caps in cream sauce

8–10 large saffron milk caps
butter
cream
finely chopped onions

What I was reading was making no sense at all. My eyes moved further down along the paper, but it didn't get any better.

extra-fine flour
broth
vinegar
allspice, pepper, caraway seed, bay leaf

I turned the sheet over and turned it back again. I couldn't figure it out.

Stew the cleaned, sliced milk caps with the onions . . .

This simply couldn't be it. I took the envelope in my hand, pulled it open and looked inside to see if there was anything else. I also checked the lining of the envelope. Nothing.

Maybe Milan was just teasing me and had slipped in an old recipe that had been tucked into a cookbook. The page was in fact missing a date and a salutation. The sealed envelope, however, had my name on it and there was no doubt that it was my mother's handwriting.

Or maybe it was a coded message. My mother might have been afraid that my brothers would open the letter and discover something that they weren't supposed to know. Maybe my mother was using the recipe to communicate something that was meant only for me. I tried to remember when we had eaten saffron milk caps with cream sauce. Had something significant occurred on that occasion that my mother wanted to remind me of? Something that would shed new light on what had happened in our family?

But if memory serves me, we rarely ate saffron milk caps at home, one year our mother had pickled them, and five years later most of the jars in the cellar were still untouched. As for cream sauce, I had no memory of it whatsoever.

Had my mother perhaps tried to hand me down a precious recipe? A family secret passed down from generation to generation exclusively to only daughters?

But there was nothing about the recipe that struck me as being mysterious.

Add the broth and cook the saffron milky caps until softened. At the end, add the cream and thicken with the roux.

If she had sent me a page torn from a journal or a plain white sheet of paper it would have made more sense to me.

Serve with bread dumplings or Carlsbad dumplings.

It had been exactly fifteen years since my mother had caught my father in my room. She could have pulled me out of there, confronted my father, called the police, moved away with me and my brothers, there were so many things she could have done, but she chose silence, and beneath her smiling mask, squelched her tears as if they were intrusive ants.

I remembered how at the theatre my mother would cover her eyes with her hands. When something terrible was taking place on stage, she would look straight ahead through the narrow slits between her fingers. The image before her paled and receded, she could see only the dim reflections of what was happening in the drama, and it no longer frightened her.

In real life she behaved much the same way. She had always been accustomed to observing the world through half-closed eyes, she wore blinders like a horse hitched to a wagon and saw only the limited area in front of her. She filtered the world through her fingers and treated what was left of it like modelling clay. She smoothed out all the sharp and jagged edges, she wanted only soft, rounded curves.

Today I understand why she did it. It was so easy, so tempting to close one's eyes to everything. Maybe later on she truly believed that it had been just a bad dream, merely a horror film on a screen that she could turn off with the click of a button and dismiss with a wave of her hand.

And finally, what liberated her from the incubus that would sometimes visit her at night was illness.

'Where am I? Where the hell am I?' she screamed at me when I visited her in the hospital that winter. She was sitting on the hospital bed with her legs dangling over the edge. She was forcing down a banana that the nurse had brought her for a snack. She wasn't biting into it but was breaking off small pieces, which she then placed inside her mouth. The way a proper lady does it. The ribbons down her back had come undone, the patterned hospital gown was hanging loosely and revealed her massive, lumpy shoulders and her arms, covered in bruises. She was so confused that she wasn't even aware of my presence, nor did she seem to know who she was herself. I wasn't surprised, this would often happen during my visits.

'We see this in patients with cirrhosis. Disorientation is one of the concomitant symptoms of liver failure,' the attending physician explained to us when they hospitalized our mother that winter. This had made Evžen literally fly out of his chair.

'What kind of nonsense is that? Why, our mother never touches alcohol!' he began to shout as I looked silently at the piece of paper that lay on the table in front of the doctor: blood alcohol level 2.37, it said on the admission report.

'The liver is so badly scarred that it most likely will not regenerate itself. The only option is a liver transplant. The earliest we can put her on the waiting list is after six months of documented complete abstinence and a strict hepatic diet,' the doctor calmly informed us.

'How come you never noticed anything?' I dared to ask both of my brothers out in the corridor, although I myself knew the answer long ago. Our mother never let it show. She would sip on vodka, which had no scent, in small quantities throughout the day. When she began to stagger, she would lie down on the sofa and pretend her hip was hurting. The dark circles under her eyes, the yellowed skin and the swollen face didn't strike anyone as odd. Nor did anyone stop to wonder about the fact that our mother kept on gaining weight even though she hardly ate any more. Her stomach had become so bloated, she looked as if she were pregnant again.

Nobody could have noticed because our mother managed to conceal every problem. She smeared her sallow face with makeup, hid her bloated belly under an even looser fitting dress, kept her trembling hands folded in her lap, and when company came, the pot of coffee and cookies were already on the coffee table, so that she wouldn't have to get up and stagger into the kitchen.

My brothers were in shock. Not me.

They kept her in the hospital because she began to bleed in her stomach and was retaining too much fluid in her abdominal cavity. I went to see her in Plzeň every Sunday. Went to see my mother who no longer recognized me. I visited her in the hospital, although I was sure that she would never come out of her delirium and tell me what I needed to hear. She was lying there in the hospital bed, a few sparse tufts of hair left on her head, her forearms riddled with needle marks as if she were a junkie. Apart from her corpulence, which even after weeks of being on a diet didn't want to release its hold on her, she really looked like one. Her eyes were bloodshot, her face jaundiced and full of sores. She would sink into a slumber, doze off for a while, and then jerk awake and start to shout fragments of sentences that made no sense, bawl like a child and then burst into giddy laughter.

The explanation behind the nonsensical letter might have been entirely prosaic. Perhaps it was around that time, in a state of profound delirium, that she had pieced together the letter which she then sent to me through my brothers.

I tried gently to raise her and do up the laces on the back of her gown, but she started to resist, shielding her face with one hand and pushing me away with the other. 'Don't touch me, it hurts, please, let me be,' she sobbed. She looked into my eyes and from her blank expression I realized that she was speaking to someone else entirely, someone from beyond the grave whom she was soon to meet. 'Don't ever touch me again,' she added, this time in a firm voice and looking me straight in the eye. She was completely out of it and yet at the same time it seemed to me that she had never spoken more clearly.

And then she began to whimper again: 'Where am I, where the hell am I?'

When she died, she was only one month away from being admitted to the transplant programme. She was not even fifty years old.

For the last time, I picked up her letter and placed it among the papers in the drawer. I walked out into the garden and sat down beneath the mulberry tree, whose branches by now had reached all the way to the ground. I hugged my knees with my arms because I was freezing cold. Through the dense foliage I couldn't see the garden nor could anyone see me.

29

'Not today,' came the gruff voice of a woman even before I could manage to ring the bell. I had to lean over the fence in order to see Vojta's mother. She was taking down the laundry from the drying rack and folding it into a large wicker basket. She was wearing a pink nightgown that had Snoopy on it and a scoop neckline from which her left shoulder was peeking out.

'Vojta can't make it today?' I asked.

'Not today,' she repeated and turned her back to me. She removed the clothespins from a red and white striped tank top, folded it loosely, holding it against her chest, and added it to the basket with the other bright colours. Then she took down one of Vojta's T-shirts and folded it carefully on the plastic garden table. Afterwards she ran her hand over it to smooth out any wrinkles.

I stood by the gate a bit longer, rocking back and forth on my feet, until I realized that I wasn't about to get an explanation.

At least with the mushrooms I got lucky. Plenty of ungnawed red cracking boletes, some lurid boletes, brittlegills and blewits, and in Annín I snagged several strapping cornflower boletes. And finally, a stone's throw from Sušice, I came across a giant puffball. It was so big that I couldn't add it to my basket, it would have crushed the other mushrooms. So I tucked it under my arm like a ball.

As I approached the Toadstool, Ruda was standing on the doorstep and waving at me. 'Heeeeey, *gutes team*,' he patted me on the back. He was beaming at me like a kid about to get on a merry-go-round without a trace of his former resentment. The Austrians must have left him a big fat tip yesterday.

Together we stepped inside the kitchen, where the Walrus was just sprinkling marjoram onto a mushroom goulash. On the cutting board next to the stove, he had already prepared the chopped garlic.

'We still have more than three weeks left before we get to the end of August. Do you think you and Vojta can handle a few more tourists between now and then?' Ruda asked me, not wiping the eager expression off his face.

He was all pumped up at the thought of the money that, thanks to me, would come pouring in. He started to cavort around the kitchen as if the springs from the sofa were fastened to the soles of his shoes. He used his hip to nudge the Walrus away from the stove, lifted the lid of the pot on the burner, sniffed, and then broke into a grin, grabbed the wooden cooking spoon and the whisk and started to drum with them on the stainless-steel surface. It was obvious that if he didn't stop soon, the Walrus was going to have a heart attack.

'Can I ask you something in the office?' I said to Ruda, feeling sympathy for the Walrus, in whom the pressure was building like steam in a locomotive gearing up for departure.

'Sure, OK.'

'How . . .' I searched for the right words, 'How exactly is it going to work with the money?' I asked Ruda who had sat down in front of his altar. I remained standing in the doorway.

'Like what do you mean?'

'Well, how much are you actually going to pay me for the tourists?'

He stretched his mouth into a grimace and tilted his head from shoulder to shoulder, as if doing an exercise. But still he said nothing.

'What I mean is, are you going to give me a bonus like you did for that first family?'

'Hmmmm,' Ruda responded. He leaned back in his chair and laced his fingers behind his head. 'How about two hundred a day, plus more on the spot for what you gather?' he proposed his generous offer.

'Three hundred,' I said as calmly as I could.

Ruda tried to whistle, but all he managed to emit was a sharp hissing sound, and then he scratched his head and cautiously nodded. 'Fine. But you're starting first thing tomorrow. It's a group of some Dutch people, supposedly they speak German. In the square, same as always.'

He held out his hand and I forced mine to return his high five.

'I've started growing button mushrooms at home,' I added. 'The home-grown ones are much better than those from a store. If you like, I can pass by my house one day after I'm done mushroom gathering and bring you a bag.'

'Sure, why not,' answered Ruda. Then he scratched his head, cleared his throat, and sheepishly asked: 'Hey, when I was over at your place the other day, how much did I actually drink?'

'Why?' I blurted out.

'Let's just say afterwards I felt a little lousy,' he snickered. 'It was that anniversary.'

'Anniversary?'

'Yeah, yeah, anniversary . . .' he waved his hand. 'One year ago, they took the old man away to the nursing home. So I indulged in his honour,' he added.

Had it already been a year? I marvelled to myself.

'And just imagine how he's ended up,' Ruda went on, an amused expression spreading over his face. 'His arthritis is so bad that he's in a wheelchair. He can't even get himself to the can, let alone get a beer.

So he sits there and whines, and any time a nurse passes by, he begs: Siiiister, please be so good as to buy me a shot . . . but I gave them strict instructions. That's karma!' he chuckled.

I shrugged my shoulders and lied: 'There was no beer left over at our place.'

'Yeah, well,' he waved his hand again. 'Nothing like a yearly reminder of what booze can do to you.'

It was probably the first time that I agreed with him.

I didn't go straight home but continued on for a few blocks to the library. Out of the three emails, one had been answered. 'Your email interests us, please call me,' wrote the manager of a warehouse with stationery supplies. And that's exactly what I did. I went out into the street, positioned myself in front of the glass door, pulled my cell phone out of my pocket, punched in her number and introduced myself. I stated my name and why I was calling, and I didn't stutter even once.

'How about the day after tomorrow in the morning, let's say around ten, will you have time?'

'I'll make the time,' I declared, in a voice that never wavered.

That afternoon I still stopped over to see Vojta.

'Come on in,' boomed a familiar woman's voice. Vojta's mother was sitting on a plastic bench on the doorstep wearing the same pink nightgown, but with the other shoulder exposed. It was Saturday, so she wasn't about to get dressed. The loosely hanging nightgown revealed a tattooed lizard, with a tail that coiled from her shoulder along her collarbone all the way to her neck. The outlines, which must once have been sharp, were now indistinct and the colours seemed faded. On the small table in front of her was a cup of steaming Turkish coffee, and next to it a full ashtray on which rested a smouldering cigarette stub.

'Go on, you'll find him upstairs, yesterday the post office delivered a package to him.'

When I stepped inside Vojta's room and saw the chaos, my eyes grew wide. The entire floor was strewn with books, some were open to the copyright page, and out of others protruded colourful bookmarks. The books were in various stages of disassembly, on some the binding was coming apart, others had damaged covers, whereas still others looked almost new. Vojta sat cross-legged in the middle of the room, holding a book in his hand. He caressed its cover, opened it, ran his fingertips over the text as if reading in braille, then brought the pages up to his nose and sniffed them.

'You're organizing them, right?'

Vojta turned around and nodded. I walked over and knelt down next to him.

'I put one aside for you.'

He handed me a slim volume with a pale green cover. Boris Vian, *I Spit on Your Graves*. I looked at his face. Had I not known him, I would have said he had a mischievous look.

'Thanks. Ruda made me an offer. I wanted to ask if you would join me.'

Vojta smiled, as if he'd known all along why I had come to see him.

'And how's the job search going?' he went on to ask.

'Pretty well,' I answered truthfully. 'Actually, that's why I'm here, because I need help with something.'

Vojta looked up from his books and his eyes met mine.

I left his house in a better mood than the one in which I had arrived. His mother was still sitting on the porch. When I said goodbye, all she said was 'Thanks.' She didn't get it at all, I was the one who should be grateful.

Back home, my cell phone was flashing at me reproachfully. One missed call from Evžen and three messages from Milan. I had no desire to spoil a nice day.

30

It takes just under two hours by train from Sušice to České Budějovice. Long enough for the nerves to kick in. Yet at the beginning it looked promising. I boarded the train with a clear head. I'm on my way to a regular job interview, it's something people do all the time, it's for a job that is just right for me, a person with no qualifications or experience. The lady on the phone seemed very pleasant. No reason why I shouldn't nail this. But then the bad memories began to eat away at my self-confidence. How at eighteen, I would drag myself past the warehouse reception every morning, my head pounding from lack of sleep. How I had to hold on to the handle of the utility cart to keep myself from collapsing to the floor with exhaustion. How my supervisor used to shout at me that I was a good-for-nothing who would never make it anywhere. And over the past seven years her prophecy had come true.

Getting off the train, my head was buried between my shoulders and my eyes were fixed on my feet. Any hope that I might walk off my nervousness soon evaporated. With each step I hunched over more.

Mrs Soukupová, the company manager, was waiting for me in front of the entrance to the warehouse, an enormous grey box with a flat roof. When she saw me, she moved her cell phone away from her ear, slipped it into her jacket pocket, waved at me, threw her unfinished cigarette to the ground and stubbed it out with the tip of her shoe. She offered me her hand and I forced myself to smile.

She came across as someone who doesn't like to waste time unnecessarily. She didn't ask me what I expected from the job, what kind of work experience I had, or why I wanted to work specifically for her company, but immediately motioned for me to follow her: 'I'll show you around and then you can tell me what you think.' She led me into an enormous shed devoid of any daylight and with pallets stacked three stories high. The space was basically identical to the warehouse in which I had worked in Plzeň, the only difference was the merchandise. Warehouse workers walked past us, pulling large crates on wheels. Two others moved around on forklifts.

'I'm grateful for every female asset to the team,' Soukupová gave me a wink.

'Around here we work in three shifts,' she added and I just nodded. At that point the manager reached into her pocket for her mobile that was ringing and started to discuss something, apparently with her distributor. She spoke matter-of-factly and brusquely.

A man in blue coveralls passed by and the manager waved him over. 'Fanda, this is your new co-worker. Show her around.'

I disliked Fanda on sight. The zipper of his coveralls was open and his chest hair was showing. He looked at me in surprise and raised an eyebrow. Then he shrugged his shoulders and came out with an: 'OK, then.'

'First-name basis, OK?' he asked straight off but didn't wait for an answer. Together we walked around the stacks of pallets and he explained where things were stored, where goods were sorted and where they were registered. It wasn't anything that couldn't be learnt in a few days. Except that my stomach was once again already in knots.

'Apart from the boss and her secretary, you'd be the only other woman here. But those two don't count, they mostly sit in the office,' explained Fanda. 'Come to think of it, we have a shared locker room, but that's OK, isn't it?' he smirked.

I was incapable of answering him.

We came to a stop in the middle of the storage building. I could see and sense the warehouse workers on the carts and by the pallets, stopping one by one and turning towards me. Dozens of eyes on me. All the men staring at me. And then I caught sight of one of them running his tongue over his swollen lips. I bolted for the exit.

The manager rested her phone on her shoulder and called out to me: 'So when can we expect you to start?'

But I just shook my head noncommittally and kept going without looking back.

As for the boarding house nearby that I had found on the internet, I never even set foot inside. I stopped on the pavement across the street and watched the people going in. Most of them looked like foreign labourers. Here and there among them would be some woman, who judging by her looks had been through a lot. From a partly opened window on the second floor came the sound of a woman's drunken laughter. I turned on my heel and made for the train.

'So?' asked Vojta back in Sušice. He was waiting for me on a bench on the platform. He had placed my basket full of mushrooms underneath.

I shrugged my shoulders. 'Not much.'

I wasn't in the mood to talk. Together we made our way towards the Toadstool.

'So now what are you going to do?' asked Vojta. The question sounded matter of fact and impartial.

'I don't know. I'll try to look around for some temp work. Or I'll make myself call that warehouse back. And instead of the boarding house I'll find something to rent. But really, I have no idea,' I reached for the door handle and turned to him. 'It's better if you don't wait for me. I need some time alone.'

31

The next day Vojta didn't come with me to go mushroom hunting. Maybe he was annoyed, because the day before I hadn't thanked him for the basket of mushrooms. I waited for him on the footbridge, but after he hadn't shown up for a quarter of an hour, I headed into the forest without him.

It was no big surprise that I didn't make out too well in the forest. In my mind I kept going over yesterday's fiasco. Ruda, who had a knack for sensing my every weakness, looked into my basket and snorted.

'Come on, Sisi, what's wrong? You're not starting to slack off on us, are you?'

I winced a little, wondering if Ruda suspected something, and shook my head.

'It hasn't rained in a while, nothing I can do . . .'

I bought myself two rolls and slowly dragged myself back to the shack. By the time I reached Dvorce, I could already see from far away that there was a tall man standing by my gate. I was in no mood to argue with Evžen, which is why I was about to turn on my heel and head back to the footbridge to enter the garden through the bushes growing on the other side of the fence. Fortunately, I noticed the fluorescent shoelaces in time.

'I have something for you,' announced Vojta instead of saying hello. His face had the same expression as always, but I noticed a slight tremor in his voice. In his hand he held a dark cardboard folder, tied with two ribbons. I invited him in, but before we had a chance to step inside the cottage, he blurted out: 'You have a job.'

He untied the ribbons and handed me the open folder.

I scrunched up my forehead quizzically.

'You're going to be the porter. I called our librarian yesterday to ask if they had found someone to replace Mr Hajný who retired, but they still don't have anyone.'

Again, he stuck the papers under my nose. 'She sent me an application for you. I stopped by at the library and printed it out. All you need to do is fill it out and your job is guaranteed.'

He caught me completely off guard. I just stood there in front of him, unable to say a word.

'You can start in September, when the library is back in full operation.'

He sat down on the bench and placed the folder on the table. As if reading my mind, he announced: 'And don't worry about housing. I have a two-room flat.'

Before I had a chance to protest, he added: 'Two non-communicating rooms. The kitchen is set apart and the toilet is separate from the bathroom. You can sleep in the living room on the couch.'

Uncomprehending, I looked back and forth from Vojta to the papers.

'I...'

'Of course the pay isn't much,' Vojta interjected and squirmed a bit, 'But you can stay with me for free, just pitch in for expenses...'

'That's not it, Vojta.'

'Or you can live somewhere else, I'm not forcing you,' he declared, with a hint of a stutter.

'Vojta, I have to think about it,' I said barely above a whisper.

'Mr Hajný liked his job. He was in no hurry to retire . . .' Vojta said in a quiet voice.

'Anyway, thank you, really, I'll consider it.'

He bit his lip and shrugged his shoulders.

At home, on the table, my mobile was blinking again. A missed call from a number that looked familiar. The warehouse manager.

I climbed into bed already around eight and stared at the ceiling. For hours, I went over in my head all of the reasons why I needed to turn down Vojta's offer. I had only been to Prague once on a school trip. It's a big and dirty city. Much bigger than Budějovice, which already seemed huge to me. I would have to leave Dvorce sooner than I expected, so I wouldn't have much money. And above all, I would have to live in a flat with another person. What's more, a man. Share a bathroom and the toilet.

I could call the manager back, she certainly hadn't phoned just for the sake of calling, she was still counting on me. I'll say I didn't feel well that day, which is why I had to leave. Or I'll make up something else. I'll try to ask her if instead of changing in the locker room, I could change in the office. But then I remembered the warehouse worker who had licked his lips. I sighed and shuddered in disgust. It was clear to me that I couldn't take the warehouse job. It wouldn't work.

I climbed out of bed, got dressed, and went out into the garden. I paced from fence to fence. Back and forth.

In my mind I went back over Vojta's offer. I had to admit that working as a porter was a job that was tailor-made for me. Sitting in a booth somewhere at the entrance and presenting those who came by with a notebook, in which to sign themselves in. Every now and then to make a phone call. To have a small space all to myself. It sounded ideal. A once-in-a-lifetime offer.

Among the job listings I was looking at in Budějovice, there wasn't a single opening for a porter. But maybe I could try my luck in a different city. Not in Plzeň, I had no intention of going back there, but what about.... Again, I found myself thinking about the position that Vojta had offered me. It wasn't an entrance for the general public, but one that led to the archives, in a depository away from the main building. It was used by academics and students.

No warehouse workers, smacking their lips at the sight of a female.

But what about housing? Maybe it would be manageable for a few months after all. With Vojta, there was definitely no danger. Whenever I've been in the forest with him, I have always felt safe in his presence. I could stay out later in the evenings and come home after Vojta was already asleep. And in the mornings, I could disappear quickly. As soon as I got my first paycheque, plus the money from the tea tin, I'd have enough to go find my own place.

I went back to my room and lay down again. The reasons why I needed to refuse Vojta's offer hadn't disappeared, but they no longer seemed so fundamental. As I fell asleep towards morning, I felt clear about my decision.

The next day I handed Vojta the signed papers. He nodded without batting an eyelash.

32

Over the course of the three remaining weeks of the holiday, we refined our collaboration to perfection. The four of us—Ruda, the Walrus, Vojta and I—truly became a *'gutes team'*. Almost every morning Vojta and I would pick up our charges at the fountain and head south together. We led a group of Prague folks into the woods, who originally had wanted to go canoeing but due to the low water level of the Otava had to quickly come up with an alternate activity. Two older widowers who, due to vision problems, couldn't go mushroom hunting on their own, and one hipster couple. A small group of young Germans who weren't interested in ordinary mushrooms, but the magic kind. Two young families with children.

Those expeditions wore me out, I still couldn't get used to the idea of going mushroom hunting in a group, the obligation to make conversation with people made me tired, but the outings with the fungi tourists had their upsides as well.

Sometimes Ruda would join our excursions. It was always such a strain on my nerves that after just one day with him I felt as though I deserved a merit badge for self-control. He was constantly getting in my way. He always walked directly in front of me, whipping his head around, as if he had a radar implanted in his neck. But not even the most assiduous scanning of the ground ever led to any results. 'Hey, do you see anything?' he would whisper, jabbing his elbow backwards into me. As soon as I spotted a mushroom, I gave him a nudge, motioned with my chin, and whispered 'bolete' or '*Xerocomellus pruinatus*'. Sometimes I even had to point him to the right mushroom with the tip of my foot, because instead of a brittlegill, he was capable of pulling a polypore off a tree stump.

When things went well and Ruda squatted down beside the correct sporophore, he lit up and let loose: 'See him trying to hide, the little bugger? But with me, not even the cleverest mushroom can get away with it. Not with meeeeee!' And then he would brandish his knife with such bravado that the members of our group would come close to losing their ears.

Walking through the woods, he would tell the tourists outrageous nonsense. For example, he told a small group of programmers who had come to Sušice all the way from Prague for a mushroom-themed team building activity, that every mushroom that had been nibbled by slugs was edible. According to him, if they could survive, it meant that the mushroom couldn't harm people either. Fortunately Vojta always intervened at the right moment. 'Mister Vobořil, you are mistaken, gastropods have entirely different digestive enzymes!' Of course he was right. A slug can savour even a death cap unharmed! It was as much of a fallacy as saying that worms wouldn't take a bite of a poisonous mushroom, or that silver, upon contact with a toxic fungus, would turn black.

Another time Ruda claimed that the remedy for mushroom poisoning was to drink milk. Fat chance, I thought to myself. The only thing that could help, apart from a hospital, might be black tea and charcoal, but that's only if it's not a serious case of poisoning. I always listened to his long-winded lectures rolling my eyes, and when Vojta didn't interject with his 'Mister Vobořil . . .' I was quick to set the record straight just moments later. The tourists in general didn't pay much attention to me, God only knows what bits of knowledge they took back home with them.

Fortunately, Ruda came along just a couple of times, and always a few days apart, so I had a chance to take a breather.

When Ruda couldn't round up any tourists, Vojta and I would meet in the morning at 7.30 a.m. sharp by the footbridge over the river and would make our way south along the Otava. We no longer had to make plans in advance, suddenly it seemed only natural to go mushroom hunting together. We set off through the thicket and soon peeled away from the riverbed and continued up the hillside. We spoke little and mostly walked in silence, heads bowed, so as not to miss anything.

As always, when we got to Hartmanice we would begin to slow down and veer eastward, as I had always done. Then from there on to Annín, past the double stump, and continuing along the river until we got to the square in Sušice. And so it went on, until one Sunday in late August.

It happened without being planned. Moments before, nestled in the moss, we had found a little family of young shingled hedgehogs, which had lifted my spirits, as I don't come across them that often.

When we reached the edge of the forest grove, Vojta was ready as always to go left, but I stopped him. I took a few more breaths and then set off, right foot first, in the direction of the woods near Hartmanice. Vojta joined me, saying nothing.

It was like entering a foreign country. I left my motherland behind and could feel her reproachful glare on my back, so I quickened my step to get away. We reached Hartmanice and sat down on a bench in the triangular square hemmed in by streets, and suddenly I felt overwhelmed. But after a little while I managed to pull myself together, and to move on to where Vojta was leading me. He had become my guide in an unknown land.

It felt like throwing off a heavy backpack after an all-day trip and sticking my swollen feet into a cool stream. A feeling of relief, freedom and happiness. I was proud of myself, and the next day stepped across the boundary between my path and Vojta's with much more confidence.

In short, it was simply a brilliant summer in every way. An excellent year for boletes, brittlegills, blushers and pleasant experiences. I didn't even notice the spiderwebs that brushed against our faces with increasing frequency. I didn't observe the shadows growing longer and longer. As we strode through the tall grass, the chill drawn in by the earth during the ever-lengthening nights brushed against our feet, yet all we felt was the warm sun rolling down our backs.

33

One time towards the end of August, as Vojta and I were returning from the Toadstool, some bad memories slammed into me full force. We had done our usual 25-kilometre trek, but still didn't feel like going home. From the Otava riverbed, some paddlers who had got stuck in the shallow water and were dragging their canoe over the rocks, waved at us. 'Heeeeey!' they called out, but we didn't even bother to turn around. We continued along the river all the way to Sušice. It was only about four o'clock so we decided to stay in town a little longer. It occurred to us to go up to the Chapel of the Guardian Angel, and then come back down to the Otava and soak our feet in the river. For the end of the holidays, it was unusually hot and muggy.

We were standing at the traffic light by the Šumava Museum, waiting for it to turn green so that we could cross directly to the bridge over the Otava, when suddenly I felt someone's hand on my shoulder. At first just a timid caress, but then a firm grip. I even felt sharp nails digging into my skin through my thin T-shirt. Startled, I nearly shook off the hand in revulsion, but then I turned around. Vojta was staring at me, his eyes wide, his mouth slightly open. The look of a frightened child.

I shuddered. This was exactly where it happened, fifteen years ago.

It was towards the end of the holiday, just before my tenth birthday. That day we were supposed to head back to Plzeň. By then, there was practically nothing left of who I had been before the summer holidays. What remained was just a tired little soul that allowed a wasted body to drag it around against its will. I had become a shrivelled and withered old woman, who longed only to be left alone.

My brothers and my mother and I were planning to stroll along the bank of the Otava for a bit and then sit down in the garden of a pub. We did this every time we were ready to return home at the end of the holidays. My father dropped us off in Sušice and then drove back to Dvorce to do one final sweep of the house, close the shutters, turn off the electricity, disconnect the gas cylinder and go through the rooms, in case we forgot something. He always liked to inspect the family property himself. Then he would get back in the car and join us, and by then we were already warming ourselves in the sun, sipping lemonade. He sat down with us, ordered a Viennese coffee and treated us all to an ice pop as a farewell to Sušice.

I don't remember exactly how it happened. All I know is that I was standing and staring at the traffic light. The little red man didn't peel his feet off the ground for an endlessly long time. Suddenly, instead of the red light, I saw grey shadows flitting around me. The world spun, and a blue sky dotted with wispy clouds unfurled before my eyes. The clouds weren't moving at all, as if someone had glued them there. Somebody's hands were touching me but I hardly noticed them. I suddenly felt very light, and all the misgivings that had been weighing me down over the past few weeks seemed to fall away. I was looking up and completely oblivious of what was going on around me.

And then suddenly someone's hand pinned me back to the ground. I wanted to look around, but could barely move my head. I caught sight of my mother above me, looking terrified, she was holding up her arms as if shielding herself from something. Evžen stood beside her, supporting her so that she wouldn't fall.

I felt warm palms on my chest. They belonged to Milan.

'Come on, sis, damn it, breathe!' he was shouting and pressing on my chest, until I thought it would snap under his weight.

And then abruptly he stopped, leaned down and hugged me. I mustered all my strength and placed my right hand on his back. His behaviour struck me as being absurd, this was not at all how I knew him. What are you nuts, I wanted to say to him, but all that came out of me was a strange gurgling sound.

'Damn, sis, what a bitch,' he began to sob, smiled at me and wiped some blood off his forehead with the back of his hand.

Then I saw a yellow car with flashing lights and two men in uniforms running towards me. As a girl I had always wanted to take a ride in an ambulance with its siren on. Except that my eyes closed before they managed to take me on board.

I don't recall Vojta being around then. But somehow, he must have heard about the accident, because in a small town news like that travels fast. I didn't shrug his hand off my shoulder, but instead took it gently in my palm.

'Sára ...' he whispered, still with the same frightened expression.

Sára, I repeated to myself, as if it were a foreign word.

With that name he breathed life back into me. For a moment it really did feel like mouth-to-mouth resuscitation. I didn't let go of his hand, even after the light turned green. Not even as we stepped into the crosswalk and made our way across the Otava. Vojta tolerated it until we reached the opposite bank, and only then slipped out of my grasp, wiped his hand on his trousers and stuck it into his pocket. But even that was progress.

Back home, I opened the kitchen drawer and put both envelopes on the table. For a moment I looked from one to the other, and then I went to get the matches. The first one, the smaller of the two, I lit and threw into the sink. I watched the yellow flame licking at the white paper covered in writing, my disappointment dissipating with the smoke travelling up the chimney. When only a corner remained, I threw in the paperwork Milan had brought me. Even that tiny flame was enough to set the contract on fire. As the blaze died down, so did the feeling that there was anything left to bind me to my family. I emptied a full pitcher of water into the sink and watched as the curling ashes dissolved and disappeared down the drain.

I went up to the second floor, pulled my military duffle bag out of the closet, and started to pack.

34

As I sat on the steps putting on my hiking boots, my cell phone rang. For a moment I hesitated, but then I removed my right boot and went back into the kitchen.

'Hey, sis, I've got something for you!'

'Hi, Milan.'

I tried not to sound too annoyed.

'I've got a great tip. Get this, yesterday I just happened to turn on the TV. And they were doing a story on mushrooms, about how they're really growing right now, as you probably already know . . .' he chuckled. He was talking fast and furiously, and one could hear the noise of the street in the background. It was still early for him to be on his way to work, he must have been standing on the balcony or in the little garden out front, smoking his morning cigarette. 'Anyway, they were showing footage of people, and how much they'd collected, stuff like that, and there was this old lady, who in a single morning had found forty king boletes, and get this . . .' It was at least the twentieth time he had called me this month. I wasn't used to him paying me so much attention. At one time I had been the needy one, that's why I was always tagging along with him and pestering him with all sorts of questions. The fact that the tables had turned gave me a sense of smug satisfaction. ' . . . That old lady was from Kašperk, so I figured you might be interested, you could swing by there and have a look around, and then at the pub you could really shine, huh?'

'Hmmm,' I replied.

'So, what do you think?'

'Kašperk is too far away, as you yourself know. Besides, there are masses of tourists there right now, but thanks anyway.'

He sighed. There followed a pause. I imagined him taking a drag on his cigarette, squinting as he always does, then blowing the smoke upwards across his protruding lower lip.

'And actually I also wanted to ask you about those papers, did you have a chance . . .' I detected a hint of nervousness in his voice.

I remained silent.

'So, Sisi,' he cleared his throat, 'Can I drop by to pick them up?'

I bit my lip and took a breath: 'I didn't sign them.'

'What?'

I was looking out of the kitchen window towards the fence. A silhouette darted past the gate. Vojta must not have found me at the footbridge so had come by to see what was up.

'I simply didn't sign them and I'm not going to sign them. I don't even have them any more, they're burnt. I'm not interested in your offer. And now I have to go.'

'Sis, what the hell is wrong with you? What about Evžen . . .'

I hung up, waved to Vojta, who through the hedge of overgrown roses couldn't possibly see me, and ran back to get my shoes. I double knotted my laces, grabbed the basket and made for the gate.

For the end of August, it was pretty hot. While we were still on Santos, my sweaty T-shirt began to stick to my back. The trek southwards was gruelling, and as for mushrooms, there were barely any. As we were passing by some fencing below Krušec, we heard a desperate bleating. A dozen sheep were huddling in the shade of three young saplings. We wanted to continue, but the sheep literally started screaming. We climbed over the wooden planks and our feet hit the parched ground. Their water tub was completely dry, and not a well in sight. We hung our half-empty baskets on a tree and Vojta grabbed the plastic tub. We carried it down to the creek and then together hauled it back up, full. It wasn't far, but the way back was uphill and with the tub full of water, we got pretty sweaty. The sheep lunged for the tub, stumbling over the packed soil, butting their heads. The ones who managed to get through practically choked on the fresh water. It was clear that it wasn't enough for them, so we had to repeat the entire exercise. When I went back to grab my basket again, the handle almost slipped out of my sweaty hand.

'Come on, I'll show you something,' said Vojta. Back on the main road, he motioned to me to climb over the guardrail and led me further along a stream down a dirt path. The creek had receded from us a bit, but we could still hear its gurgling. Then, we abruptly swerved and beat a path through some saplings and bushes and descended all the way to the water. We arrived at a small beach with fine white sand. Directly ahead was a little black pool, created by the confluence of two small streams. It must have been deep because one couldn't see the bottom. I wondered how it was possible that I didn't know about this place. I touched the water with my finger and it was ice cold, like all the rivers and streams in the Bohemian Forest.

I sat down on the sand, took off my shoes and socks and wet my feet. Vojta did the same, except that he removed his shoes while standing up. It was refreshing. How lovely it would have been to immerse oneself completely into the cool water. It occurred to me that the last time I had gone swimming must have been in high school. Maybe I wouldn't even know how to do it any more.

Vojta seemed to read my mind.

'Shall we have a swim?'

I quickly shook my head. I wasn't about to undress. Not even in front of Vojta, to whom my nudity would certainly be of no interest.

He noticed my discomfort and turned to the water. He took a step, paused briefly, then continued. I watched him in surprise. A moment later, the dark water swallowed him completely, beige corduroys, striped T-shirt and all. Only his shaggy head was sticking out. He was waving at me to follow him.

I lingered on the shore a bit longer, then mustered my courage.

The water was terribly cold, I had to hold my breath. Suddenly it seemed foolish. I'd probably end up with another bladder infection. I wanted to return to the shore, but then my gaze fell once more on Vojta, just his happy face on the surface of the water. I took a step towards him. I felt the icy wave moving up my body, and finally plunged in, head and all and opened my eyes. The rushing water seeped through my clothes, washing away sweat, dirt and all the heaviness. In my ears all I could hear was the swoosh of the current. I lifted my feet off the bottom, became one with the river and floated in my ethereal body. Everything around me dissolved, no gravitational, centrifugal or any other kind of force existed, I was just completely alone, nothing at all around me, except for Vojta's blurred silhouette. He had buried his bare feet into the sand at the bottom right where the two streams converged, the water rushed over him but he didn't budge. I closed my eyes. And then the current seized me and swept me away from the confluence. I struck my head on a boulder, spun around in the water and suddenly saw only darkness around me, my foot had caught in an eddy that was dragging me to the bottom. I couldn't tell where the surface was, I was floundering in the current. And then I felt Vojta's hand on me. I stopped flailing my legs and let myself be pulled up. I was gasping for air.

We clambered out onto the shore and sat down on the sand with our feet still submerged in the water. Once we had caught our breath, we grabbed our baskets in one hand and our shoes in the other and returned to the forest on tiptoe, so that the sand wouldn't stick to us. We lay down in our wet clothes on the moss and the grass, head-to-head, a space between us. Only our hair touched—lifeless, insentient tissue.

I was looking up at the treetops, and had to squint my right eye more than my left, because the sun was flashing through the branches at me from that side. There was a soft breeze, the woods rustled and the moss and the pine needles gave off a pleasant smell. My body grew heavy, my arms and legs became numb, the tension drained from my fingertips, my open palms pointed to the sky. My left eyelid also began to droop, but before I closed both eyes completely, I heard a voice.

'He'll never to do anything to you again. He is dead. You don't need to be afraid of him.'

I wasn't sure whether it was Vojta or just my imagination, but I didn't have the strength to lift my heavy eyelids.

When I next opened my eyes, the sun was directly over my head. In the clearing, amid the pinching ants and pine needles prickling my back, I must have slept a solid hour in my damp clothes. I turned over onto my side and felt Vojta's curls right in front of my face.

'Good morning. Actually, good afternoon,' he said. And then, without changing the expression on his face, he added: 'So, it's tomorrow.'

Of course, he had only stated what I already knew. At home my duffle bag was packed and my ticket for the bus from Sušice was ready. Even so, my heart began to pound wildly, I felt as if my chest was going to explode at any moment. I lay on my back again, closed my eyes and said nothing.

When we got up I was almost dry. It was only along the way to the Toadstool that it dawned on me that I was walking through here for the very last time. That never again would I get up in the morning and head for the footbridge past Dvorce. That my scuffed hiking boots would never again touch the trail. I felt myself shrinking more and more. I felt a tingling in my arms and legs, and a throbbing in my temples.

Ruda wasn't at the Toadstool, so I handed my mushrooms over to the Walrus and shook his hand to say goodbye. He just waved and repeated exactly what he had said two weeks ago. 'You'll see, you'll change your mind.'

'You've got some plums-and-custards in there, for pickling, first ones this year,' I tried to cheer him up, but he turned his back to me and brought his fist down on the stainless-steel countertop.

I accompanied Vojta all the way to his house, a prefab wooden building with white walls and a red roof. I thought I saw a curtain stir behind the window. 'See you tomorrow, then,' I whispered so softly that Vojta couldn't have heard me.

The roses at the gate scratched my hands and caught on my jeans. I had to set down the basket and pull off the tendrils one at a time. I walked into the hall. The familiar smells wafted to me from the kitchen. Beside the shoe rack my duffle bag was ready. I walked through the rooms, one by one. As I went, I caressed the furniture and the walls. Meanwhile outside it began to grow dark. Finally, I sat down at the kitchen table, opened the drawer, and pulled out the tin box. I counted the money into little piles—8,670 crowns, not bad for starters. I hid the money in my pocket and poured a cup of tea. I looked at the clock—it was almost nine o'clock at night. How many hours did I have left to spend in this shack? Suddenly I realized that Vojta hadn't told me what time we would meet the next day.

I pulled on my boots in the hallway and walked out into the garden. I left the door ajar behind me.

The light was on in Vojta's room. Quietly I slipped through the gate, stood in front of the prefab and gazed into the light on the second floor. Somewhere behind the window, beyond my field of vision, he was there. No doubt on his bed was a suitcase into which he was packing his carefully folded clothes. The books he had received in the package had long been arranged on the shelf, only the most interesting ones would travel with him to Prague.

I imagined I was in the room with him. I am not standing outside in the darkness, but inside, in a room flooded with light. I am sitting with him at the same table, looking at a book, watching television, or maybe we are dining together like that time on the porch of the shack. And then suddenly Vojta appeared in the window. He was standing behind the glass, looking out. I backed away in fright, although I knew perfectly well that in the darkness he couldn't see me.

He was wearing a striped cotton pyjama jacket in which his slight silhouette loomed. I could see his bony shoulders, the fine hairs on his neck, his narrow hips. From now on I would see him this way every day. Once I'd settled into his two-room flat, we would meet in the hallway every morning in our night clothes. We would take turns in the bathroom, do our laundry at the same time in one washing machine, brush our teeth together in front of the mirror and afterwards our toothbrushes would nestle side by side in a cup.

You're only going to stay with him for about six weeks, just until you get your first paycheque, I tried to calm myself down. Six whole weeks. That's more than forty days, and my heart sank. I could feel my body stiffening. A metal band was tightening around my chest. I gasped for breath.

I turned around quickly and headed back home.

I sat down at the table. You can do this, I repeated to myself. What was it that Mouchová had said? You are a healthy twenty-five-year-old young woman with a life ahead of you. So listen to her, damn it! You have a unique opportunity to get yourself out of here, so take it and run! There's nothing wrong with you, you haven't done anything. It's not your fault that your parents died. You are not responsible for what your father did to you. The whole world lies at your feet, just take the first step.

At the same time, the opposing side was whispering to me that it would be a terribly foolish thing to do. You don't have it in you to go out into the world. You won't be able to keep the job, after all, you've got it on record that you're unable to work. Remember the fiasco in Budějovice. After a few weeks at the most they'll fire you from the library and in the meantime, you'll have lost your job at the Toadstool. Why risk losing the only thing you have? Ruda's not going to kick you out. And what's more, you can call Milan and ask him to swing by with a new contract. You'll stop making trouble for your brothers and you'll sign. At least you'll know for sure that you won't lose the house. The shack is your destiny, your home, without it you are nothing. You're not about to move into a flat with a strange man.

Outside, it was slowly beginning to grow light. In the morning twilight, the contours of the objects around me began to emerge. The rumpled cot with the sleeping bag tossed over it. The tattered curtains and grimy windowpanes. The small stove and the gas cylinder. The radio and next to it the non-working television. And finally—the framed photograph on the wall between the windows. I was sitting right across from it. My mother with her big belly, at which my dad and my brothers are pointing their index fingers. They look like a happy family. Because I hadn't yet come into the world.

When Vojta came by in the morning, I was still sitting there. He knocked three times gently on the door and then there was silence.

Through the chinks in the door and the windows and the cracks in the walls, a suffocating sense of expectation began to infiltrate the space. It was like a poisonous gas that infested the entire room.

There was another knock on the door.

I wanted to call out that I was coming, that I had everything ready, I was just putting on my shoes, but my throat was dry and I could only wheeze. I was unable to get up from the chair. My palms were glued to the table.

Move, damn it, I shouted to my inert body from above, get up and go to him, you can do it. What the hell is the big deal?

It was as if my father was still here with me. Three years after his death he still had me in his power. He was behind me, gripping my shoulders and pinning me down to the chair.

Let me go! Don't ever touch me again! Leave me alone!

I turned and looked towards the front hallway. He was so very close, I needed only to reach out my hand. He knocked again, louder this time. Vojta, my lips moved but nothing came out. He went around the house, tried to look in through the window, but couldn't see me through the thick curtains. I could hear his hand on the door handle, but the door was, as always, locked with the key on the inside. Through the glass I could see his slender silhouette with his big curly head, which he was scratching uncertainly.

He knocked one more time. And then just the sound of footsteps.

Yet again my body had betrayed me.

I sat there for another hour or so, then got up, went into the hallway, pulled on my hiking boots and grabbed my basket. Without turning to look towards Vojta's house, I hurriedly crossed the footbridge over the river and headed straight south. I knew that I wouldn't make it to Hartmanice this time. Waiting for me was my usual route through Kundratice and Vatětice, and then on to Annín, with a brief stop at the double stump on the piney slope. It was perfectly clear to me that from this day forward I would not deviate from my route by even a millimetre.

Overnight, autumn arrived. Outside it was lightly drizzling, the clearings were thick with fog. I walked into one patch and let the fog swallow me up. The white darkness cut me off from the surrounding world. Whatever was happening around me, I remained oblivious.

'You see,' the Walrus said to me in the kitchen. 'You belong here.'

When I returned home in the afternoon, a large envelope with Milan's handwriting was sticking out of the postbox. I placed it on the table, opened it, flipped to the last page, and signed without the slightest hesitation. When Milan next drops by, I'll hand over the contract.

35

I woke up in the hospital with no idea where I was.

Something similar happens to me sometimes even now. I wake up in the morning and for a moment I don't know where I am. In fact, I have no idea even who I am, and would be unable to respond to the simplest of questions.

Back then it was much stronger. It was complete emptiness. Not only did I not know the answer to any question, no question came to my mind. Who, when, where, these were all total unknowns. I was in the grip of pure nothingness. A white darkness was spreading around me and I floated in it without a body.

As I later learnt, I had sustained serious injuries during the accident. In addition to a concussion, a bruised coccyx, lacerations and scrapes, I had a complicated compound fracture of the femur. The operation went on for a long time, apparently the head surgeon spent several hours picking out bone fragments from my muscles. Along with them, he extracted every feeling and bad memory. All that remained was an infinitesimal spore, detectable only under a microscope. It had taken refuge from the scalpel in an innermost cavity and had encapsulated itself there.

Above me, faceless blurs of colour danced before my eyes. Only gradually did they assume human forms.

Mom. Dad. Evžen. Milan.

Their presence evoked nothing within me. It was as if they were perfect strangers to whom I later learnt to assign proper names and roles. Over time I got used to them, the same way I got used to the faces of the nurses and the doctors.

A long and arduous rehabilitation followed. I remember how I howled in pain when, a few days after the operation, they forced me for the first time to raise myself in bed. It was as if someone had stuck a knife into my leg. To this day, when I run my thumb over the scar on my thigh, I am reminded of that searing pain. Back then, physical pain stifled the agony of the soul. Every day they would transport me from my room to the physical rehabilitation ward where I had alternately to bend and extend my knee, exercise my toes and raise my leg, while lying prone. At least twice a day. Later they stood me up between parallel bars and forced me to put weight on my foot. Each time the sole of my foot touched the floor, a sharp pain shot through me. That pain brought me, step by step, back to life.

It took almost four months before they let me go home. They did everything possible to make sure I could enjoy Santa Claus.

'You don't want to be hanging around here on Christmas Eve, you can't do that to us, hurry home,' the chief physician gave me a wink.

I couldn't care less. Everything that was going on around me I perceived as if through opaque glass, sounds were muffled and colours muted.

All four of them came to fetch me from the hospital. Dad was driving, and this time I was allowed to sit up front, so that I could extend my sore leg. It was the morning of the 24th of December. The streets were full of zigzagging dads in search of last-minute Christmas gifts, the last of the sickly carps lolled lazily in the tubs, and coloured lights twinkled in the windows of the houses. Up until last year it had been my favourite day. Now it was no different from any other date.

At home, a decorated Christmas tree was already waiting, plates with Christmas cookies were out on the table, and my mom ran straight from the entrance hall into the kitchen and lit all four candles of the Advent wreath. She had dark circles under her eyes, she must have been up all night preparing everything.

I sat down on the sofa that, until recently, had been the domain of my obese mother. Now it was reserved for me, the cripple, who could barely hobble to the bathroom. I put my crutches down on the floor beside the sofa and lay back on the cushion against the armrest. I gingerly propped my sore leg up on the coffee table. No one objected. Nor could they have, because in fact no one noticed. The entire family was caught up in the Christmas frenzy. Out of the corner of my eye I watched them all darting back and forth. Mother was stressing out in the kitchen, turning the carp fillets in the pan, and stirring the soup on the other burner. Now and then she would disappear from my field of vision because she would run off to the pantry. No one asked why. When she came back, the tension in her face would be gone for a while and her eyes would be misty. Every so often she would turn to me and absentmindedly ask: 'Do you need anything, Sisi?' without waiting for an answer. Meanwhile, Evžen was setting the table, Milan was bringing out the food and even our father was putting finishing touches on the decorations, straightening the star at the top of the tree, sweeping up the fallen pine needles and polishing the silverware with a cloth.

I tried to convince myself that I belonged among them. That I had just stepped away for a brief moment and would shortly rejoin them. I would take my seat at the festively set table, drizzle some lemon on the fried breadcrumbs and then chew carefully, lest a carp bone get stuck in my throat.

Mother tinkled the crystal bell, put on the CD with Christmas carols and clapped her hands. Everybody sat down and I, like a good girl, hobbled over on my crutches to join them. The illusion of Christmas cheer was perfect. The formally set table positively radiated a holiday atmosphere. Arranged on the tablecloth embroidered with candles decorated with holly and boughs of spruce was the traditional 'Blue Onion' china. The soup tureen was steaming, the golden-brown fillets of carp glistened with butter, the potato salad was a kaleidoscope of colours. In the centre of the table stood a three-armed candelabra on which the candles were lit. All of the food and beverages were, as always, ready on the table, because one didn't get up from Christmas dinner, or someone would die within the year.

I stirred the yellowish creamy soup with my spoon. The brownish gobs of roe floated to the surface and bumped up against the pale, motionless lumps of milt. I felt like throwing up. I forced down the soup and made myself move on to the fillet. The carp was neither too fatty nor too bony, my father pronounced with satisfaction, the best we'd ever had. Yet, all I could smell was the stale fishiness. It tainted every bite. I chewed the white flesh and tried not to gag. I hoped that a bone would get stuck in my throat and liberate me from this dinner.

Finally, after a long struggle, I was able to let myself slowly be drawn into the present by all those smells. I soaked up the scent of nutmeg, star anise, pine needles and lemon.

When the little bell jingled in the living room, I hobbled, on unsteady legs and noticeably more slowly than my brothers, over to the tree and obediently sat down to unwrap presents. I played at Santa Claus along with the rest of them, handing out gift bags to the others and opening my own. As I tore away the paper, I smiled at my mother, who evidently yearned for this, as she always did, and as was always done. With the untying of each successive ribbon, I felt myself slowly rejoining the family again. Once more I was a daughter and a sister, and not someone standing on the sidelines.

36

In January I began to return to *normal* life. My mother would drive me to school every morning. Because of me, she had paid for brush-up lessons at the driving school, as she hadn't been behind the wheel since her nineteenth birthday. It was only a few blocks, but even so the trip to school turned into quite the drama. My mother would scrape the side of the car against the bushes that grew along the street, came close to running into pedestrians in the crosswalk and would need to look down to check not only what gear she was in, but also which of the pedals she was pressing. The only thing missing was for her to stick labels on them.

She would drop me off in front of the school, where my classmates were standing around the entrance. She would open the car door for me, hold my French crutches while I clawed myself out of the back seat, and then try to kiss me on the pavement. At first, I had hoped that she would realize how much she was embarrassing me, the crutches were bad enough, let alone my mother's sprawling backside. In class I got teased about her, the obese Slovakian, who even after twenty years in Plzeň still had a foreign accent.

'Mom, let me be,' I said as resolutely as I could, rolling my eyes so that she would finally understand and wrenching myself away, but still she would pucker up her lips and blow me a kiss as I practically broke my neck on the steps, scrambling to avoid it.

At first it seemed impossible, but then in the end it went well. I managed to make up the missed classes and didn't have to repeat the grade. And it was no wonder, really, since every afternoon after school I would hole up in my room and study. I wasn't left with much of a choice, I didn't know what else to do with so much time. I couldn't go outside much because of my sore leg, my mother was planted in front of the television, and my parents hadn't yet bought me a computer. So every day after school, in my bedroom, I would hop over to the armchair and hoist my leg onto an inflatable ball that my parents had placed there so I wouldn't have to struggle to sit on a regular chair. I would stack my textbooks on the bed beside me and pick them up one by one: history, Czech language and English. I would memorize poems by heart, circle the globe with my finger and sing along with English songs on the CD player.

Everyone walked around me as if on tiptoe, afraid that if they upset me, I might do something rash again.

'Boys, leave Sisi alone,' my mother would say when they rattled the door handle of my room, 'She has to study.' And after a while the boys really did leave me alone. They stopped teasing me, locking me in the basement and tying me to the tree, they walked around me as if I were an unexploded mine. As if I were encased in a fragile shell, that could break at the slightest disturbance.

As for the *bullshit*, as Milan once haplessly termed it, that I had been up to at the end of the summer, it was referenced at home only obliquely and in hushed tones. Mother referred to it as *that Sušice thing*, but for the most part never mentioned it at all, it was long past, best not to speak of *it* any more.

It was as if once I got back from the hospital the whole house went silent. There was no talk about why our father came home from work only after dark, and then locked himself in his study. About why our mother spent hours sitting at the table with a glassy-eyed look, getting up only to fetch something from the pantry. On the outside, though, we looked like a respectable family. The house was tidy again and our mother didn't spend her days lounging on the living room sofa. My brothers, like me, stopped loitering about outside. The arguments between our parents ceased. Everything seemed to have gone back to normal, back to before our mother's accident on the stairs, the only difference being that the newfound communal space was not filled with anything at all. We treated each other with mutual politeness, perhaps with excessive consideration, as if we were strangers on a social visit. On a physical level, the closest we got to each other was when we ate dinner together, but once we had eaten, everyone would scatter, as if a bomb had exploded in the centre of the table and jettisoned us in all directions. We would shut ourselves up in our rooms and would see each other only the next day at breakfast.

When my mother, as an exception, would ask me something, I would answer in monosyllables or with a gesture. I had no desire to discuss anything with her or with anybody else. I preferred to be alone. In the presence of other people, I felt a strange uneasiness. I was perpetually on guard, as if danger lurked everywhere. Even now I can vividly recall the feeling, which back then haunted me relentlessly— of someone's eyes fixed on my back. I would turn around constantly, and even when I saw that it wasn't the case, the relief was short lived.

And so, not long after my return from the hospital, I limped over to the closet under the stairs, opened a shoebox that held keys, which had accumulated in our house over many years, and took it up to my room. And then I tried them out, one by one, some were suited to an entirely different type of lock while others fit, but wouldn't turn. After about thirty attempts, one finally worked.

Whenever I was in my room, I double-locked the door and left the key in the lock, and anytime I left the room, I kept the key with me in my pocket. Although up to that summer I had always been rather distracted, I never lost that key. The feeling that no one could enter my room gave me a sense of security. I needed somehow to safeguard my solitude, outside of my locked space I felt anxious.

That key may have saved me. One night, as I lay in bed, I saw the door handle move. Slowly, without a sound, the shiny metal handle tilted downward and then returned to its original position. I lay there in silence, without moving, and stared at it until dawn. Maybe I had only dreamt it.

I avoided my father deliberately, without any explicit justification. Of course, we greeted each other and exchanged a few generic phrases from time to time, but when we went out as a family, I never took his hand, let alone climbed into his lap on the sofa, as I had done in the past. When he entered the living room, I often made up some excuse and shuffled off to my room upstairs.

In May, three-quarters of a year after the accident, I celebrated an unexpected triumph. Despite the adverse circumstances I had successfully passed the entrance exams for the academic secondary school, or the Gymnasium.

'Welcome back,' my father patted me on the back. He took half a day off from work in my honour. We went to the pastry shop to celebrate together. He bought me a cream puff and a hot chocolate, and nibbled on a piece of rum cake with his coffee. He looked pleased, and although he tried to hide it, I could see he was moved. Finally, one of us had made it into the St Nicholas Gymnasium. It was high time, the family tradition had been in danger of being broken, for neither of my brothers had passed the admissions exams. Evžen was attending an ordinary technical college and Milan hadn't made it past junior high school. Only I had succeeded. On the 1st of September, now without crutches and with a backpack over my shoulder, I entered the building that was to be a springboard for further success. My grandfather, my father and now me.

A bright future lay ahead of me. The past remained locked away behind a demarcation line as thick as a fat slug.

Everything that came before was entirely obscured by a void. I remembered nothing of what had happened the previous summer. It was as if someone had ripped those two months out of the calendar. Only occasionally, when at night I would spend too long watching the headlights of cars travelling across the ceiling, would my thoughts stray into some deep place, all the way to the edge of a bottomless black pit, and spill into my dream. But they never fell in, they were deflected by an invisible membrane, which covered it, and bounced back up. When I awoke the next morning, I wouldn't remember the dream at all. All that was left in me was a very faint nebulous feeling, a mere whiff of something unpleasant.

37

September is usually my most successful month. Most of the tourists go back to work in the city, so on weekdays mushroom hunters in the woods are scarce. The earth in the Bohemian Forest is warmed through after the balmy summer and it rains more often, in short, the perfect climate for mushrooms. Practically all the boletes, russulas, blushers and parasols are growing, and add to those the milkcaps and blewits. Towards the end of the month, I usually spot the first clusters of honey mushrooms growing on old stumps. For the most part, I do so well that the earnings are enough to last me for the next few months.

There tend to be so many mushrooms that they get under my feet. They grow right next to the trail, sometimes directly on it. I really don't care for this type of mushroom hunting, there's no challenge. Sometimes I even half close my eyes to make it a bit harder.

In the last few years, I've gone out right after the summer holidays and just outside Dvorce, have stumbled across a patch of boletes or milkcaps so vast, I could simply have turned around and walked back along the Otava with a full basket straight to the Toadstool. By noon I would have been done for the whole day. The first time it happened, I hesitated for a moment about which direction to take, but in the end I grabbed the heavy basket, reached into my pocket for a canvas bag into which I could toss more of my conquests, and descended as usual into the heart of the Bohemian Forest. The money was always secondary, first and foremost, I needed to complete my route.

This September, however, was entirely different. Just like the whole year. On the trail I came across some matte boletes, added a few brittlegills and two milkcaps. In the Annín woods my heart leapt for joy when next to a stump I spotted three handsome king boletes, but when I pulled one up and turned it over, I noticed the gills and flung it furiously to the ground. How could I have confused a velvet roll-rim with a king bolete? I arrived at the Toadstool with my basket half empty. Again. The last two weeks it hadn't rained at all. The weary sun struggled to find its way through the thick branches of the conifers, its feeble rays just lightly dabbing at the chilled moss.

But the bad weather wasn't the only reason that I arrived at the Toadstool every day with a long face. As I surveyed my usual spots, I had a feeling that many of the best finds were eluding me. Every day I would pass several mushroom hunters who, judging by their appearance, I would have thought under such conditions were unlikely to find even a half-gnawed puffball. A discreet glance into their basket, however, had me completely floored. I was glad that my basket was as always covered by a dishcloth, otherwise I would have died of shame on the spot.

'You're too late,' a mushroom hunter once called out to me as he approached.

It made me furious. Under normal circumstances that should have been my line. I would walk past the others with my basket so full that the dishcloth would be bulging and nonchalantly shrug.

A couple of times I scoured my usual sites and found nothing at all, or at the most some remnants. I moved a few steps away and then returned, knelt down, laid my cheek against the cold moss, and examined the spot from an ant's perspective. I, who could find mushrooms practically with my eyes closed, suddenly discovered that I had overlooked a few specimens in the grass. In places that I had meticulously searched before.

Maybe it was due to my exhaustion. After Vojta's departure I would fall asleep only long after midnight, a few times dozing off only at dawn. The fatigue turned everything before my eyes into a grey smudge.

I felt as though the forest had turned its back on me. As I entered among the trees, the spruces pulled away their boughs, as if I were a leper. I picked my way through the bristling and wary branches, over ground that cringed at every snap of a twig. I felt like a soldier who had inadvertently strayed behind enemy lines. I could sense apprehension in the air. In the bowels of the forest something was lying in wait for me.

I was completely unnerved by this change. Up to now I had only felt this way among people.

38

I was just getting back to Sušice, the bottom of my basket showing through beneath the mushrooms I had gathered. At least, for the very first time this year, there were a few honey mushrooms. Hopefully the oyster mushrooms would start coming up soon, so the Walrus could show off with something new on the menu. Ruda would be pleased, oyster mushrooms are all the rage right now, supposedly they boost the immune system. All he talks about is drying them and turning them into capsules that he will sell as a miracle cure against the common cold.

My head was prickling from lack of sleep,, the previous night I hadn't slept for more than three hours and the night before that hadn't been much better. I was unsteady on my feet and after walking all day, was very short of breath.

As I stepped off the pavement in the square, my foot landed wrong and I fell onto the kerb. The mushrooms spilled out onto the ground, and a driver passing by was forced to jerk sharply on the steering wheel and swerve wide to avoid me. I knelt down on the dusty asphalt and gathered up the mushrooms. Apart from the honey mushrooms and a few nibbled saffron milkcaps, I only had half a dozen small button mushrooms, half of a russula cap and several field blewits in my basket. I looked like a total loser, and the worst part was that I felt like one, too.

After I finally managed to gather up the mushrooms, I heard my name behind me.

'Sisi!' someone called out to me tersely.

Evžen stood with his fists clenched and his arms held away from his body, as if he was ready at any moment to strike me.

'What the hell do you think you're doing?' he hissed. He was purple in the face and only two smouldering slits remained of his eyes. This was the expression on our father's face, when he would come home from a faculty council meeting and our mother would greet him with a glassy stare.

He raised his hand and I instinctively ducked. Instead of striking, he threw a stack of papers down in front of me.

'Sign!'

I was kneeling on the pavement with the basket full of dusty mushrooms beside me. The knee onto which I had fallen was hurt and the fabric of my corduroy pants was torn. My hands were scraped. I grabbed the contract by its edge so as not to soil it.

'So, are you going to sign it or not?'

'Sure,' I would have liked to say, and ask him for a pen, but no sound came out. I only gasped.

Evžen stuck out his lower jaw and clenched his fists even tighter.

'This is your last chance, you goose. I am giving you three weeks. Either you sign or you'll even lose your shack,' he was practically shouting.

He turned on his heel and strode away from the square towards the river.

'But Evžen, those papers, I've already . . .' I finally began, but my weak and tired voice didn't carry far enough to reach him.

I thought about running to catch up with him. I would tell him that I wouldn't make any trouble, that I accepted their terms. If he gave me a ride home, I could hand over the signed contract right then and there. Or I could sign the papers he had tossed at me on the spot. But I knew full well that my tired body wasn't up to it.

So I just stood there and watched as the corner of the building swallowed Evžen up and then sucked up his shadow. I'm an expert at ruining lives. My own and the lives of others. In the past few years alone, how often have I heard it said. *How could you do this to us?*

I got to the restaurant, climbed the steps to the back entrance as usual, and knocked on the plywood door.

When I reached for the handle, someone on the other side forcefully grabbed it and pulled it shut. A moment later the door opened a crack, and Ruda poked his head out through the narrow opening and glowered at me.

'Damn, the shit's hitting the fan, you didn't check your cell, did you?'

No, in fact, I wasn't even sure where it was.

'Go wait for me somewhere else.'

'Where?'

'Maybe the wine bar,' he hissed and slammed the door in my face.

I slowly descended the steps and made my way three blocks down. In front of the entrance to the dive bar stood an old leatherette baby carriage with two small boys in it. Twins, who must have been a little over a year old. They sat opposite each other, strapped into the carriage. They looked sullen. I didn't want to go inside, nor could I even afford to. I stood about a metre away from the carriage, leaned back against the peeling facade, raised my head, and let the soft rays of the sun caress my face.

'What's that?' I heard Ruda's voice a moment later. He was pointing to the carriage and shaking his head.

'Those must be Chochola's kids, their dad is probably inside knocking back a few,' I explained.

'I see ... Hold on a minute, I have to take care of one more thing.' He darted off to the side and for a while was yelling something into his phone, gesticulating wildly.

'Come inside ...' he hollered at me, once he had finished.

He waved to the waiter and ordered a sparkling water. I had him bring me black tea.

'The health department is over at the Toadstool. Deep shit. They've been there all morning, apparently yesterday several people vomited after eating the soup.'

I gave a slight start in my chair. My blood ran cold.

'That's impossible, it couldn't have been because of my mushrooms,' I whispered. It had to be nonsense, I had never yet picked a bad mushroom. But even so, I started to fish around in my memory for what I had gathered that day.

'And can you really be so sure?' he scrutinized me. 'What if just this once you made a mistake?' He glared at me.

I shook my head, annoyed. Still, his question had planted a seed of doubt within me. In my mind I tried to remember what I had picked two days earlier. I had delivered to the Toadstool three red cracking boletes, two blushers, one birch bolete, a few button mushrooms and half a dozen brittlegills. Some of the mushrooms weren't the freshest, and under normal circumstances I would have let them be, but they certainly hadn't started to rot, so it couldn't have been that. Nor am I stupid enough to confuse a blusher or a button mushroom with a toxic amanita. Besides which, if that had been the case, not just the health department would have shown up, but also the police. No, I certainly had not made any mistake. Even so ... I couldn't get it out of my head. I remembered how I had found three small bog russulas in the grass. Since I hadn't been sleeping well I was so tired, it was as if there were a haze before my eyes. Could I possibly have confused them with a sickener? I replayed in my mind how I was holding the mushroom by its cap and turning it over in front of my eyes. The colour was not as deep a red as a sickener, it had to be an edible russula, I couldn't have mixed those up. Or had I?

'Rubbish, to this day I've never in my life made a mistake. Ask anyone,' I said, trying to look as confident as possible.

'I certainly hope so,' Ruda declared, visibly somewhat relieved.

'Even so, it's not good. They're trying to figure out where I get my ingredients, luckily, I sometimes buy them wholesale, so I have some documentation, and hopefully I'll manage to work something out. They can't find out about you, and besides, do you even have a food handler permit?'

I grimaced.

'Ruda, I don't even have a trade . . .'

Just then two officers burst through the door.

'So, Mr Chochola, where might we find you this time?' asked a young policewoman, her eyes surveying the room. The guests at their tables looked down in unison, as if they'd been caught red-handed.

Finally the policewoman's gaze landed on a table in the far corner of the room. Chochola's head was resting on the table, a glass of wine in front of him. Smoke was rising from the still-lit cigarette in the ashtray.

The policewoman approached him, grabbed him from behind by the collar and pulled him up against the back of the chair.

'Come on, pay up, and then you're coming with us to the station,' she said aloud to his puffy, flushed face. 'You left the boys unattended again. This time we're going to have to call social services.'

Ruda watched as the policewoman led the ruddy faced fellow out and her colleague followed with the baby carriage and both boys in tow.

'That's how it was with my dad,' said Ruda, his narrowed eyes fixed on the door after it had banged shut behind them. 'I had to drag him home from here a few times. You can't imagine the shame, when instead of a schoolbag, it's your old man covered in vomit on your back.'

He took a sip of soda water and tapped his fingers on the table.

'No, no,' he continued our conversation, 'You'd better stay away for a few days, besides, you could use a break, this summer was intense. Just let it be for a couple of weeks, and then we'll figure something out.'

I nodded vaguely.

Ruda tossed down the rest of the water and threw a 100-crown note on the table.

'So long, let's hope for the best, otherwise we're screwed,' he gave me a wink and patted my shoulder on his way out. As for the basket of mushrooms, he didn't even dignify it with a glance.

I paid at the bar without looking the bartender in the eye, because I hadn't left him a tip, shoved the remaining change into my pocket and set off for home with the basket. I had no idea what I was going to do with the mushrooms. It occurred to me that I could eat them myself, but at that moment I thought of Vojta. Back to that afternoon on the porch of the shack, with the festively set table. Again, that familiar pressure behind my eyes. I quickened my pace.

I brought the mushrooms to Zatloukal. He thanked me and asked if I had changed my mind about the roof. That he wasn't one to be giving me advice, but there was no way to get around its needing repair. It was a bit of a shambles, that shack of mine, but even so it would be a shame, after all the work my father did on it, to let it fall apart. He had a bit of time now, if I wanted, he could look around to see where he could buy some sheet metal and stuff for cheap.

'That would be kind of you,' I said and kept my eyes down.

39

In my class, there wasn't a single person who didn't find me annoying. They called me all sorts of names: ultra-nerd, kiss-ass, collaborator. And I didn't get mad at my classmates. In fact, I couldn't care less about them. Besides, they were right, I did justice to all of the nicknames. I was in every way the perfect pupil that every teacher wished for.

While others sat in front of the television, played videogames, met up at McDonald's and hung out at the mall, I spent every afternoon in my bedroom behind my locked door, reading in my biology textbook about the differentiating characteristics of leaves. If I couldn't name every type of lamina, I would start over from the beginning, repeating type after type, over and over. While the others were trying to memorize the states of the European Union, I already knew all the capitals of the world and could point them out on a blind map. I spent several hours every afternoon studying, and often would leaf through the textbooks even at night, when I couldn't fall asleep, which over time happened more and more frequently. In the evenings I would go to bed afraid I wouldn't sleep anyway. After a half hour I would get up and sit on my bed. With time, I didn't even bother putting away my schoolbooks, after brushing my teeth I would change into my pyjamas, sit down at my desk, switch on the lamp and go back to my open book.

Most of all, I devoted myself to reading. While others were ploughing through *Aesop's Fables*, I had already read *Myths and Legends of Ancient Greece*. Instead of Jan Neruda's classic poem about his grandfather, I started listening to Vladimir Vysotsky, and while others were flipping through Foglar's *Mystery of the Puzzle*, I was already done with *A Clockwork Orange*. I set myself a personal reading goal: a minimum of two books per week, to be adhered to no matter what. In a few weeks, I read the complete works of Jirásek; *The Good Soldier Švejk* took me less than a month; in my third year I immersed myself in Dostoevsky; and in my fourth I took on Goethe. I read at night, on the tram, while walking and even under my desk. My father, himself an avid reader, noticed after a while my passion, and tried several times to draw me into a conversation about books. I, however, would try to get out of these exchanges as quickly as possible, without knowing why.

I soon outgrew our family library, so I got myself a municipal library card and most importantly, found favour with our Czech language teacher, nicknamed 'The Box' because of her boxy torso and spindly legs. When she was explaining something, she would often pause for a moment by my desk and tap her fingers on the tabletop. 'I'm sure I don't have to explain this to you,' she would declare, and I could see all the peeved faces turning in my direction. Little by little, something resembling a secret romance developed between me and The Box, although our passion was reserved exclusively for literature. During breaks I would sneak up to her office. Before knocking on her door, I would surreptitiously glance over my shoulder. I would borrow books from her, or have her write down recommended titles on a slip of paper with which I would then dash over to the library. Her suggestions never disappointed.

In Czech language I always got an A on my report card. Just as I did in every other subject, for that matter. Everything could be learnt.

Except for physical education from which, due to my injured leg, for the first few years of high school I was excused.

The broader my knowledge, the wider the gulf between me and my classmates. With every A plus, the distance between us increased. In terms of class popularity, I ranked at the very bottom, the level of a zero, even lower than the perpetually sweaty, huffing-and-puffing Radek. And that was fine by me. I didn't need to have anyone by my side, I no longer saw my old friends from elementary school and hadn't made new ones, I was fine on my own.

I probably would have continued like that right through graduation and then gone on the same way in college had it not been for one innocent question.

'What are you reading?'

There were about ten minutes to go before the start of class, I had arrived in the classroom early and was sitting in front of an open book. The voice wasn't at all familiar to me. I closed the book to show what was written on the cover and looked up.

Beside me stood a kid I had never seen before. He wasn't exactly a hunk, just a hair taller than me and rather stocky, his hair reddish and his skin too pale, but something gleamed in his eyes that caught my attention.

'Excellent book. Have you also read *I'm Not Stiller*? I think it's even better, I can lend it to you if you want,' he added.

I was stunned. Among my other classmates, not only did no one know Frisch's *Homo Faber*, but they also made fun of me because of the title. *Homo*.

'I'm Martin,' he held out his hand, and I gingerly shook it.

And so between me and this new kid, who had just moved to Plzeň from Žďár with his mother, there began something that at least initially could be called a friendship.

He was completely different from my other classmates. Although he was in high school, he was still in the Boy Scouts, which normally would have discredited him, except that in his boy scout shirt, a block away from school, he'd be quietly rolling a joint. He always seemed to be on top of everything, he would ask the teachers probing and complex questions, and although he was new to the class, he didn't force himself on anyone, and made it clear that he was fine on his own. And above all, he wasn't interested in classroom hierarchies, he had no clue about where people ranked on the popularity scale, and even if someone had told him, he couldn't have cared less.

It wasn't long before we began to meet up after class. Martin was crazy about poetry. Although until then I had been mainly into prose, I borrowed his Apollinaire, just to make a good impression. At first it was a struggle, I couldn't always decipher the deeper meaning, but eventually it grew on me. After that more borrowing followed: Eliot, Nezval, Hrubín and Sylvia Plath.

In exchange, I lent Martin a few of my favourite books: *Sophie's Choice*, *The Joke* and *One Hundred Years of Solitude*. A few times, I caught myself trying to think of which book I might impress him with. It mattered to me that he liked the books I lent him. When he returned my Waltari saying that it reminded him of a 'well-written soap opera', I in turn denigrated his Bokowski as 'porn affecting to pose as art'. We didn't speak for several days, and then during recess I nonchalantly slipped him *Mrs Dalloway* and the following day he placed Kainar on my desk.

It went on like this for the next few weeks, we would get together even over the holidays, and try to outdo one another with new additions to an imaginary reader's journal.

Only in hindsight did I realize how obtuse I had been in the early days of our relationship. Looking back on it now, I actually admire him for how much patience he had with me. It took me several long weeks to realize that, for Martin, being initiated into the mysteries of prose had for quite some time ceased to suffice. The initial manifestations were subtle. When I would pass him a book, he would fleetingly stroke the back of my hand, smile, cock his head to the side and look me in the eye. They were timid touches, perhaps overly innocent for our age. I would bet that our peers had long since indulged in entirely different kinds of games. In me, however, his tender romantic advances sparked a sense of panic.

40

What most people designate as a mushroom is merely the part they can see above ground. The fruiting body they find in the moss or in the grass, and that they toss into their basket or steer clear of if it doesn't suit them. But the mushroom kingdom is much more diverse. Most mushrooms are such minuscule organisms that they are visible only under a microscope. Others in turn have fruiting bodies that are so large that they can be used as umbrellas. And furthermore—that which protrudes from the earth represents only a tiny part of a giant organism. A much larger part of the mushroom is hidden beneath the surface in the mycelium, a network of fine fibres that spreads through the soil in breadth and depth. The sporocarp itself, which mushroom gatherers bring home in the form of a parasol, bolete or blusher for their scramble, is merely the fruit of the vast kingdom that lies beneath, a sexual organ that appears for a moment to allow the mushroom to reproduce and, its purpose fulfilled, dies away.

Many mushroom gatherers believe that if they pluck a mushroom, nothing will ever grow in that spot again. Many of them, therefore, cut off the mushroom at the very base, leaving the end of the stipe in the soil. Still others claim that it is important to pull the mushroom out in its entirety, so that it makes room for others. In fact, it makes no difference at all. You can pick a mushroom by twisting it, wriggling it loose like an embedded tick, or by pulling it up—the mycelium will not be affected in any particular way. The only way to preserve the underground realm is by not treading too heavily on the soil around the fruiting body and by carefully covering up the hole left by the extracted mushroom, so that the mycelium doesn't dry out. Apart from that, it's important to let a fruiting body mature now and then so that the mushroom can continue to propagate. But the mycelium, when its time comes, will always find a way to the surface. At times it pretends not to exist. Not even the best mushroom hunter can discern its presence underground. It can lie low, cautiously waiting for months or years at a time, sending up just a few barely visible fruiting bodies here and there, and then a few alternating days of rain and sunny weather suffice for the mycelium to reveal its might. The mushrooms practically leap out of the ground, one day you pick them and the next day they are back in the same spot.

At the beginning of my last year of high school something started to surge up inside me as well. I had recently come of age and for the first time had kissed Martin in the park. I remember feeling uncomfortable at the time. Strange processes were taking place inside my body. It was as if I had contracted a serious illness. I would get out of breath just by walking, was often so dizzy that I would have to steady myself against a wall, and every meal made me feel nauseous.

The first attack came in September. That morning, as I was putting on my shoes in the hallway, the smell of shoe polish that my mother had left open on the shoe rack crept into my nose. It occurred to me that my father had used the same polish to shine his boots back in Dvorce, I swung my backpack over my shoulder, called out 'Ciao, Mom' towards the kitchen, when suddenly a sharp jolt struck me in the chest. Someone threw a black shroud over my head and wrapped it around my neck with duct tape, I could see nothing, and I couldn't breathe. I felt my heart start to crumble, my arms and legs went limp, and a moment later I was sinking to the ground. This is what it's like to die, flashed through my mind. After a while the image before my eyes lightened and I saw my mother, who was slapping my cheeks.

'What happened, Sisi?' she asked me, her voice trembling. 'Are you all right?'

'Yes, just a bit dizzy,' I nodded once I came around, and made an effort to smile.

The second time I didn't get off so easily, instead of school, my mother took me straight to the doctor. He gave me a general check-up, drew some blood, but found nothing. It will be fine, this sometimes happens during puberty. The next time I felt an attack coming on, I was supposed to sit on the floor and breathe for a while into a paper bag, which would calm me down. It was bound to be from an excess of oxygen. If it got worse, I was to come back and see him.

Such an attack never recurred, but soon my joints began to ache excruciatingly and to swell. I shuffled to school like an old geezer and suffered through every gym class. And then the pain migrated from my joints into my stomach. I was writhing on the floor in convulsions, unable to get up.

My doctor was at his wits end. He would send me to specialists and I would keep coming back to him like a boomerang with new problems. EKG, EEG, thyroid exam, neurology, rheumatology, ultrasound, spinal tap, Lyme disease, I shuttled from one doctor to another, each one focusing on his or her area of expertise, and briefly suppressing the pain. I would heave a sigh of relief, but the agony was just taking a break somewhere in my bowels and soon the pain would resurface elsewhere. Sudden cramps, stabbing pain and heart palpitations came on without any warning. They could be triggered by a gesture, a seemingly familiar fragrance, or even a snippet of a song.

None of the specialists could help me, such a thing was not even possible. The problem was not in my body, but rather buried deep beneath the surface, in my brain. Memory locked away in a dark dungeon was sleeping a restless slumber, tossing and turning, awakening and banging on the heavy metal door. The reverberations of the blows were spreading through my entire body. The locked-up memories needed to break out of their cell.

'You're as fit as a fiddle. It's just nerves, that's all—school, boys, it's simply too much for you, you need to stop taking it all so seriously,' declared my primary care physician after months of futile investigation. He prescribed Xanax, saying 'Go easy, though,' and gave me a stern look. I was to use it only as a last resort, it was addictive.

He handed me a report officially stating that I was fine. I didn't protest. But even so I felt like an infested mushroom, one that appears shiny and smooth on the surface, but when it's cut open, reveals itself to be riddled with worms and mould.

'What nerves?!' exploded my father at home, upon reading the doctor's report. 'What do aching joints have to do with nerves?!' he fumed. He was a longtime member of the Czech Skeptics' Club Sisyfos, and considered anything that could not be scientifically proven to be quackery.

'She's just making stuff up, that's all,' and that was that.

41

When it rains, it pours. Literally and figuratively. I got the message loud and clear this morning, just as I was about to leave the house. Last night we had a downpour, finally—after more than three weeks of drought, we needed it. Except this time, it backfired on me. When I sat down on the stool in the hallway and pulled on my boots, there was an ominous squish. I kicked off the soggy shoes, looked up and discovered a trickle of water that ran from the corner of the ceiling along the wall all the way to the window. The roof was in even worse condition than I had suspected. Yesterday I met Zatloukal in front of the house. He said he couldn't get anything for under 15,000 crowns. Even with the money from the tea tin, I still came up 6,000 short. On top of all my other troubles, I needed this.

I went to the pantry to fetch a bucket, set it under the windowsill, emptied the water out of the shoes, dried them with a dishcloth, pulled on dry socks and put them back on. Outside it was still pouring, I stuck my head into my hood and made a dash for the shelter of the woods. My socks were soaked by the time I had passed the first few trees. I immediately began to sneeze.

Beneath the full-grown spruces, a little further on, I straightened up a bit. The raindrops, beating down furiously on the branches, hadn't yet managed to break through the dense canopy of needles to the woods below. The ground was still dry. I sat down on a stump and, propping one foot up on my knee, inspected my sole. In the faded treads I found a worn-out hole. Same thing on the other shoe. Dad's boots were on their way out. In addition to everything else, I'd need to get a new pair.

I needed money. I could no longer put off purchasing the sheet metal for the roof. I reached for my cell phone to dial Evžen's number. I would ask him to come by for the papers and to bring me an advance, so I could get the roof fixed. And buy new shoes. And maybe some wood, too. I didn't have enough to last me even through Christmas. Usually, I drag home bits of dead wood all summer long, but this year I had brought back only a little. By now I was supposed to have been long gone. In Budějovice. Or with Vojta in Prague. I sighed.

I pulled my cell phone out of my damp pocket. I pressed the central button under the display. Nothing happened. The display was completely blank. Condensation on the inside. I pressed one button after another. Useless. I would have to call my brothers from the Toadstool. But then I realized that I only had their numbers saved in my cell phone.

Now what? Until one of them showed up again, maybe I could ask Ruda for a loan. True, I hadn't been doing all that well lately, but the summer had been worth the effort, maybe he would give me a break. Today, though, I needed to make a good showing.

It was the first time I had gone mushroom hunting in a week. Yesterday Ruda had called to say that everything was all set with the health department, you know what I mean, he chuckled, he knew how to deal with such people. And that we could start up again.

Just past Santos I almost collided with someone. A figure with the hood of her raincoat pulled so far down that I couldn't see her face. Her hands were shoved into her pockets but her zipper was half open so I could make out the tail of a lizard on her bare neckline, coiling from her collarbone to her neck. Meanwhile, the raindrops had penetrated the thick branches and were softly drumming on her back. I wasn't surprised to run into her here. It was Sunday, she had nothing to do, so she had set off along Vojta's path.

'You won't find anything out there,' she said in a somewhat rueful voice.

'Oh, no,' I countered, 'I've got my own spots in the forest, I'm bound to find some mushrooms for sure.'

'Yeah, right . . . for sure,' she hissed irritably, as if she meant something else entirely. Then she shook her head and took off without saying goodbye.

I shrugged my shoulders and continued on my way. I couldn't afford to experiment and stuck to the places I knew. I crawled on my knees, peeking under every leaf and separating the grass.

The forest noticed the humiliation in my bearing and, here and there, tossed a handout at my feet. I discovered a nest of red cracking boletes, next came a handful of small porcinis and by the stream I even snagged a group of soggy slippery jacks. Near Kundratice I almost tripped over a family of overgrown parasols—I half-closed my eyes and tossed three into my basket—and by the double stump I spied a cluster of blewits that were trying to hide. In the clearing beyond Annín there were a few puffballs rolling around, just enough for a couple of fried schnitzels. I covered my basket with the dishcloth and hoped the rain wouldn't drench the mushrooms completely.

I didn't get to Sušice until about five o'clock. By then the rain had stopped, but it was so cold that my wet clothes were steaming. My face was still tucked inside my hood, my hands and knees muddy, my waterlogged shoes making squishy sounds.

Ruda, who was just coming out of the back door of the Toadstool with the trash, almost burst out laughing.

'Damn, if it weren't for the basket, I'd almost think you were the Lord of Mordor.'

'Keep the jokes to yourself.'

He gestured for me to follow him into his office. He sat down at the desk with the computer, behind him an altar of binders, and lined up beside them, paper bags tied with colourful ribbons. 100 grams of dried porcini mushrooms, hand-picked by me, for exactly 100 crowns, superior quality, not a single worm. I got 10 crowns per bag—after all, didn't I realize how much electricity the dehydrator consumes, not to mention the cost of marketing? It all adds up.

Ruda pulled the basket closer and peeked inside. 'Well, considering the slim pickings lately, it's not half bad. And what about those white balls, aren't those champignons?' he asked. If his knowledge of mushrooms continues to improve at this rate, a few years from now he should be able to distinguish a parasol from a wood cauliflower. Just a couple of months ago he would happily have classified a puffball as a bolete. I didn't disabuse him of his error, the Walrus would sort the mushrooms out.

'So how much?' I asked.

He assumed, as always, an air that was both important and desperate at the same time, after all, he had to let me know who is boss and that gastronomy was on the rocks, and that if his heart wasn't in it, he would have turned his back on the pub long ago. Following the inevitable dramatic pause, he slipped his hand into his vest pocket and placed two 100-crown banknotes in front of me. 'All right?' He then dug into another pocket and produced six 10-crown pieces that he stacked up next to the paper bills.

'That's for the dried ones.'

I nodded. It wasn't so bad. Except that I needed several times more.

'Things have picked up around here lately,' I tried to butter him up a bit and made a real effort to keep my mouth from twisting too much.

'Thanks,' he said.

'Will there be any more fungi tourists?' I asked tentatively.

Ruda leaned back in his chair and clasped his hands together above his head.

'Zippo, mate,' he shook his head. 'Now that TV Nova announced that nothing's growing, no one is coming out to go mushroom hunting any more. I put an ad on a couple of mushroom sites, we have a promotion on a discount website, a mega offer half-price voucher, plus kids for free, and nothing.'

He fixed his gaze on the fogged-up windowpane.

'Yeah, well,' he declared thoughtfully. 'Maybe next year. Let's hope things improve a bit, so we don't end up losing our Toadstool. Listen,' he made a face, shaking his head, 'Not even I know how it's going go. Pops left behind a pile of debts. I'll do whatever I can to hang on for another year.'

I swallowed my question about a loan.

'You can definitely count on me for next year,' I said in a half whisper.

'Hey, take care of yourself,' he said while I was still in the doorway. 'You're looking a bit off.'

As I left Ruda's office and went down the narrow corridor, I noticed the door to the freezer room next to the storeroom was ajar. Before I closed it, something caught my eye. On one of the shelves there were several bags of frozen mushrooms. I picked one of them up. On the label it said something in Cyrillic and underneath was written: *Tiefgefrorene Stockschwämmchen*.

On the way home I looked at myself in one of the shop windows and had to agree with Ruda. My face was an unusual greenish-yellow colour. And even the whites of my eyes were far from white. I felt a dull pain in my lower abdomen. As if someone was squeezing my bladder in the palm of their hand. My legs grew heavy and my back felt rigid. This couldn't just be from lack of sleep.

From the square I went down a narrow lane. I passed the public library. I remembered how not quite two months ago I had been sitting at the computer there, looking up job listings. How confidently I had answered the ads. I tried to dredge up from memory the excitement I'd felt reading the email from the owner of the warehouse in Budějovice. And the pride I'd felt when I called her without stuttering. Not a trace of either remained.

Right outside Sušice it started to rain again. I pulled the hood over my head and shoved my hands into my pockets. The empty basket hung from my right elbow.

What now? ran through my head. The less than 300 crowns Ruda had given me wouldn't get me out of this. Fortunately, I still had a glimmer of hope. By now surely a few little heads had popped up, and home-grown champignons are always better than imported ones. Back home I would rest a bit, find an umbrella, and then take them to Ruda. He would give me a few hundred crowns for them. And hopefully my brothers would show up soon.

At the door to the pantry an unpleasant stench hit me in the nose. I leaned over the bag of substrate and through my puffy eyelids spotted some whitish little lights. I reached for the first one, but instead of a soft nub, what remained in my hand was cold slime. The same thing happened with the second mushroom. I went back for a torch, shone it in the corner, and froze. The entire bag of substrate, along with the mushrooms peeking out, was covered in white mould. The fuzzy, whitish blanket had spread from the substrate all the way to the wall. My efforts had gone down the drain. I broke out in chills.

42

The last year of high school had turned into hell. I floundered between the role of a conscientious student and the demands of being a teenage girl. After school I would meet up with Martin, we would go to the movies, for coffee, or to the park, and in the fall when it got chilly, he started to invite me to his house.

He had grown tired of making out on a bench with his frozen hands stuck inside coat pockets, and moved lower and deeper.

I tried to oblige him as far as my strength and imagination would go. I no longer flinched when he grabbed my hand or put his arm around my shoulders, and I let his kisses slip from my face to my neck. I did not allow my body to go limp in his arms, but I played with his hair and stroked the nape of his neck. But not even that was enough, I needed to make an even greater effort and, most importantly, allow Martin to conquer more bases. I crammed for our dates as if they were a major exam. In the evenings, after our house went quiet, I would surf teen websites and study the rules of the game. How to handle a horny teenager. I myself, however, felt nothing. So at least I tried to pretend I liked it, and pressed my cheek against his, breathing heavily—I had read that it turns guys on. I closed my eyes and sighed obediently while I battled waves of nausea. Afterwards, back home, I would spend a long time in the shower, scrubbing the places he had touched until my skin itched.

I felt like an imposter. A fraud, who keeps pulling aces out of her sleeve, but they're all fake. Something was missing, while something else was overflowing. The carcass in my bowels was forcing its way ever closer to the surface. And Martin, despite my thick skin, sensed its presence.

'Sára, what's your problem?' he snapped at me a few times. 'We've been together for almost six months. Do I gross you out or what?' and I shook my head, even though it wasn't far from the truth. In moments of intimacy, I truly felt nothing but revulsion towards him. Martin, who for the most part was always in control of things, in the dim light of the bedroom turned into a bristling tomcat trying to coax the pussycat into lifting her tail. Suddenly, he was just like all the others. A poor guy unable to control his libido. A pesky little dog, wheedling his mistress into letting him rub his balls against her leg.

Other times he tried blackmail: 'If you want to break up, just say so!'

No, I did not want to break up. I wanted to be with him, but not in the way that high school conventions and his growing libido dictated. I knew that all I had to do was to lie on my back, close my eyes, and leave my body to his mercy, but I just couldn't do it. And I had no idea why. At eighteen, I was probably the last virgin left in the grade, even though I was far from the ugliest.

Martin and I flopped around like fish out of water, all while I was plagued by pains and nausea, on top of struggling to keep up with the demands of school. As I often devoted the whole afternoon to Martin, in order to have enough time to study, I had to cut out even more sleep. I was sleeping less and less and growing more tired and sluggish than before. In class I had trouble following the lectures. The books I read in the evenings no longer made sense.

But that wasn't everything. When I got my mid-term grades, the entire class seemed to gasp. Something absolute had collapsed. My report card showed three Bs. And one of them, on top of that, was in Czech.

43

For my parents, the graduation ball was nothing short of an extraordinary event. My mom had been preparing sandwiches and snacks all morning, there was a huge vase of roses on the table and the champagne flowed. I noticed my father downed the sparkling wine as if it were a shot, and then refilled the same glass with whisky. And then he did it again. He was nervous, soon the elections for the academic senate would take place. For a long time now, he had been breathing down the rector's neck. Maybe this time it would work out. Maybe his irritability was also in part due to the fact that he would have to appear in public with our mother. Her satin dress was so tight that the fabric between the buttons down her back was all puckered. Her instep bulged out of her pumps.

Milan was acting as our father's drinking buddy, pouring his twenty-five-year-old whiskey straight into a mug, not even bothering to add ice. Even our mother's glassy eyed look suggested that she was diligently preparing for the ball in her own way. From the kitchen she would run off to the pantry and then return smiling ear-to-ear to continue preparing more delicacies. Evžen, on the other hand, took an ascetic approach to the whole evening and settled for black coffee.

I wasn't in much better shape than my nervous father. In my new dress I felt like a mannequin in a Chinese shop. For this solemn occasion, my parents hadn't bought me an ordinary off-the-rack dress but had one made for me by a first-class ladies' seamstress. In my one-shoulder dress, fastened at the waist with a simple sash, I was apparently supposed to evoke Helen of Troy. Instead, I looked more like a country bumpkin.

I had noticed during the fittings that the seamstress was a little uneasy. She kept darting around me with the tape measure, measuring and remeasuring my back, shoulders, waist, mumbling to herself through her tightly pressed lips in which she held several pins. It sounded to me something like 'I don't get it' or maybe 'I can't do it'.

It was only at the final fitting that I understood what she meant. I examined myself carefully in the mahogany-framed full-length mirror. I turned from side to side, studying my reflection front and back, bending over, then straightening up again. I held the hem of the skirt between my fingers and twirled. Like a porcelain ballerina being propelled by the mechanism of a music box. Simply put, something was wrong. It wasn't that the seamstress had made a mistake. Everything looked fine. The fabric neither wrinkled nor pulled, it didn't gap under the armpit or at the neckline, the skirt was the perfect length. In short, everything seemed just right. And yet my body did not fit the dress. I felt like a vagrant who had been picked up off the street, washed, shaved, given a haircut, doused with expensive perfume and dressed up in overpriced clothes. And it was in this outfit that I was supposed to undergo one of the most important rituals of my youth.

The icing on the cake was when my mother, just as we were about to leave for the ball, tripped over the living room carpet and fell, knocking over a glass of red wine that my father had left on the table.

'Shit,' she blurted out as she clumsily picked herself up and looked at me. A few red droplets had landed on my snow-white dress. She immediately covered her mouth, 'It slipped out, I'm sorry,' and took charge of removing my dress. 'Sorry, sorry,' she repeated. Having unzipped the back of my dress, she practically tore it off. With one hand she waved the stained fabric, with the other she clasped her head, apologizing again and again. 'What a silly goose I am, I'm so terribly sorry.' Finally, she dashed off to the bathroom, 'I need to soak it,' she called out to me as she ran. The sound of running water in the bathroom blended with bursts of self-deprecating swearing, interspersed with apologetic exclamations. Eventually her words were lost in the hum of the hairdryer. Dry dress in hand, my mother then ran upstairs to iron it.

The entire operation didn't take more than fifteen minutes, during which time I put on my bathrobe, polished off two open-faced sandwiches and gulped down two glasses of Coca-Cola.

When my mother returned with the dress cleaned and pressed, she was still carrying on, as full of remorse as if making a last confession. It seemed to me that she wanted to hear some words of absolution from me: 'No big deal', or even 'I forgive you'. Subconsciously, I sensed that this might stop the torrential flow of her words.

But I was fed up with all of it. The whole thing was ridiculous, I could have soaked my own dress, or even just kept it on, those three tiny droplets were on the side and would have been hidden by the pink sash that fastened the dress at the waist. And even if the ribbon had moved, the three specks the size of freckles wouldn't have bothered me all that much. I couldn't understand why she was carrying on this way.

Besides, what was weighing on my mind had nothing to do with the three spots on my dress. 'Tomorrow,' I had said to Martin the day before. We had agreed that after the ball, we wouldn't join the others for a glass of wine, but would make our way together to the flat belonging to his grandmother, who was away at a spa. I had told my parents that I was going to stay out with my classmates, so I wouldn't be getting home until the next morning. But now, I was having second thoughts, and I was hatching a plan to avoid having to spend the night with Martin.

When my parents, brothers and I reached the family Passat, I headed for the back door behind the driver's seat as usual, but my father grabbed my shoulder. 'On a big day like today, you don't want to sit in the back,' and he pressed the keys into my hand. Puzzled, I stared at him unsure of what he meant, then finally slid into the front seat and inserted the key into the ignition. My mother climbed into the back and my brothers, who struggled to get into their seats, had to wedge themselves against the doors so that all three of them would fit. Milan fidgeted in his tight suit and Evžen made no effort to hide his annoyance. Because of me he'd had to come all the way from Prague. Moreover, our dad kept taunting him with comments such as: 'So, did you get that illustrious degree added to your ID card? Evžen Tichý, BSc?'

The motor started up and my dad winked at me from the passenger seat: 'Let's go.' When I placed both of my hands on the steering wheel and we slowly started to move, my dad abruptly reached his hand across to press the headlight button to the left of the steering wheel. As he did so, he brushed against my thigh. It didn't hurt, but I flinched, as if he had jabbed a needle into my leg. The engine died, there were a few comments about how retarded I was from the back seat, I had to restart the whole process—key-brake-clutch-accelerator—and then repeat it two more times, before I finally managed to peel away from the parking spot.

Our homeroom teacher was already waiting in front of the banquet hall, wearing a green velvet dress. Due to my nervousness I kept staring at the tips of my shoes, and only later did I notice, with surprise, that she had shaved her hairy legs for the occasion.

'You look nice,' she said and shook my hand. Either she says that to everyone or she has no taste, I thought as I caught sight of my stiff posture reflected in the glass door.

We had a table reserved on the second floor right next to the balustrade, the champagne was already chilling in an ice bucket with caviar and a French baguette beside it and a bowl of fruit on the other side. My father had clearly done things in style.

We queued up at the edge of the dance floor. Martin stood beside me, in his dark suit he looked older and taller. He took my hand and I winced a little. As a result of the constant washing, painful red patches that looked like burns had formed between my fingers and on the backs of my hands. To the strains of *Gaudeamus igitur*, we processed into the hall.

Along with our class there were two other classes, and then came all the teachers, so by the end there were more than a hundred people on the dance floor. There was a lot of commotion, but I had a feeling that all eyes were on me. A sea of twinkling will-o'-the-wisps urging me to flee from the building and follow them. There is still time, they told me.

After our entrance came the principal's droning speech, full of good-natured admonishments and condescending superiority. By the time sashes were given out and photographs taken, some students were no longer even trying to pretend that it was possible to survive the entire ceremony.

Someone at the microphone announced the parent's dance. Suddenly, my father appeared at my side, gripping my shoulder with one hand and my palm with the other. We stood facing each other on the dance floor. The hall fell silent. I noticed how nervous he was, but even so I could see he was pleased. In his eye there glistened what might even have been a proud tear. It took an interminably long time before the opening chords resounded through the hall. Louis Armstrong, *What a Wonderful World*. We stepped out too soon and bumped into the couple next to us. On the second attempt we succeeded, step sideways, step backwards, promenade, I repeated to myself from memory, sideways-backwards-turn, slowly we made our way across the room amid the crowd of other couples. I looked down at my feet that were obediently executing the learnt steps, kept my body nice and straight, held on to my father, everything was going exactly by the book, but my mind had long since danced away. Thousands of thoughts were swirling in my head, everything that had happened that day was going through my mind, my mother's apologetic face, my fingers in Martin's palm, my father's hand on my thigh.

I looked up to our table on the balcony and saw a dark figure. I couldn't see its face, but even so I could feel it staring at me. It was a massive, mighty shadow that was pinning me to the ground, I tried to wrest myself out of its grip but it was stronger. My eyes wandered over the guests in the room, the spectre lurked behind each column, it was everywhere I looked, its eyes so piercing that I could feel them stinging my face.

Step sideways-backwards-solo-turn, 'Hey, what's wrong with you, idiot?' I heard to my right. My body had begun to rebel against the prescribed steps, it stopped where it was. My dad tried to force me back into the double line. 'Sára, don't be silly, you know how to do this.' I looked him straight in the eyes and in that instant they changed from light brown to the dark, brutish orbs of a wolf. Our gazes locked. Everything around me fell silent.

Suddenly I was back there. A dark room. The branch of the walnut tree rapping on the window. The moth flapping its wings. On my shoulders, the grip of bony hands.

I broke through the bars and fled the dungeon.

'What are you doing, Sára?' my father shouted after me as I forced my way through the dancing couples and made for the steps. 'Sára, please, come back!' But his shouting merely slipped across my back, the dancers leapt aside, the ones who got underfoot I pushed away, several fell to the ground.

I ran for the exit, but my father caught up to me, seized my hand, and dragged me up to the second floor and to our table.

'What's this supposed to mean, Sára?'

I wanted to tear myself away, but my mother jumped up from her chair, grabbed me by the shoulder, and pulled me back to our table. My brothers sat there, frozen, no one was able to utter a single word.

I looked from one to the next, my gaze darting from my mother's bewildered face to my father's stiff expression, my brothers staring at me, mute.

I wanted to run away, but my father grabbed me by the shoulders and held me back.

'Sára, what happened?'

'Leave me alone!'

I broke free but he caught me again. He dug his nails into my shoulder. Just like back then. I wrenched myself away. His nails left red marks on my skin. I turned to face him. 'You . . .' I began to shout. 'What did you do to me?!' I shouted at him as if deprived of my senses. My father stared at me, uncomprehending, everyone was looking at me as if I had gone mad, and in that moment perhaps I truly had, because I hurled myself at him and slammed into him with all my strength. My dad fell backwards to the ground and hit the table as he went down. He pulled the tablecloth with him, the glasses went flying, the champagne spilled all over my brothers' and my mother's clothes. My mother fell off her chair. The bottle rolled to the edge of the table, then over and down towards the balcony balustrade. It fell onto the dance floor, the shrieking dancers scattered and the music abruptly stopped.

'How could you have done that to me, I wasn't even ten years old!' I bawled. I was lying on top of my father, pummelling his chest and face with my fists. Suddenly he was the one flat on his back, he should have defended himself, but he was in such a state of shock that he made no attempt to dodge my punches. 'Please, Sára, please, please, be quiet, shut up, dammit, shut up . . .' he whispered. A trickle of blood ran down his cheek from a cut at the corner of his lip, his face was red from my blows.

'How could you do it to me . . .' I shouted at him.

My mother, both of my brothers, the guests at the surrounding tables, Martin, who had come running upstairs after me, and my classmates, all stood petrified. Their eyes were filled with anger, revulsion and contempt. And all of those eyes that should have been looking at Dad were fixed on me. My mother pulled a handkerchief out of her purse and pressed it to her mouth. In the place where just a moment before a proud tear had glistened, only deep lines in her makeup remained.

I'm not sure how things would have turned out had it not been for two strangers who pulled me away from my father.

My mother burst into loud sobs.

I sat slumped on the floor, my back against a column, 'You . . . you . . .' I repeated over and over again the beginning of a sentence that I could not complete.

'Easy does it, young lady' one of my father's two saviours grunted at me.

Through my hair that had come undone from its French twist, I stared at the devastation, at my father, at my mother, and wiped my father's blood from my hands onto my white dress. Out of the corner of my eye I caught sight of Martin. Our eyes met for an instant. He was standing there with his head to one side, his mouth slightly open. Then he slowly backed away a few steps among the shocked spectators, turned and disappeared into the crowd.

For me, the rest of the evening dissolved into a grey haze.

44

I had squandered my fifteen minutes of fame so stupidly, I kept repeating to myself again and again in the days that followed. In the meantime, I managed to recall a few details that had escaped me amid the frenzy. I remembered that as my father and I were flying across the table, the singer had just finished crooning the last bars of the song.

And I think to myself what a wonderful wooooorld! echoed through the hall as the glass around us shattered and my father knocked the back of his head against the wooden floor. Some ham was stuck to his ear next to a smear of blood on his cheek, which had been sliced by a shard of glass—he looked practically decadent.

In the bed with the blue-striped white sheets where I lay in isolation for the next three days, I must have replayed the whole scene in my head at least a thousand times. Pills–food–personal hygiene–pills–beverage–pills, those were the only times that I got out of bed . . . and immediately lay back down like a vampire at dawn. I lay there without moving, and although the next day they unfastened my arms and legs, I didn't abandon my position of a mummy in a sarcophagus.

When three days later, having revealed myself to be a quiet, still, and thus harmless patient, they released me from the isolation unit and moved me to another ward, I remained silent.

I don't know if it was intentional, but in the room where they placed me there were two other girls around my age. The first was a slight blonde named Kamila, who looked like she had just come out of a concentration camp. She greeted me with a wave and smiled. 'I'm not in top shape at the moment, I haven't shed the extra pounds I put on at Christmas yet,' she said, smiling, as she patted her belly that resembled an inverted basin.

The other girl, a stocky brunette with large freckles on her cheeks, was much less chatty. Her hair was cut short and she looked more like a boy, even in her thick-set physique. It was only on the second day that she confided to me that she was called Eda. Maybe short for Eduarda, but she never told me her real name. I didn't discover the reason for her stay in the asylum until sometime later, when, as she was sleeping, the sleeve of her pyjamas rode up. Her left arm was covered in scars at various stages of healing. Her forearm resembled a ruled sheet of paper, the lines were perfectly straight and of exactly equal length. This was no work of a novice, but of a master at her craft. I got out of bed and drew closer to Eda so that I could examine her wounds, but she rolled over and tucked her arm under the comforter.

I felt like I was at Girl Scout Camp. As if I'd been randomly assigned to a tent with whoever was left on the list. And both girls were obviously well-versed in camp rules, they had occupied the best two beds, the ones closer to the window, and I was left with the bed that was in full view of the door.

Soon after my arrival, my jailmates set about initiating me into various gimmicks and ploys. Kamila introduced me to the mysteries of the world of anorexics and bulimics. She told me that she had started at fifteen, when she got tired of people calling her fatty. 'It was easier than I expected,' she explained. 'Suddenly ten kilos were gone, and with them my nickname was gone forever, too. The ones who used to make fun of me were suddenly falling all over me.' She said she liked how she was suddenly in control, how she could exercise self-restraint. But in the end, things had got a little out of hand. This was already Kamila's second time at the clinic, because her mom, when she had last visited her, had caught her flushing food down the toilet. But now she had learnt her lesson, and when she got out, she would be cleverer about it. 'This place sucks, they're not stupid, they know all the tricks, but as soon as I've gained enough for them to let me go, I'll get back to it,' she gave me a wink. 'Last time I blew it, this time I'll be smarter.'

'How?' I asked with curiosity.

'There are all kinds of tricks. For example, swig down two or three litres of water, and your stomach gets so bloated, you have to loosen your pants. Or every now and then, take some food out of its wrapper and leave the packaging on the table, so it looks like you've eaten it, or smear a bowl with some food, hit yourself in the stomach when it grumbles, bulk up with clothing. I tell you, it's a real science. I'm so good at it, I could be a coach. In fact, I have my own pro-ano blog!'

As for Eda, she set about introducing me to cutting techniques. Apparently, she first started with an ordinary knife, but it didn't work very well, even if the blade was sharp. 'It makes a mess, and the results are sloppy,' she shook her head. She had also tried with a razor blade, but often would cut her fingertips, which was hard to hide. 'And then I figured out what works best is an ordinary box cutter. Open, cut, wipe, retract, done.' She had studied different parts of the body, but the thighs and forearms remained the best, because according to her: 'You feel it just enough and it's easy to hide.'

Aha, so this is where I am supposed to arrive at the right thoughts to bring me back to the world of the sane, went through my head as I tried to fall asleep after such conversations.

My two guides, however, were only communicative at rare moments. Mostly all three of us remained silent. In the dining room we each sat on our own and didn't even seek each other out during group activities. At night we would curl up under our comforters and stare at the greyish ceiling. Each of us saw something different projected there.

I could understand them, we were all so caught up in our own problems that we no longer had any interest in delving into the difficulties of others. Furthermore, I had to admit that I wasn't a very good conversation partner myself. The drugs they poured into me made me groggy, formulating a coherent sentence was for me often a superhuman task. I perceived the world around me as if I were in a moving car with fogged up windows. The motor roared so loudly that I couldn't hear what was going on outside.

As time went by, I realized that Eda and Kamila were among the mildest cases in the ward. Perhaps half of the other patients were women whose illness had made them withdraw completely into themselves. They barely interacted with the outside world, shuffled silently down the corridors, occasionally breaking their own silence with a shriek. They performed various activities that had been prescribed as part of their therapy, opened their mouths on cue to ingest pills and then obediently closed them again. These were the inmates I preferred. They didn't ask anything of me, nor did I want anything from them. We would pass each other in the hallways like travellers on escalators going in opposite directions. It was worse with the other, more outgoing group. You had to stay on your toes so as not to get caught. One time, for example, in the dining room, I sat down in good faith next to an elegant looking lady and from that moment on had to listen to her endless lectures about the nano agents that were all around us. They were being sprinkled onto our food, released into the air through the air conditioning system and emitted through electromagnetic waves. And then a woman in her forties somehow got it into her head that I was her daughter. She would sit in front of the door to our room on a chair that she would bring up from the dining room and call me 'Hedvička'. Fortunately, her outbursts of affection were limited to verbal displays accompanied at most by hand holding.

When after one week I took stock of my hospital stay, I first came to the conclusion that I needed to get out as quickly as possible, preferably that very evening. But then I realized what was waiting for me at home. So, I ended up staying at the institution for another three months.

45

Everything was coming together. My accident in Sušice, the psychosomatic problems, insomnia, panic attacks, health issues with no apparent cause and Xanax. The collision, crisis, turning point and finally, in the hall of the Měšťanská beseda, the spectacular debacle worthy of a Greek tragedy. The shattered glass, the smudged caviar, the bloodied ham. All that was missing was a deus ex machina, a higher power to pull me out of this. And that's why they put me in here, in the loony bin, to get me out. In reality, what they needed was an alibi for themselves.

I imagined my father and my mother sitting in the chief physician's office, my father dressed in a perfectly fitting suit, every so often adjusting his tie, speaking matter-of-factly, quietly, clearly, my mother fumbling with her handkerchief, now and then dabbing at her eyes.

'In hindsight, it started a long time ago, it must be about nine years. Back then, Sára was delirious, suffering from insomnia, becoming increasingly withdrawn, there was no way of talking to her. And then there was the accident,' says my father, while my mother stifles her sobs against the back of her hand.

'Back then we thought, actually we tried to convince ourselves, that she stepped out into the road from carelessness, that she simply wasn't paying attention, but now we know that it wasn't the case, suddenly it all makes sense,' my father continues, while my mother nods between sobs.

'Over the course of last year things got much worse, Sára pulled away from us, the situation got completely out of hand, she was making up lots of stories, not sleeping night after night. She was constantly locking herself away in her room, looking around as if she were afraid someone was coming after her. She was always having health problems, but in the end, these turned out to be delusions. We saw a bunch of doctors, went running from one specialist to another, but the examinations showed nothing, they told us it was psychological. Even now we still find it hard to believe, but . . .' my father clears his throat in embarrassment, 'She made it all up.'

The psychiatrist stares fixedly at my father, making notes in the chart.

'But most importantly,' for the first time, it's my mother who speaks, and my father lowers his eyes to the ground, as if this is very unpleasant for him. My mother's tentative voice falters but she bravely continues, searching for the right words: 'Lately she has been attacking her father. What happened at the ball . . .' she has to pause for a moment to wipe away the tears streaming down her cheeks, 'It was nothing compared to what was happening at home. We were even a bit scared of her, I hate to think what she might have done. I think . . . We feel that Sára could . . .'

'We were simply hoping,' my father interjects, 'That we could handle it on our own, she is, after all, our only daughter. But now we know that we underestimated the issue. We should have dealt with it already a long time ago. Now we're afraid we can't. We are concerned that she might do something. To someone else, but above all to herself. We're afraid for her,' my father says in a firm voice and his final word is lost in my mother's loud sobs.

The psychiatrist nods his head with an air of understanding. He has plenty of such cases here, she's just another daughter who, on the cusp of adulthood, has been seized by delusions and a persecution complex. Only time will tell if it turns into schizophrenia or remains a simple psychosis. The doctor still asks if anyone else in the family has had similar problems, and goes over my medical history with them. At the end he gives my parents an encouraging smile: 'We'll do all we can, here she is in the best of hands, and I personally will oversee the course of her treatment,' he assures them. As they say goodbye, they shake hands at length.

'It cannot be ruled out with certainty that the patient may harm herself or others,' he finally types into the computer.

How could he have reacted otherwise, everything my parents claimed was written down in black on white: the report from the emergency room, where I had run towards an open window and resisted the orderlies to such a degree that they were forced to strap me to the bed; the attempted interview during which I had kept my eyes closed and remained stubbornly silent; the notes in my medical record about my health problems without any established cause; and the police report from nine years earlier. 'Any culpability on the part of the driver was ruled out during the investigation.'

That's more or less how I imagined it.

Visiting hours took place every day, but families most often came to see their deranged relatives on Sunday afternoons. Starting early in the morning, a general sense of unease prevailed throughout the pavilion. In the smoking lounge, twice as many cigarette butts were piled up in the ashtrays, the patients would knock into each other walking down the corridors, there was a queue for the bathroom. Everyone shuffled along, hunched with shoulders drawn up, as if bracing for a blow to strike their backs at any moment.

At lunch an almost funereal atmosphere set in. Even the notorious shriekers kept their screeching to a minimum. In the canteen all the women sat in silence, slurping their soup. By the time the first visitors began to appear, some of the patients hadn't yet managed to finish their dessert. It wasn't uncommon for inmates to choke on their last bite when their eyes fell on a visitor.

It took my folks almost three weeks before they ventured to come see me. I wasn't particularly keen on them coming to visit. Yet every Sunday I would look out for them, feeling tense.

I took my time going down the hallway towards the dining room. I stopped just before the open door and peeked inside.

I spotted Kamila at a table not far from the door. She was sitting across from a full-figured fifty-something-year-old woman with a perm who was droning words into her. Kamila was all hunched up, her arms crossed defensively over her chest, looking even smaller than she really was. 'Would you cut this nonsense out already,' came a shrill female voice. Her mother's breath threatened to blow her away.

Most of the other patients had also adopted a defensive pose as they faced their relatives. Their heads were bowed, they bit their lips, the hands resting in their laps were trembling. I didn't blame them. Their relatives looked as though they too could be locked up here on the spot.

I practically had to stick my head through the door before I spotted them. My mother sat slouched on the cushioned chair, her fingers smoothing the vinyl tablecloth along the edge of the table, my father, ever slim with a slightly protruding belly, sat bolt upright. I observed them for a while, hoping they wouldn't see me.

Kamila, not far from them, cleared her throat and pulled a handkerchief out of the pocket of her sweatpants. The outline of her ribs on her curved back was visible even through her T-shirt. 'Why the hell do you keep this up?' her mother hissed at her through clenched teeth. Her daughter, meanwhile, had shrunk to the size of a garden gnome.

I glanced once more at the mismatched couple in the corner of the dining room, turned on my heel and went back to my room. I positioned myself by the barred window. Most of my body was concealed by the wall, from the outside only half of my face was visible. It must have taken a full hour before I saw the pair descend the front steps by the main entrance and step onto the dirt road. They weren't holding hands, but they walked side by side, rubbing shoulders as they went, a closeness that they surely hadn't experienced in years. It was my *illness* that had brought them together, it had turned them by necessity into accomplices, they had made a pact of silence. I watched as they stepped off the road onto the withered lawn and made their way among the trees, on which a few twisted yellowish-brown leaves fluttered in the wind: a lone couple in the corner of an old, faded painting. I stared at them through the window until all I saw before me was the landscape. I don't remember if on that day I cried.

After a while a nurse knocked on my door: 'Miss Tichá, I'm bringing you your pills.' She wore a slight smile, as did all of the nurses and doctors, apparently there must have been some internal regulation about it—along with the uniform, the job description included an appropriate facial expression. They always walked past us with the same fixed smile, and when they spoke to us, they carefully articulated each syllable.

'How are you feeling?' was the question I heard most frequently at the clinic. It was addressed to us every morning by the nurses, the doctors, even the orderlies, and accompanied by a politely concerned expression, and most importantly it was posed to us in every group activity, therapy session, or one-on-one interview with the psychiatrist. The question was more insidious than it seemed, as it was a little psychological test that I mostly failed.

'How did you feel when . . .' was one of the other questions that I heard several times a day. I had trouble answering, as I wasn't used to analysing my feelings on command while modelling animals out of clay or sweeping the deck of the veranda.

Our treatment consisted mainly of a ritualization of our behaviour that was to result in our resocialization, namely our return to society in a state that conforms to its social norms. We were supposed to become decent people, in other words, those who don't defecate on the street, don't hurl expletives at others and don't strip naked in the middle of the square. The entire day consisted of precisely prescribed activities from which we were supposed to fashion a safety net in case of a lapse. They established a fixed daily routine for us: wake-up call, morning hygiene, breakfast, group activity, occupational therapy, lunch, conversation with psychiatrist, art, music, drama, God knows what other kind of therapy, dinner, wash-up, sleep. We had to be engaged in some kind of activity from morning to night. Down time between activities was therefore minimal, so that our thoughts wouldn't wander into forbidden zones. The repetitious daily activities were supposed to drown out the voices coming from within us, strangulate our destructive impulses, stomp out the memories from our previous life. The sequence of individual activities varied only according to the group to which we were assigned. I was placed in the red one, and when I asked if that meant anything, I received an ambiguous answer. Suddenly, I simply was red, while the others were perhaps green or yellow, regardless of our diagnosis, in this there was absolute egalitarianism. It was a community devoid of any prejudice, our colour did not discriminate against us in any way, we were all equally badly off.

When it came to the cure, I had only one reservation—I did not wish to be cured. I wasn't about to accept the idea that it wasn't what surrounded me that was sick, but that I was. But since I couldn't rebel against the treatment programme, I went on being the diligent student who blindly followed instructions. Without a word, I stuffed myself with pills, tried to cooperate during therapy and in art therapy crocheted blankets according to the pattern. The outside world grew more and more distant, it seemed to me that the low wall surrounding the clinic was growing taller, and that someone had fortified it with watchtowers and razor wire. I sank ever deeper into a strange lethargy, the hospital routine was seeping into my bones. All of those psychotic, self-destructive and borderline individuals suddenly seemed to me to be kindred spirits, as if we shared a blood bond. Soon I'll be braying alongside the others, I thought to myself one day as I was working in the kitchen and, like my neighbour to the right, rolled and re-rolled my dough at least ten consecutive times, convinced it was never flattened evenly enough.

46

Every night it was the same story. When the lights went out, I would get into bed, pull the comforter up to my nose, close my eyes ... and nothing. Because of the pills they were giving me by the bushel, I was constantly half-asleep, but never managed to be fully asleep and get a night of proper rest. I would toss in my bed as if I were on a carnival ride, my comforter mangled, my arms, legs and back gone numb, all to no avail. Most of the time I would get up and roam the corridors, back and forth, from wall to wall, like a caged animal, but not a tiger, more like a mangy hyena.

Sometimes I would go over to the lavatory, sit on the toilet, lean back against the water tank, prop my feet against the door frame and start to read. Twenty or thirty pages before going back to my room and starting from scratch.

Once as I was working my way through Sartre's *The Wall*, I caught a glimpse of Eda's artistry through a crack in the door.

She came into the bathroom, peed in the stall next to mine, then went over to the sink, rolled up the left sleeve of her pyjamas, and struck a pose in front of the mirror like a bodybuilder. Her gaze travelled from her wrist all the way to her shoulder, and then she moved to the other arm.

I shifted on the toilet, the seat creaked and Eda quickly let down her sleeves.

When she discovered who it was, she was clearly relieved.

'Want to see?'

We sat down on the cold tiles, Eda rolled up her sleeves again and then moved to the legs of her pants. I was pleased. Up until now I had only seen her scars from a distance, but suddenly I could look at them as closely as if they were on exhibit in a display case.

The skin looked as if it were covered with railroad ties onto which the tracks hadn't yet been mounted, but one could easily see where the ties began and where the tracks would end. On the left leg the ladder stretched from the groin down to the knee, on the right it went halfway down the thigh. The cuts by the groin were a bit lumpy, Edina's hand must still have been a bit shaky back then, though by the end the lines were already more confident. On her left arm each line was already identical to the next. Practice makes perfect.

Eda ran the palm of her hand back and forth a few times over the roughened skin. As if she were caressing the strings of a guitar. Her gaze was distant, dreamy, she reminded me of an artist contemplating what to paint on a white canvas.

'May I touch?'

It surprised her, but she obligingly held out her arm. My fingers traced her lacerations, bumping over them in a steady rhythm. It was as if I were caressing the severed trunk of a tree, running the tips of my fingers over the rings—this a bad year, this a good one.

'If someone asks me why I wear long sleeves in the summer, I tell them that I have problems with my circulation and so I'm always cold,' she said, and in her voice, I sensed a twinge of regret. She would certainly have been happy to show off her handiwork to the world and must have felt like a misunderstood artist, born at the wrong time. I closed my eyes and let myself wander further along her corrugated skin.

'And what is it about this that you actually enjoy?'

Eda thought for a moment, she probably hadn't been asked a question like that in a while, everyone was always asking about her childhood and her parents and her relationships, and now this, out of the blue.

'I remember when I was about three or four years old, I had a middle ear infection. I remember the terrible pressure, the throbbing in my ear, I felt as if at any moment a bomb was going to explode inside my head. My dad took me to the emergency room, where they punctured my eardrum. It was such a relief! Like popping a water balloon with a pin. For a moment, terrible pain, when they jabbed me, but then that congested, painful crud in one's skull rushes to one place, gushes out, and is gone. Like when a volcano erupts, for a moment everything's on fire, but then peace returns for a while. Cutting is the same. It's just a release valve through which the crap flows out.'

Altogether it sounded like a logical explanation.

'And does it work?' I asked.

'The first time it did. An explosion of euphoria. Now it's weaker, I cut myself but it's just shadows of the earlier sensations. Sort of like when a pressure cooker gives a little fart, the pressure drops, but it's back up in no time. And then the wound heals, so I have to find another spot and go deeper, and every so often I go too far. Or for a while I'll stop, and then the pressure really builds up and it comes close to that original feeling. It takes discipline,' she chuckled.

'Listen, given the alternative ... well, you know,' she went on smiling.

She summed up her stint in the clinic with the obligatory: 'I can't wait to get the hell out of here. Actually, it's not so bad here, at least when I get out, I really enjoy it. The wounds are already healed on the surface, I'm feeling the itch all over,' she giggled again and her eyes sparkled.

'Hey, so why do you actually do it?'

'I already told you, to get relief.'

'But from what? What made you start?' I wasn't about to be dissuaded.

'Because I enjoy doing it, so there,' Edina retorted and slapped her forehead.

The she looked me straight in the eye: 'And why are you here?'

'Well...my father, my mother, sort of like everyone else here...'

I shook my head and made a face. This wasn't anything I wanted to be sharing in the women's bathroom between two and three in the morning. In fact, I didn't want to talk about it at all. The thought of putting that horror into words, or even attempting to do so, struck me as completely absurd.

The door to the bathroom opened, I was saved by a patient with a prolapsed pelvic floor. Eda hurriedly stood up. She gave me one last pat on the back and added: 'I'm telling you, the pus has to come out, otherwise no wound will ever heal.' She adjusted her pyjamas, gave me a wave, and left.

I leaned over the sink, rinsed my face with cold water and returned to the room. Eda was already burrowed in her bed, turned on her side, her back towards me. I lay down and closed my eyelids. The barcodes of her scars kept flashing before my eyes. It seemed to me that those lines represented a cipher of some kind. I couldn't get her words out of my head. On some level, that crazy girl was absolutely right. It was as if I had a giant wound inside my body that had been sewn up in a hurry, but had never been properly cleaned out. I needed to reopen that wound, disinfect it and only then sew it up.

Confusing images began to flash before my eyes. The little red man on the traffic light, the impact in my side, the terrified eyes. A blur of red, grey and blue. Scenes like in the paintings of Edvard Munch. *Breathe, sis.*

I turned on my side and reached under the headboard. With my fingers I felt along the inside of the wooden bedframe. At last. With all my strength I pried off a splinter, gripped it between my thumb and forefinger, turned over onto my back, and took a few deep breaths. I channelled all of my strength into my right arm and then stabbed my thigh as hard as I could. I pressed my lips together and stifled a moan. Munch and his banners of intense colours billowed even more, fluttering before my eyes, tangling together and unfurling again. Now, now it must come. A sharp pain throbbed in my right thigh, spreading from my groin to my knees.

And that was it.

I'm not that crazy after all, I thought to myself, relieved, I would have to find another way. I covered the confusion of colours with my white comforter and waited to see if the bite of sleep would lift me out of the painting.

47

The first thing I did was to get off the meds. Most of the time it was no problem to spit them out right away. They monitored us only superficially, and in my case usually didn't bother at all, because I was considered to be a generally conscientious and harmless patient. If the nurse happened to be more attentive, I had to go to the bathroom. Kamila had initiated me into the secret of how to stick my fingers down my throat correctly in order to vomit.

During the one-on-one visits with the doctor and in group therapy I didn't cooperate. I would hang my head and hum songs to myself to avoid hearing what they were telling me.

I didn't want to dance to the choreography prescribed for me in the clinic, so very soon I began to make up my own steps. During art therapy I drew pictures of my family using my left hand, during drama therapy I rolled my r's and in music therapy I sang two tones lower as a matter of principle. Occupational therapy in the garden towards the end of winter was difficult to sabotage, I couldn't pretend not to have raked the leaves that I had already long since raked, so I preferred to direct my subversive activity to boycotting psychotherapy. As part of our treatment, we were required to keep a diary, at least half a page each day, and after one week the journals would be turned over to the psychiatrists who would study them and give us advice on how to live. 'I see that you have made considerable inner progress,' or 'Don't be afraid of your new feelings,' Eda and Kamila would mimic the therapists before bedtime, laughing out loud at their rote one-liners. If we didn't complete the minimum number of pages, there would be sanctions, for example we wouldn't be allowed to watch TV or play football. But they couldn't get wise to me, I was an ace. 'Today for lunch we had *knedlíky* with tomato sauce, it was too watery, but I liked it, it made me think of my grandmother,' I wrote in letters so large that they went over the top line. 'My pyjamas have got too tight around my stomach, I'll need a new elastic or a new pair.'

With the help of such gimmicks, I frittered away all of March and April at the clinic. In my spare time I would sit in front of the television and flip through books. I had no interest in postmodern novels or surrealist poetry. I read about what I couldn't bring myself to speak about. Or I would just lie in bed and imagine what my brothers were doing back home. Most of all I thought about Martin. I wondered what he was reading right then, apologized to him in my mind for the scene at the ball, and I even wrote him a love poem. Every Sunday, after lunch, I would sit on my bed crumpling up the piece of paper with the poem in my hand, and then come evening I would slip it back into the drawer of my nightstand.

Slowly I was beginning to experience changes. The blurred world around me started to come back into focus. In order to be free of that morass completely, one more deep cut had to be made.

How could I articulate what had happened to me all those years ago? How could I describe the darkness deep inside me? How could I possibly try to translate that horror into words?

What I had experienced that summer was beyond my verbal capacity. Every time I took a breath to voice what had happened to me, the words remained trapped behind a wall of glass. They would reach that point, but then would ricochet off and fall back down.

The pus must come out.

As I ate breakfast, spat out pills, went to group therapy, even as I scrubbed the toilets, I would rummage through memories, link them together into a coherent chain, which I would then break apart and start over. Several times I had to give up because of the pain and ran away crying. At night when I shut my eyelids, the yarn of words would writhe before my eyes like a snake, in the darkness it would slink into remote corners, and come morning I could barely gather it back up into a ball.

I was so caught up in myself that it wasn't until afternoon therapy one day that I realized I hadn't seen Eda that entire day. Her bed had remained empty all night.

'She didn't come back from her walk yesterday afternoon,' explained Kamila without a trace of agitation. As an experienced patient, she knew that making friends in a psychiatric institute could only lead to disappointment.

'They're letting me go next week,' she added.

There's still more for me to learn, I thought to myself as I took off my pyjamas.

I threw myself even more intensely into my work. The painstakingly formulated words began to arrange themselves into sentences, which in turn coalesced into clauses and paragraphs. I filled in the gaps by educating myself in the on-site library where I went in my spare moments. One Thursday, when I came back from art therapy and walked into the dining room, the drawings of pink ponies with rainbow-coloured manes and tails slipped from my hand in surprise. Seated at the table was none other than Edina. My first instinct was to run over to her, but then I caught myself wondering where this sudden feeling of joy at seeing her again had come from. Eda was seated at the table, in front of her was a plate with a piece of cheesecake on it that she was slicing with a spoon and stuffing into her mouth, which in and of itself was perfectly fine, except that she was doing all of it ten times slower than usual. Her lips were smeared with cream cheese, the corners of her mouth full of crumbs, and her eyes as if veiled by a moist membrane. Her left arm was bandaged from elbow to wrist.

I sat down opposite her.

'Edina...'

Slowly, very slowly she looked up from the plate, it took an interminably long time before she looked into my eyes, after which her pupils slid back down. She hadn't recognized me at all.

Long into the night, I couldn't get the image of Edina out of my mind. I lay stiffly in bed, my arms and legs urging me from my immobile position, but I didn't budge. It was as if once again I had been strapped to the bed like some dangerous lunatic.

The next day I knocked on the door of my attending physician's office.

'How much longer am I going to be here?' I asked when the doctor invited me to have a seat.

'According to the treatment plan you should be here for at least another three months.'

'What do I need to do to get out sooner?'

The psychiatrist looked at me with a tired expression.

'If you leave during the course of treatment, you may experience a relapse and your psychological problems may become chronic. I would recommend that you...'

What followed was a long litany on the theme of highly qualified psychiatric care and the irresponsible patient. I feigned interest and nodded my head to the rhythm of the syllables pouring out of his mouth.

'... But basically, if you want to leave, we can't stop you.'

My eyes grew wide.

'What?!'

'It's not as though you are here by a court order, you're an adult, so you can leave at any time. Just sign the waiver.'

And so, the next morning I paid my last visit to the doctor's office. Before leaving the clinic behind me, I asked the doctor if I could make a phone call.

Once outside, I skimmed through the medical discharge papers.

Psychiatric Hospital in Dobřany

Ústavní 341, 334 41 Dobřany

Ward XII

HOSPITALIZATION PROGRESS REPORT

Surname and name: Tichá Sára
Personal ID number: 9158310341
Address: K Bezovce 1727/3, 301 00 Plzeň 3
Insurance company: 211
File no.: 3212/17

Date: 15.5.2010

Dx: F23.3 acute psychotic disorder
Lab.: Biochemistry normal range, toxicology neg.

Admitted: 14 Feb 2010, 10.12 p.m. Involuntary admission, escorted by paramedics.

Case history: Female, 18 years of age, hospitalized for acute psychotic attack. She verbally and physically assaulted her father, who suffered lacerations to his face and finally had to be hospitalized for a suspected concussion. On admission, uncooperative, aggressive behaviour, borderline suicidal, stabilized by administering clonazepam 2 mg PO and diazepam 10 mg IM.

According to her parents, the patient first manifested psychological problems around 9 years of age, and in recent months, her atypical behaviour has significantly worsened. The patient suffered from insomnia, appeared distracted, invented illnesses, verbally and physically attacked her father. It can be inferred that she was developing a paranoid disorder (she was hypersensitive, locked herself in her room, avoided her parents and her siblings, became withdrawn), evidently suffering from the delusion that someone wanted to cause her harm. Genetic load is not to be discounted (paternal grandmother and aunt exhibited similar behaviour, although without a diagnosis), also possible is the presence of a prenatal disposition (severe case of influenza during mother's second trimester of pregnancy, difficult birth), a direct trigger for the psychosis could have been stress (approaching graduation exam and relationship problems). During consultations the patient is non-communicative, does not react to questions, is introverted, covers her ears, closes her eyes, behaves as if she were living in her own inner world. It cannot be ruled out with certainty that the patient may harm herself or others.

Discharge summary: The patient is leaving the facility after three months of hospitalization at her own request, despite the explicit recommendation of the attending physician not to discontinue treatment. Condition at discharge is lucid, mildly apathetic, level of orientation completely normal, observes social conventions, communicates normally, intelligible speech, coherence in manifestation, psychomotricity rate slightly low, euthymic affect, in touch with reality, risk of suicidal behaviour low, but not to be discounted.

Therapy: Risperidone 3 mg a day 1-0-0, PO for a period of at least one year, preferably two depending on the evaluation of the outpatient psychiatrist, to rule out a relapse of psychosis.

Recommendation: Psychiatric visit within and no later than one week following discharge from the psychiatric clinic. Should problems arise, it is necessary to seek outpatient help immediately.

The patient was informed about the nature of the illness, its typical course, treatment options, and the importance of cooperation during treatment. She understood the instructions and had the opportunity to ask questions. The patient agrees to present the discharge summary to the outpatient physician.

In Dobřany, 15 May 2010
Dr Jan Netolík
Attending physician

I rolled up the papers and tucked them into my winter coat, beneath which my back was sweating under the spring sun. I walked across the grass, in which the first daisies and sunflowers were blooming, and didn't look back even once at the peeling building with washable tiles. It was a Tuesday morning, my father would be at the college.

48

I climbed the four steps and caressed the inlaid beech-wood door. I ran my hand over it as if I were a blind person, reading a book. The dark wood suddenly sprang away from me.

'I'm so glad that you're back,' burst out my mother and quickly pulled me inside by my sleeve. She slammed the door on the curious stares of our neighbours.

She had changed. She looked even more corpulent than she had three months ago, deep wrinkles had formed around her mouth, not the joyful kind from laughter, but dark furrows caused by drooping corners. Her misty eyes had long since lost their girlish sparkle. She looked withered and worn.

'Come, sit down.'

She placed a hand on my shoulder and pushed me into the living room. She tried to plant me on the sofa but I sat down in my father's armchair.

'But that's . . .' she whispered, then caught herself and placed her palm over her mouth. Then she quietly sat down on the sofa beside me.

For a while we just sat there, I staring at her face, she at the floor, rubbing her hands on her thighs.

'I'll make you something, you must be hungry.'

'No, thank you,' I uttered my very first words since I had arrived, but my mother leapt to her feet anyway and ran off to the kitchen.

'So how are you?' she called to me as she opened one cupboard after another, surely there had to be something with which to consume the silence.

She placed a plate of lemon cookies on the table.

'You got here a bit sooner than I expected, it's still in the oven...'

I almost hadn't noticed. The entire living room was suffused with a sweet fragrance. I smiled slightly. I felt as though I had come back from summer camp and my mom had baked me something to welcome me home.

'I'll make you some tea,' she got up and ran back into the kitchen.

'No, thanks,' I called after her and a moment later heard from the kitchen the sizzle of the electric kettle.

I looked around, and my eyes landed on the remote control on the table, which in our house was never called anything but 'the button,' and I contemplated the bookcase: *Talks with T. G. Masaryk*, Eco, Vančura, Alighieri, Goethe, all classics that make an impression, evoke tradition and a classical education and don't stir up controversy. The other books, those by Šabach, Kotleta, and Danielle Steel, huddled on the shelves of the second floor.

From the kitchen came sounds that I associated with home. The opening of the oven, the baking sheet scraping against the oven's enamelled inner walls, the clinking of porcelain.

After a while my mother emerged, pushed aside the dish of lemon cookies, and set a plate down in front of me with a piece of cake sprinkled with powdered sugar and a cup of tea beside it. Then she made another trip to the kitchen and returned with the same for herself.

It was my childhood plate with three little girls on bicycles riding around the perimeter. The cup was one of the fancy ones, with a gold rim. We were sitting so close to each other that we could have embraced. I in my father's armchair and she to my left on the sofa. In our enormous villa there were just the two of us, no one could see us, no one could overhear what mother and daughter were saying to each other. All had gone exactly according to plan.

I brought the plate closer to me and touched the cake with my index finger. After three months of eating a non-fat, low-salt, bland diet, I was craving something of substance. Something homemade. My mother's cake. On the surface it had already cooled, but if I took a bite, I was sure I would burn my tongue.

My mother was resting her elbows on her thighs, looking straight ahead and smiling.

'I missed you so much,' she declared into the fragrant silence.

I clasped her hands in mine and inclined my head so that our eyes would meet.

'Mom, I need to talk to you.'

She remained silent, but continued to smile slightly, lowering her eyes to the cake on the coffee table.

'Mom, I . . .' My throat was dry. I had to swallow several times before I could start again. 'I keep having to go back to what happened back then . . .' I continued. 'To what he did to me back then.'

She nodded as if she understood.

'I can't get past it,' I went on. 'It's horrible,' I added, wanting to describe all of my feelings to her. That for eight whole years I felt as though I didn't exist at all. As if I were completely frozen, empty, maybe even dead. That I didn't wake up until the ball and didn't want to go back to that zombie-like state. And that only she could help me. I had intended to tell her all of this, but instead all that came out of me was: 'I need your help.' I looked at her, still smiling softly, the wrinkles had faded from her face, in her eyes I glimpsed understanding. Finally, she understood me. Again, she nodded, not saying a word.

There was nothing to add to what I had said. It was perfectly clear that this time she wouldn't abandon me.

'He can't get away with this. I would like you to come with me . . .'

From outside I could hear footsteps and then the jingle of keys in the lock. I practically leapt in fright. Strange, could it be Milan already coming home? Wasn't he supposed to be at work or in school?

I saw the keys flying, they landed right in the wooden bowl on the dresser under the mirror. It had always been like that, first the keys, then Dad.

My father walked into the living room, he must have prepared his smile already in the hallway. 'There she is.' By way of welcome he even held out his arms.

I was petrified. I couldn't even manage to shut my mouth after the unfinished sentence.

My father took the hint that I wasn't in a hugging mood, stood by his armchair not knowing which way to turn, and finally sat down across from me. My mother kept on smiling, but in the meantime had pulled her handkerchief out of her pocket. Just in case.

A moment later she scrambled up and ran back to the kitchen. As if she kept a magic potion hidden there that she went to sip from when she didn't feel well. My father and I stared at each other in silence. A moment later a plate with a slice of cake landed in front of him as well. The china scraped ominously against the glass.

My father crossed his legs, rested his right arm on the armrest, his left hand remained suspended in the air, he wasn't used to the sofa. He tried to look self-assured, but was rubbing his hand on his thigh. Even so, I noticed that his fingers were trembling.

'So, Sára, how did you make out over there? Are you feeling better?' asked my father.

I swallowed hard but didn't look away. I knew how I could overpower him. All of my memories were neatly arranged in meticulously labelled folders. All of the data carefully examined, classified, recorded, registered and filed.

'You're going to go to jail,' I whispered. My heart was pounding, beating all the way to my tonsils.

'We're glad you're home already, we missed you,' he went on.

'You're going to go to jail,' I repeated, and then, three being the charm, once more: 'There's no statute of limitations, I made sure, they're going to put you away.'

I turned to my mother for support, but her gaze slid away. Her eyes were bleary, misty.

'Let's go ahead and eat, shall we?' she uttered in a half-whisper.

I looked at the piece of cake on the plate. It lay there motionless, like my father sitting across from me. My mother, on the other hand, couldn't stay still for a moment. She kept nudging the plates towards us: 'Go on, have some, it turned out really well today, the dough rose beautifully,' she spoke in a voice that was barely audible, but not everything, Mom, can be patched up with food. This was not at all how it was supposed to be. Nothing was going the way we had agreed by phone the day before. This was when she was supposed to stand up and confront him. I was supposed to walk away the winner, and my father the loser. I was still jammed full of words that were extremely difficult for me, rape, trial, punishment, but those words were stuck inside me, they wouldn't come out. And even if they did—it was useless. There was no point, it was as if there was a fortified wall between us and we found ourselves in parallel worlds, in different time zones, the questions and answers out of sync, each of us leading an isolated monologue.

I glanced back and forth from one to the other, from my mother, who with practised fingering had practically shredded her cloth handkerchief and was sipping a tea lighter in colour than mine, to my father, who had assumed a self-assured air but nonetheless appeared much smaller than last time and kept rubbing the corners of his mouth with his thumb and forefinger. His shoulders were stooped, his cheekbones etched in his gaunt face, and the elastic band of his therapeutic socks was visible beneath his trousers.

My anger slowly began to drain away. It occurred to me that all I needed to do was to keep silent. To pretend that nothing at all had happened, and maybe it hadn't, and it had all just been a too vivid dream. To pick up where those eight silent years had left off. Those trembling hands could barely even hold a cup of coffee any more.

'Go on, Sisi, have some,' my mother urged again, pointing at the cake. 'I made it with ricotta, you like that, Evžen and Milan will survive for once . . .'

I smiled without meaning to. Of the three of us, I was the only one who liked ricotta. Milan liked poppy seed and Evžen plum jam. I picked up the spoon and poked at the cake. The aroma was impossible to resist. We would sit around and have cake and tea and chat. I'll stop with this madness already, everything will be explained away, it had all been a terrible mistake. We will forget everything, embrace and have ourselves a good cry. We will be a family again. I'll go back to school, get my diploma and go off to college in another city. In the end, this was what we all wanted.

Or maybe I'll give it a shot after all, I'll grab her by the shoulders, dig my nails into her flesh, find the solid bone buried deep beneath the layer of fat, Mom, it's me, Sára, your daughter, I need you to help me, I'll shake her so hard that she'll be forced to get up. We'll go away together and leave this dark place, just you and me.

'Ma . . .' I took her wrist gently, but her hand was cold and clammy and slipped easily away.

She stared into her lap and said in a half-whisper: 'Be careful not to burn your tongue . . .'

I remembered that my mother had said the identical phrase to me all those years ago in Sušice, after the night she had come into my room. She had cut me an end of the sponge cake and then swung at me with a knife.

I felt I was sinking. My mother had not reacted to my words in any way. There was nothing I could say that would wipe the insipid smile off her face, my thoughts couldn't get through to her at all, there was too much flesh. So I did the only sensible thing that it was possible to do in that moment. I flung the spoon onto the plate and raced upstairs. I ran into the bathroom, bent over the toilet bowl and vomited. I retched for a long time, to get everything out. I stood over the bowl long after there was nothing left in my stomach. Then I rinsed out my mouth, slammed the door of my bedroom shut and double-locked it. Fortunately, they hadn't hidden away the key. I lay on the bed, completely empty inside. A hollow being.

The summer solstice was just over a month away, it was getting dark late. From downstairs, an endless stream of unintelligible words drifted up to me. It was obvious they were discussing a single topic. What to do with me? I imagined myself going to the police, presenting my ID card at the reception desk, explaining why I had come. Answering all the questions: when, where, who?

Why hadn't I filed a report long ago?

Did I have any evidence?

Was there anyone who could testify?

Sooner or later, they would discover where I had spent the last three months. Maybe I would have to go back there.

I waited until after dark, packed my military duffle bag and tiptoed downstairs. I couldn't turn on the light so I held on tightly to the railing, to avoid tripping on the steps. Every knot in the wood I ran my hand over was etched into my memory. In the front hallway I grasped the door handle and heard something drop to the tile floor. A small cloth pouch. In it I found several banknotes and two keys, one a patent key and the other a brass cylinder key. I recognized them immediately. They were the keys to the cottage in Dvorce. My parents had hung the pouch on the handle for me to find. I attached them to the house keys, slipped the whole bunch into my pocket, and grasped the handle one more time. The door was unlocked. From outside I felt a rush of hot air. Summer was already in full swing.

I took a first step but stopped once more. It was the very last time I felt a longing for someone to touch me. To feel another's skin on mine. My mother's. Or Milan's. I stood where I was for a moment longer, but there was no one far and wide who could embrace me, turn me away from the gate and bring me back home.

I shut the door behind me and plunged into the darkness. I sat down on the bench at the bus stop and threw my duffle bag under my feet. Couples in shorts and miniskirts bustled around me, the girls licking ice cream cones and the guys sipping beer from bottles beaded with condensation. They laughed and draped their arms over each other's shoulders. It was the first tropical night of the year and I, my pants stuffed into my socks and wearing a heavy sweater, sat with my teeth chattering on the wooden bench. I could no longer go back for my jacket. When daylight came, I fished a slip of paper out of my pocket with Kamila's telephone number.

49

It has been raining for two weeks straight. The raindrops have long since found their way through the branches and soaked the ground. Crossing the footbridge, I felt the cold water running down my neck. It wasn't long before all my clothes became damp. My fingers and toes were frozen, and in my lower abdomen I felt thousands of needles. My hands and feet swelled up, my taut skin itched, my swollen feet in the drenched leather boots hurt. I had to cast them off and go barefoot. I also took off my heavy, soggy jacket and tossed it aside so that I could continue. I felt terribly cold, my teeth were chattering, but on the inside of my body I felt a strange heat, my cheeks were on fire.

During the night I hadn't slept at all, but I could no longer stay awake either. I had fallen into a state of semi-consciousness, on the edge of sleep and wakefulness. When I closed my eyes as I walked, images of rotting mushrooms riddled with crawling worms darted beneath my eyelids. And when I opened my eyes again, all I could see were the vague outlines of things around me covered in greenish slime. The forest had turned into a mysterious enchanted jungle. Everything around me was burgeoning, flourishing, proliferating. The full moon drew the fruiting bodies out of the ground, the viscous, whitish stipes forced their way to the surface through the waterlogged pine needles and bark and rubbed against my feet. From the rotting stumps, devoured and decimated by parasitic fungi, the soggy bark was peeling away. I myself am nothing but a parasite, sustained by the forest and the state, in return I give nothing, I only take. I am no better than Ruda, who just plunders nature, I am like a wood-decaying fungus that destroys everything. The trees that have been growing here for decades will collapse, and all just because of me. The forest has seen through my paltriness as well, it wants to swallow me up and spit me out in some unknown place, partly digested by acidic gastric juices, a bloated yellow carcass with fish eyes.

Among the tree trunks flashed the faces of the people I had failed: Milan's big eyes, my mother's averted countenance, *help me*, long shadows falling across me, *damn it, breathe*, shouting at me, *I don't know what you're talking about*, a shadow glued to my back, *eeny, meeny, miny, moe, it's all your fault!*

I'm the one who killed my parents. It was because of me that my mother drowned in alcohol and that my father was destroyed by a malignant tumour.

They found him two years ago in his office. Who knows why the hospital called me: 'You must come immediately, it's serious!' By the time I got there, Evžen had already taken charge. He shouted at me in the hospital corridor and I turned and fled.

I used to go to Plzeň to see him almost every week. I no longer dared to go inside the hospital, I stood outside in front of the pavilion and stared at the window of his room, but he never appeared. Until one time I saw him on a bench in the garden. A nurse had taken him there so that he could get some fresh air. He had got there with very short, shaky old man steps. With one hand he was leaning on a cane while the nurse held onto to his other arm, and she had trouble getting him seated on the bench in a way that he wouldn't fall off. His entire body was withered and listless, his arms hung limply along his sides, saliva was dribbling from the corners of his mouth. He looked completely harmless. Then he turned slightly in my direction and I quickly ducked behind a bush.

It took several more months before death liberated him. *It's all your fault*, Evžen's words rang in my ears as I stood in the corner of the crematorium. He was right. Why hadn't I just let it go? Why hadn't I kept quiet?

I was stumbling over broken branches, falling to the ground and struggling to get back up. I scraped my knees and a dark brown stain seeped through the wet fabric. The soles of my feet were bleeding and I winced at every step. The air was heavy with rot, the cold, wet branches brushed against my face, beneath my fingers I could feel soggy mushrooms. They were growing absolutely everywhere, I was tripping over red cracking boletes, honey mushrooms and even brittlegills. They were all infested with mould.

I'm not sure when I got lost. The forest was a labyrinth and I couldn't find my way out. The thread had snapped. My path had only a beginning, but no end, it had all just been an illusion, there had never been a trail, it was impossible to get out of the woods and back home. I will never make it to zero, I'll be forever a zilch. My legs gave way. I tried to continue on all fours, to drag myself to a stump, but I had no more strength.

I leaned back against a wet trunk from which the waterlogged bark was crumbling. I struggled to breathe. The entire forest was at my back, coming after me. I could no longer keep my eyes open, my chin dropped to my chest.

50

I must have been lying there for months, years, entire centuries, an infinitely long time. In my head shadows weaved in and out, figures wandered, an echo resonated.

When I opened my eyes for the first time, all I could see was a mushroom-like grey nothingness. A cloud that had swallowed sky and earth. The second time, the murky grey was joined by other colours, white, yellow and blue, all pallid shades that portended nothing good. It occurred to me that perhaps I was back in the room with washable walls, but strangely enough this did not particularly upset me, I closed my eyes without concern and fell back asleep. On the third awakening the pastel haze around me began to take on shimmering contours. But those soon dissolved as well. It was only on the next attempt that I could distinguish individual shapes. I could see a bright room, in front of me a glass door, above me a contraption with a tangle of tubes and wires, and on the ceiling a row of lightbulbs.

'Miss Tichá . . .' I heard, but I wasn't sure if I was hearing that voice from outside or just imagining it inside my head.

'Miss Tichá, are you awake?'

Standing next to me was an elderly nurse. She placed the palm of her hand on my forehead, it was a routine yet at the same time gentle touch. Her palm was pleasantly warm. Had I been able, I would have liked to take her hand and press it to my cheek. My entire body was paralysed, non-functional, all of my muscles flaccid, a living mind in a dead body.

'What day is today?' were my first words. I managed to get them out that same day, after much coughing and swallowing. It felt as though someone else had spoken them, my voice was strangely crackling and raspy.

'It's the third of November,' the nurse told me.

I started to calculate how long I had been lying here. It must have been a mere seven or eight days.

It had been an infection of the kidneys and urinary tract, as I later learnt. 'Sepsis had set in, both kidneys were affected, but luckily the failure was only temporary and we were able to save both of them,' the doctor explained to me during her visit the next day. 'That infection must have been there for quite some time,' she went on, 'I'm surprised you let it go for so long. Had it not been for the lady who found you in the woods, God knows how it would have turned out.'

'What lady?'

'She was a sort of strange, tattooed lady, I happened to be on duty, I don't remember her name but if you'd like, I could check the record...'

'No,' I interrupted her. 'I know who it is.'

'Once you've recovered, you should thank her. But now you have to concentrate on yourself, you need to rest and drink a lot.' And finally, she added the inevitable: 'You were lucky, you got here just in time.'

I wasn't sure if I had all that much to be happy about, but to be polite, I assumed a grateful air. Her words must have struck home, because as soon as she left, I felt overwhelmed with fatigue and my eyelids grew heavy. I was so sleepy that even the act of yawning felt like scaling an 8,000 metre peak.

Then I had a very strange dream. Once again, I was in a forest, it resembled the one I had recently walked through, it was just as dark, damp, rotting and overgrown, but I was strolling through it like a visitor in a museum, examining static objects in a display case. It was actually just a make-believe forest, a very well-done interactive 3D exhibit for which I would purchase a ticket. I wasn't cold, I was stepping on the moss, and I knew perfectly well that I had nothing to fear, that when I'd had enough I could simply leave and walk out through the exit.

When I woke up, I felt unusually free. And my mood improved again when the nurse revealed that a young man had come to visit me several days ago. God knows why the first one to come to my mind was Martin. Or was it one of my brothers? That was more likely. Probably Milan.

'He didn't tell me his name, but he was rather odd, from the way he was dressed I wondered if he wasn't some crazy person.'

And when the nurse placed a book on my bed, I knew for sure who it was.

'We didn't let him come in, he wasn't a relative, but he left this for you.'

A pocket atlas, a collector's item for mushroom gatherers, no ordinary photographs, but with Otto Ušák's illustrations. I had always wanted it. The back cover had a white sticker on it and the inside was stamped with the initials of the national library, NKČR. I opened the atlas at random—wood blewit. It seemed to me to be a message. As I was closing the book, the library card fell out. I slipped it back inside the volume and set both down on the nightstand.

'And one more thing,' added the nurse and handed me an envelope. 'This came for you in the mail.'

It was a card with a photograph of a panda with a scarf wrapped around its neck. Inside were printed the words: 'Sweat me out! P.S. Your influenza.' And written underneath in pen: 'See you next year! Ruda.' The handwriting looked like it belonged to a first grader who had just learnt to write. It was pressed so hard into the paper that the letters bulged out on the back of the card. I put the envelope down on the mushroom atlas.

Gradually I grew more and more bored in bed. I looked forward to every change of the IV drip and each temperature check. There wasn't much stimulation in the room, I was there all by myself, there was no television, and they hadn't given me anything to read, although I wouldn't have been able to concentrate on anything anyway. There was a massive weight on my eyelids, I couldn't keep them open for more than a few seconds. I slept through entire nights and dozed off several times a day.

When I was awake, I would try to spur on the slow-motion time. I came up with a way to entertain myself—in my head I would try to guess the exact minute, I would look at the clock on the opposite wall, close my eyes, count to sixty, and open them again. I was usually off by two or three seconds, so I would have to try again. As soon as I got it right, I'd try for two minutes.

By the time they moved me to a standard room about a week later, I could time five minutes, down to the split second.

51

'What's this slop again?' I heard from beside me. I picked up the grey plastic cover and began to ponder. It truly did look strange, the deep plate was filled with a pale-yellow gelatinous mass, and on the tray beside it lay a spongy piece of chocolate cake wrapped in cellophane.

'Why it's chocolate cake with custard,' explained the nurse who had brought us the trays, 'You have to crumble the cake up and mix it in.' My neighbour snorted in disgust. I could relate. This was already her second month here, they were treating her for varicose ulcers that wouldn't heal. Her legs hurt, she couldn't sleep, so all she did was complain and take out her anger mostly on the food, but sometimes also on the nurses.

I, on the other hand, was enjoying the hospital food. What a difference from a slice of bread with sardines, a roll with a triangle of processed cheese, discounted pork liverwurst and reheated frankfurters.

Being in the hospital felt like being in a spa—nothing but treatments, massages, dining in bed, 'Miss Tichá, is everything all right?' and 'What can I do for you?'

After a week spent in a regular room in the internal medicine unit, I was substantially better. I could manage to get out of bed on my own, go to the bathroom and wash myself. They had removed the IV and were now giving me the antibiotics in pill form. My fever had come down and my pain had subsided. The doctor told me that I would be going home within a week at the most.

As my condition improved, my misgivings returned. The longer I stayed awake, the more I found myself thinking about them non-stop. How had things turned out with the shack and the leaky roof? How was I going to pay for the repairs and the electricity bill? Would I really be able to return to the Toadstool? How would I get through the winter? So far, I had only managed to drag over a couple of logs. At night I had started wandering through the forest again, trying to pull myself out of the spiral, but each time I would trip and tumble back into the centre.

Most of all, a feeling that I had not known before began to nag at me. Loneliness. As soon as people who were not wearing striped pyjamas began to appear in the hallways in the afternoon, I would snap to attention. Maybe Vojta would come. I would leave my room, lean against the wall, and impatiently stake out the exit. And when they started coming around with dinner, I would go back, like a kid who hadn't been picked up from daycare.

One Saturday afternoon, my turn finally came. I was just in the bathroom when my pudgy neighbour knocked on the door.

'You've got company.'

I leapt up from the bowl so fast that I almost went flying on the freshly mopped tiles. I flung open the door, slamming the handle into someone's back.

'Ouch,' came a voice.

'Hi, Milan,' I replied, trying not to let my disappointment show.

'Hey, sis!'

I went back to my bed, Milan sat down in a chair by the window, he had set a bag of oranges on my nightstand. He had the same broad smile our mom had once had. His face had grown rounder since the last time. He was looking more and more like our mother.

'This way you'll have some vitamins. So how are you doing?'

'Not bad. How about you?'

'Same.'

He tried to sound natural, but every so often he would rub the corners of his eyes with his index finger and thumb. He always did that when he was nervous.

'What about Evžen?'

'He's good. He's going to have a baby.'

My companion on the left reached for a small portable radio and began tuning it. Whistling and static alternated with snippets of songs and commercials.

'When are they letting you go?'

'I'm not sure yet. But I think pretty soon.'

Both of us were struggling mightily to make conversation, but we were just tormenting each other. I looked out of the window, Milan stared down at his outstretched legs, tapping his shoes together and drumming his fingers on his thigh.

'And what about you, you're not getting married?'

Milan chuckled.

The little flame of conversation was flickering and beginning to smoulder, it needed more fuel, and into the midst of it all from my neighbour came the voice of Helenka Vondráčková singing *Sweet illu-uuuuuusions . . .*

In spite of the awkward conversation, Milan's visit made me happy. After all, he was the first person to come see me in the hospital. He had schlepped himself here all the way from Plzeň, even though he must have been swamped with work. Before Christmas business is good. And besides, I also felt a bit sorry for him. He had a sad look about him. Maybe he was worried about me.

All of the bad memories were slowly evaporating and resurfacing in my mind were only the good ones. The time we tried to go down the Otava on a mattress, pushing ourselves off from the rocks. How for my eighth birthday he had bought me a Swiss Army Knife with his own savings. And how we had hidden together behind the bushes in the garden so that Dad wouldn't find us, ready to give us a thrashing because we had spilled tea inside the grand piano. But most of all I thought of his hands, which had saved my life.

'We were worried about you. Evžen wanted to come too, but something came up, he's got a ton of work to do around the house now to get it ready.'

At the thought of Evžen I frowned slightly. Could he have been the one to send him? Why had Milan actually come to see me? What did he want from me?

'I thought, once they've discharged you, I would come and visit you in Dvorce. I'd like to go mushroom hunting with you again. We could retrace Dad's old route, make a mushroom scramble, you know.'

He was looking towards the door, rubbing his chin.

'Is it too late for mushrooms?' he asked.

I reflected for a moment. It was the end of November, the bulk of the mushroom harvest had long since passed. But outside it had been pretty mild lately, certainly above ten degrees, the nights weren't yet freezing, and last week it had rained. I was sure to come across some fall mushrooms—wood ears, velvet shanks, maybe even some candy caps, and, of course, honey mushrooms. And maybe even some hardier penny buns, who knew. Last year I had scoped out some new gathering sites, in addition to the deciduous grove near Vatětice, this late in the season they would also be growing just past the Annín campground. And I would definitely hit on some oyster mushrooms. Ruda would appreciate them, and things at the Toadstool couldn't be all that bad if he was counting on me for next season. The Walrus would come up with a new menu, maybe oyster mushroom sauce to support the immune system. The honey mushrooms he could conserve, whereas the velvet shanks make an excellent soup.

I imagined myself and Milan getting up early in the morning, the woods still muffled in a grey cloak, we cross the footbridge and enter among the trees, we are completely alone. I take him on our old path, show him that I'm not the loser they think I am, I finally make it past zilch, after all I too have a job for which I am paid, there is a field in which I too am number one, the best around. I stride with confidence, whenever I bend down, I find something, I explain to Milan how every species has its preferred environment, how to clean a mushroom and what it's good for, which one is best raw and which one instead needs to be cooked. The basket is filling up in an auspicious way, by the time we get to Annín I have to be careful so that the mushrooms don't fall out, I pull a cloth bag out of my pants pocket and hand it to Milan. We get to the Toadstool already by three o'clock, it's getting dark early and it tends to be cooler in the Bohemian Forest than in Plzeň. Ruda is so pleased, he convinces us to stay for dinner.

'So what, would you go?' he asked again, looking me in the eye.

It will be a successful day, we will get back to Dvorce only late at night and will pop open a beer, which I of course will pay for, I don't need anyone to treat me, I have my own money, I will tip it out of the cup in the cupboard. We'll sit down at our table with the chequered tablecloth, full of holes. Milan will pull out the cards, we won't go to bed until long past midnight and the next morning there will be no way of waking my brother up.

We were staring at each other intently, I could see his pale-blue eyes, I knew he hated their colour because in the sun they looked like those of a dead fish. I could see his hand, too, fidgeting with the pack of cigarettes hidden in his pocket. I noted the stash of papers folded lengthwise protruding from the breast pocket of his jacket. And then my gaze fell on Otto Ušák's atlas sitting on the nightstand. Sticking out of it was the library card. There were only three days left until the due date. Why hadn't Vojta come to pick it up?

Milan wiped his palms on his jeans.

'So, what do you say sis, are we going?'

I looked out of the window, which directly overlooked the cemetery. I remembered how once, very early in the spring, Milan had convinced me to step onto the frozen creek. 'If you walk across to the other side, you'll get to be a zero.' I took two steps and fell through. The water was only waist high, so I managed to get myself out and crawled on all fours to the opposite bank. They didn't accept me into their party because, apparently, I was supposed to have crossed on two feet.

'Sisi?'

It would be so nice if it all worked out next week. If.

I turned my head back to Milan and waited for him to look up and for our eyes to meet.

'Milan, I am never going mushroom hunting again.'

With thanks to Eva Skopečková
and Markéta Balcarová
for their dedicated help with
the life and institutions of Plzeň.